A VAMPIRE BETRAYED

DEATHLESS NIGHT SERIES #4

L.E. WILSON

EVERBLOOD
PUBLISHING

NOTE FROM THE AUTHOR

This book was previously released as "Blood Betrayal" with a different cover.

ALSO BY L.E. WILSON

Deathless Night Series (The Vampires)
A Vampire Bewitched
A Vampire's Vengeance
A Vampire Possessed
A Vampire Betrayed
A Vampire's Submission
A Vampire's Choice

Deathless Night-Into the Dark Series (The Vampires)
Night of the Vampire
Secret of the Vampire
Forsworn by the Vampire

The Kincaid Werewolves (The Werewolves)
Lone Wolf's Claim
A Wolf's Honor
The Alpha's Redemption
A Wolf's Promise
A Wolf's Treasure
The Alpha's Surrender

Southern Dragons (Dragon Shifters & Vampires)

Dance for the Dragon

Burn for the Dragon

Snow Ridge Shifters (Novellas)

A Second Chance on Snow Ridge

A Fake Fiancé on Snow Ridge

Copyright © 2016 by Everblood Publishing

All rights reserved. No part of this publication may be reproduced, distributed, or transmitted in any form or by any means, including photocopying, recording, or other electronic or mechanical methods, without the prior written permission of the publisher, except in the case of brief quotations embodied in critical reviews and certain other noncommercial uses permitted by copyright law. For permission requests, email the publisher, addressed "Attention: Permissions Coordinator," at the address below.

All characters and events in this book are fictitious. Any resemblance to actual persons – living or dead – is purely coincidental.

le@lewilsonauthor.com

Print Edition

ISBN: 978-1-945499-43-2

Cover Design by Coffee and Characters

Publication Date: July 19, 2016

DEDICATION

To My Husband

Thank you my love, for being my strongest supporter and the best husband in the entire world.

I love you the mostest, Joe Joe.

1

He was dying. Literally.

Christian slammed his sweaty palm against the glass wall in front of him as his bloodshot eyes watched the woman on the other side. His silver cuff bracelet clanked against it so hard, the turquoise stones should have left chips in the glass. But they didn't, because this was no ordinary glass. It was some type of indestructible, vampire-proof glass.

Through eyes that burned with lust and sweat, he watched her: The woman who had been both his sweetest fantasy and his worst nightmare for as long as he could remember now. The girl with skin so pale and translucent he could see the delicate blue veins just underneath where her life's blood flowed. The girl with eyes just slightly darker in color than the ancient stones on his wrist. The girl whose full, up-tipped breasts made his mouth water to taste them and his hips rock to and fro uncontrollably, like a dog near a bitch in heat. The girl with the hair that had stolen all of the colors of the fiery sunset he missed so much.

He shoved his other hand down the front of his jeans, gripping himself tight at the head and then sliding up and down the swollen girth with short, hard pumps. The hypnotic beat of "Closer" by Nine Inch Nails thumped throughout the room, and his blood pulsed heavier through his veins with every beat. His fangs were bared on a hiss and his gut ached with a razor sharp hunger he had yet to experience in all of his long years — until now. But he knew it was his eyes that would surely give him away for what he truly was. From the feel of them, they would be glowing bright and eerie from under his heavy brows, the color a vivid topaz, as he tracked every move she made with an intensity that human men did not possess. Yet he couldn't bring himself to *not* watch her.

Besides, she never looked at him when she was dancing.

She was alone in the empty room of the club on the other side of the glass, her back up against a single silver pole that ran from floor to ceiling. Facing him, she writhed against that cold metal that she could work like nobody's business. But she wasn't dancing anymore. She'd stopped dancing a while ago.

Instead, one of her dainty hands was shoved up under her short, gold skirt, and although he couldn't see it, he knew that she was touching herself. Something she'd never done before; at least not for him. Her other hand was on her bare breast, manipulating the soft flesh and then pinching the dusky nipple. Her skimpy top had long since been removed as part of her striptease.

As the end of the song rose to a throbbing crescendo, she threw her head back and cried out, her body convulsing as she made herself come while he watched. Her face contorted into an erotic mien, lost somewhere between pleasure and pain and made all the more beautiful for it.

He cried out with her, his forehead smashing into the glass as his body jacked towards her instinctively. But even though he was hard as a fucking rock and rubbing himself raw, he couldn't get off. And he knew he wouldn't be able to, not until he was inside of a woman's tight sheath, whether it be hers or another's.

She wobbled in her stiletto heels as her legs gave out and she slid down the stripper pole to sit on the floor. His hand was still fisted around his cock, and he squeezed it way too hard as he collapsed to his knees, wishing he could just rip the fucking thing off. But honestly he barely felt the pain he was causing himself. He couldn't feel anything over the burn of his screaming muscles as they cramped and twisted around the acid in his veins.

He lifted his head at the same time that she lifted hers, and they stared at each other through the glass for the first time. Her sapphire blue eyes were large in her pale face; the purplish circles underneath making them appear even brighter than normal. As she stared at him, a single fat tear slid down her flawless cheek, and he pressed his forehead to the glass again as he watched it fall.

He wanted to go to her. He wanted to gently wipe that tear from her delicate face. Then he wanted to rip that flimsy excuse of a skirt off of her and bury his aching cock in her warmth as he sank his fangs deep into that slender throat. He groaned aloud at the thought of feeding from her while he fucked her senseless. He swore he could almost taste her from behind the glass. But he couldn't do any of those things, because he was trapped in this goddamned, vampire-proof viewing box with his jeans hanging open and his cock jutting out of his hand like some kind of animal.

Gritting his teeth against the pain that scorched through his body like hot acid, he slapped his palm against the glass. "Help me!" he snarled.

She blinked once, slowly, her eyelids appearing heavy. Lifting her hand from beneath her skirt, she stared at it for a moment with a frown marring her pretty features before it dropped onto her lap, like she didn't understand what it had just been doing.

Christian folded forward as the fire in his blood surged across his abdomen and down into his balls. Releasing his throbbing cock with a hiss of pain, his other hand joined the first to pound on the glass. "Open this fucking thing!"

Her bemused gaze wandered to the side, and then drifted over the entire wall of glass, as if she were searching for something but didn't quite know what it was. She closed her eyes again for so long that he began to wonder if she'd fallen asleep, but then she seemed to rouse, and slowly pushed herself to her feet. She teetered unsteadily for a moment in her ridiculous shoes. Gathering up her top that she'd taken off during her dance, she stumbled across the room and out the door in the back. The music shut off as soon as the door closed behind her.

She couldn't see him, he realized. She couldn't fucking see him.

Rearing back, he threw his head forward and smashed it into the glass wall so hard it should've shattered. But it only formed an outline of the shape of his head, and then snapped back into its former shape as soon as he pulled away.

"AHHHHHH!!!" He screamed until his voice gave out.

Collapsing onto his side, he curled up into a ball with his arms wrapped around his middle to ride out the pain. It would subside after a bit, enough so he could move about freely, though it never completely went away. And he knew that it wouldn't until his body had what it craved.

He needed blood. And he needed sex. Physically needed it. Thanks to whatever the hell had happened to him after his creator, Luukas, had been taken. Before he'd been swiped up off the street near his home in Seattle and locked in this hellhole, he'd been going through six to eight females a night — every night — for the past seven *years*. He'd fuck them, feed from them, and then send them home to their families. Safe and sound. And he'd discovered real quick that if he tried to change up that routine, he suffered the consequences. The urges would become more and more intense until he was a danger to anyone around him. Thank the gods Seattle was a large city with a rising population and had plenty of human females. And that vampires were immune to STD's.

And now, if he wasn't mistaken, he'd been locked in this place for weeks. Long enough that it wasn't only his body that was suffering. He was beginning to feel like he was losing his mind, losing what was left of his humanity, and turning into the mindless creature that the horror movies always depicted those like him to be.

Of course it was all because he'd lowered his guard and gotten himself captured because he was too busy thinking about his dick, rather than what he should've been doing.

Keeping to his usual nightly routine, he'd left his apartment building to hook up with a new girl at a nearby strip club instead of helping Dante and Shea prepare for Luukas' rescue mission. He and the other Hunters were supposed to join Nikulas and Aiden across the Canadian border. They'd only just discovered that the psycho who had taken their leader had returned to the area with Luukas in tow.

He'd let down his friends who'd been depending on him. And worse, he'd failed his creator. The male that had taken him under his wing and taught him what it was to be a male worthy of calling himself such.

He wasn't worthy of anything or anyone these days.

Christian groaned and flopped over onto his back, the pain in his body overriding everything else as it always did. God help the first female he came across when he finally got the fuck out of here. And he *would* get out of here, somehow. He only hoped the first woman he came across wasn't his dancing girl with the fiery hair, because the odds of her surviving that encounter were pretty much shit. At the thought of hurting her, a sharp, stabbing pain pierced through his heart and added to his agony.

He wouldn't mean to hurt her. He wouldn't. But in the state he was in, he didn't think he'd be able to avoid it.

And didn't that just suck balls.

2

Ryan left the performance room of the abandoned club and staggered out into the hallway. Glancing to the left, she struggled to focus on what she was seeing. An exit sign glowed over the door at that end of the hall, and before she thought about what she was doing, she lurched towards it. Even in her current state of mind, she comprehended that she needed to get away from this place, and fast. The high she was riding would wear off soon, and then she'd be well and truly fucked. When that happened, the only thing she'd be able to focus on was the mega flu-like sickness that would rapidly descend upon her, along with the reality of her psychosis that would come back with a vengeance.

A wave of helpless frustration rose up to chip at the shield of numbness that filled her, and a sob caught in her throat. She wished she had the courage to take herself out of this sorry excuse for a life. But whenever she'd convinced herself that she'd finally gotten up the guts to slit her wrists or dump a bunch of pills down her throat, something stopped her. She didn't know what. And she didn't know why. But she wished it would just let her go. She didn't know how much longer she could take this sorry excuse for a life.

However, the way she was heading, she would OD any day now. Not on purpose. But it was getting harder and harder to reach the numbness where she couldn't feel anything anymore. Couldn't hear the voices. And if she were to be completely honest with herself, she was looking forward to it.

As she neared the door, the image of a younger, male version of herself made her smile. Her little brother. His memory faded and her smile faded from her face.

She wondered what he looked like now. Was he still in school? Were their parents healthy and alive? Ryan would never know. As much as she missed him and her mom and dad, she could never go back there.

Pinpricks suddenly stabbed her scalp and her head was wrenched backwards by her hair. She tried to pry away the offending hand that was gripped around her loose bun without much success. Thrown off balance in her stupid heels, she stumbled backwards until a brawny arm caught her around the ribs. It yanked her back against a wide chest and the large protruding stomach of someone who enjoyed their *cervaza* and tacos way too much. A sour, spicy stench leaked from his pores, mingling with the ever-present smell of unwashed armpits.

"Where do you think you are going, *mi corazon?*" The voice was slightly accented and higher than you would expect from such a large man, but was one she knew all too well.

With one hand still twisted in her upswept hair and the other uncomfortably close to her bare breasts, he turned her around and marched her in front of him down the hall and to the stairway. Boards creaked as they felt their way down the old steps. A loose bulb swung overhead, casting an eerie light that was barely enough to see by as he hauled her down the narrow passage.

"Let me go," she slurred when they reached the bottom. "I can walk by myself."

He chuckled and tightened his grip on her, the hand on her ribcage sliding up to caress the underside of the full curve of her breast. Her stomach heaved. Whether from his touch, his stench, or the effects of coming down from her high, she didn't know. In retrospect, she wished she'd put her top back on, not that it covered much, but it was better than nothing. It still dangled from her fingers. If he would let her go just for a second...

Emboldened by her lack of protests, he slowed his pace and turned her towards the wall so he could shove her face against the cracked paint. His hand tightened painfully in her hair and tears filled her eyes as he twisted her head out of his way. Wet lips slurped against the side of her neck and she felt the bulge in his pants hardening against her ass. He tweaked her nipple, then slid his hand down her side. A sharp slap stung her ass cheek through her sorry excuse for a skirt and she cried out in surprise and pain.

"Think you can just walk on out of here?" he murmured, squeezing her ass so hard she was going to have bruises. "I own you, *chica*. You're not going anywhere."

Ryan's stomach lurched again and she prayed she wouldn't vomit all over his arm. He would beat her bloody for the offense, if he were allowed to get that far. She wondered what was making him so ballsy now. This wasn't going to end well for him if the drugs wore off, and he knew it. And then she wondered why she cared. "Let go of me," she gritted out.

A chilly touch slithered across her skin like a lover's caress, and her eyes widened in fear.

It was too late.

"Let go," a voice whispered in the air next to them. "Release her," another one breathed from the other side.

He either didn't hear them, or maybe he chose to ignore them, idiot that he was. His wet mouth slobbered down over her shoulder, leaving a trail of sticky saliva in its wake. Ryan squeezed her eyes shut, but it didn't keep back the flow of tears.

They were back. The voices. They were back. She couldn't decide whether to be relieved or terrified.

A loud screech suddenly rent the air, and she was slammed into the wall as her attacker released her and jumped away, crossing himself as he spun around in a circle, searching for the thing that had made such a horrible noise. "Dios mío!" Grabbing her by the upper arm, he took off down the hall again, dragging her along behind him.

Unseen entities kept pace with them, rushing past in a blur of noise and wind, only to turn around and do it again. When he still refused to acknowledge them, one shoved him from behind.

He yanked Ryan to him and gripped her around the throat with one large hand. "Knock it off, or I will break her neck. Do you hear me, *demonios*?"

"Kill him."

"Run."

"Blood. Kill."

The voices urged her to defend herself, or maybe they were just telling her what they wanted to do. They got stuck on repeat and the words got mixed up, echoing around and around until she slapped her hands over her ears. It didn't help. They were in her head.

He backed away, holding her in front of him like a human shield. It wouldn't save him if they decided to physically intervene.

Go away. Go away. Go away. She didn't know why she bothered to pray. It had never worked before. There was only one thing that helped: Shooting herself so full of opiates that her receptors shut down.

They arrived at a large steel door, and he whipped out a set of keys to unlock the large padlock. Yanking the heavy door open, he slid his hand around to the back of her neck and shoved her inside so hard she twisted her ankle and sprawled face first across the bare concrete floor. Pulling a couple of plastic bags from his pocket, he tossed them at her and slammed the door shut with a loud clank.

Ryan lay there, overwhelmed by the voices that never went away unless she was chasing the dragon. But a rustling sound just behind her had her scrambling up onto her knees. Grabbing the bags off the floor, she held them tight to her chest. Her eyes were wild and desperate as they landed on the young dark-haired girl in front of her.

The girl held her small hands up in front of her. "It's okay, miss. It's just me. I was just coming to help you."

"Jose." Ryan exhaled on a breath of relief. Holding out her hand to the girl, she waited until she'd taken it and then pulled her back into the corner with her. Staring daggers at the other four women in the room leaning against the walls in various forms of undress, she warned them away without having to speak a word.

Jose, or Josefina, was a fourteen-year-old girl. She'd been traded by an uncle of hers to buy passage across the border, and now the sons of bitches that ran this place whored her young body out to any man, or woman, who would pay. Even American tourists came across the border from Southern California to enjoy all of the attractions to be had in the red district of Tijuana, including underage girls.

They both got through each day the same way.

Ryan was shaking so bad by now that Jose had to take the bag from her. "It's okay. I'll help you." Shaking out the contents, she dumped the powder into the small tin bowl, added the water, and lit a lighter underneath until it was dissolved. She dropped a small wad of cotton into the bowl, and stabbed the needle of the syringe through it to suck up the liquid.

Taking Ryan's top out of her jerky fingers, Jose pulled her arm out straight and tied it around her upper arm. She tapped until she found a vein. "Are you ready?" she asked.

By this time, the voices were a cacophony of noise, shouting at her all at once until she felt like screaming right along with them. Her jaw was clenched against the rolling of her stomach and her cheeks were streaked with tears. Tears for the girl in front of her who was little more than a child. And tears for herself.

She nodded. "Please, Jose..."

Jose inserted the needle with an expertise that no young girl should have. Large, sad brown eyes glanced up at her. "It's okay. I know...I know..."

As she slowly pushed the plunger down, Ryan told her, "Thank you. You can have the..." She didn't know if she ever finished the sentence, for the drug took affect then, and her body became weightless as her eyes rolled back and her body slouched against the wall.

The voices faded away little by little until she couldn't hear them anymore. And she was gone.

3

Aiden stopped typing as a delicious scent drifted over to him through the open door of Luukas' office. Slamming the laptop closed, he was at the front door of the apartment within the space of a heartbeat. Feminine laughter sounded from the other side, and he yanked the door open and grabbed the nearest female. Pulling her tight up against him, he kissed her soundly on her luscious mouth as the other two walked past them and into the apartment, continuing their conversation as if they hadn't just lost one of their group. The woman he held squealed as the bag of groceries she was carrying got squished between them.

"Hallo, poppet." He let his eyes roam over her beloved face.

Grace laughed up at him. "How do you always know I'm coming?"

Ah. His female always knew exactly what to say to get him all riled up. One eyebrow lifted. "Well, you're not coming yet, luv, but I can take care of that just as soon as I finish finding the location of this van for Luukas." Grabbing a handful of her thick auburn hair, he lifted it to his nose. He loved her hair. It was long and soft and felt wonderful as it tickled his bare chest and belly.

She smacked him on the arm as a warm blush stole up her cheeks. "Dude! There are other people here!" she whispered.

Narrowing his eyes, he told her, "What have I told you about calling me 'dude'?" He kissed her again, smacked her on her voluptuous bum, and then rubbed the sore cheek. His hand may have drifted down between her legs a bit, feeling her womanly heat until she was moaning and pressing her hips into his erection.

Much as he wanted to drag her to their bedroom and ease the unbearable tightness he now had in his pants, he had some work to do first. Pulling away with a silent groan of regret, there was a teasing glint in his eyes as he said, "Grace, luv, there are *people* here."

Rolling her eyes, she sighed longingly and then left him to go join Keira and Emma at the kitchen counter.

As he watched her walk away, he felt something stir inside of him, and it wasn't just the unnatural lust he felt for her that was always simmering just beneath the surface. No, this was something else entirely. Closing his eyes and gritting his teeth, Aiden waited until his demon settled down again.

Stand down, old man.

After a few moments, it did.

Waano, the demon that now shared space inside of him thanks to a demented female's plan to take over the world, had been rather quiet since he'd failed in his attempt to goad her into killing his host — aka, Aiden — and therefore releasing him. At least in theory. They really didn't know for certain if that would have worked. Aiden was glad, as he was rather attached to his body, host or not, and would prefer to stay inside of it.

Luckily, Leeha was dead now, taken out by a werewolf friend of theirs. Aiden had added her head to his collection as a memento, for sentimental reasons. At one time he'd been quite enraptured by the female, in spite of her tendencies to run amok. Of course, that was before he'd met Grace.

Not for the first time, he wondered how her death had affected the rest of the vampires she'd possessed. It was assumed they were still alive. Otherwise Luukas, the master vampire who had created them all, would have been impacted by their deaths. Especially if they'd keeled over all at once.

At least that's what they all assumed. But then again, after Aiden had become a host for one of Leeha's demons, it had been her blood that had reanimated him, and therefore her blood that had called to him. Not Luukas'. So maybe their deaths wouldn't affect him anymore? Luukas had wanted to kill him the first time he'd seen him after Aiden had acquired his other personality. Not exactly how a master vampire would normally react when seeing one of his own. There'd been no attachment between them anymore.

However, as fate would have it, Luukas' essence flowed through him once again, since Aiden had nearly been decapitated and was only here at all thanks to Grace's healing magic and Luukas' powerful blood. Aiden still didn't know how Luukas had overcome his urge to kill him in order to save him.

"Hey, Aid! You gonna stand over there daydreaming all day? Or are you gonna come help us out with this?" Nikulas asked from the office doorway.

Aiden ran his eyes up and down Grace one last time and then headed towards his friend. "Don't get your knickers in a twist, mate. I'm coming."

Like Nik hadn't just been giving Emma one hell of a greeting himself.

Plopping back down into the office chair, Aiden flipped open his laptop and resumed typing. "Where was I? Oh yes. Right...here." Turning the Mac around, he showed the screen to the bloody Estonian bastard hovering next to him — aka his best friend. "The van that took the commander is parked in this empty lot down in Tacoma."

"Cool. Who owns that lot?"

"A bloke by the name of Jared Smith. But he's not the one we're looking for."

"What makes you think he's not?" Luukas turned from the window where he'd been listening to their conversation as he stared out at the lights of Seattle. He had quite a view from the floor-to-ceiling window of his high-rise apartment, and it seemed to calm him. He stared out those windows quite a lot.

"Well," Aiden told him. "I could be completely off base here, but being that he's ninety-two and a retired dock worker, I sincerely doubt he's able bodied enough to handle a beast like Dante."

Luukas' grey eyes were sharp as he nodded. "I agree. They most likely just dumped the van there." He glanced out the window again. "The sun will be rising soon. Let's plan a drive down there first thing tomorrow night. We can check out the vehicle, see what we see."

"I'd like to get another team together to search for Shea sometime soon also," Aiden requested.

"We've been there three times, man," Nik chimed in. "She ain't there."

"I disagree, mate. She has to be. We saw nothing indicating she left the area, and I saw her with my own eyes. Plus, you wouldn't believe the maze of tunnels Leeha has under that mountain. It is very possible she's still down there. Somewhere."

Luukas cleared his throat. "We'll get that set up after we check out this van. Nikulas and I can continue with Dante's search, while you organize another search team. Just make sure the vampires you choose from the area have sufficient training to handle the situation."

"Sure," Nik agreed and Aiden nodded. They all knew it would take an act of the gods, or his mate's life being in danger, for Luukas to go back to that mountain.

"What about us?" Keira, Luukas' mate and Emma's sister, asked from the kitchen where the girls were making their last meal of the night.

Crossing his arms over his chest, Luukas narrowed his eyes, daring her to argue with him before he'd even spoken. "You will stay here. Where I know you'll be safe."

Aiden pretended to be engrossed in the map on his laptop and hid his smirk, knowing full well what was coming.

Keira faced off against her overprotective mate. "I want to come with you."

"No."

"Yes."

Emma opened her mouth to chime in, but Nik pointed at her with a warning look and cut her off. "Don't even think about it. You're not coming either." She grinned at him impishly and went back to chopping vegetables, but Aiden knew that she had her own ways of convincing Nik to do what she wanted. He'd inadvertently heard her "convincing" him a few times when he'd innocently walked past their bedroom door.

Grace, having only lived here for a few days and being the newest addition to the group, glanced back and forth between them before turning her attention to Aiden. "I do hope you don't think you can order *me* around like that."

Gathering up his stuff, he told her, "I wouldn't dream of it, luv. I have far better ways to keep you in your place. Now come, let's go home."

She glanced around at all the food prep going on in front of her. "But what about dinner?"

"I'll feed you. Later." With a wave at the guys, he slid his free arm around her and started ushering her out the door. Turning around, he gave Keira a nod and winked at Emma. "See you at home, poppet."

Nik's low growl followed him out of the apartment.

Grace laughed and shook her head. "Why do you do that to your friend? You know it drives him insane."

"Which is exactly why I do it," he grinned.

4

"Get up, *puta*." Rough hands grabbed Ryan and hauled her to her feet. They shoved her towards the modest wash area in the back corner of the cell. "Clean up. It's time to work."

The woman was nearly as large and brawny as her husband, with a deeper voice. Ryan didn't know either of their names, and she didn't ask. It wouldn't matter anyway.

Another shove nearly sent her sprawling across the floor again.

She wondered if the woman had found out that her husband had been groping her when he took her back to the cell earlier, and if that was why she was being so mean to her. Then again, she was always pretty mean. Except for the night she'd found Ryan hiding in an alley, scared, alone, and desperate for something to make the voices go away. She'd wanted her to come with her, so she'd been nice that night, although it was obvious she thought the *gringa* was crazy. But not so crazy that she wouldn't bring in customers.

Ryan stumbled into the small bathroom before she was pushed again and closed the door behind her, sliding the lock firmly into place. The tar Jose had shot her up with was still in her system, so it couldn't have been that long ago since her last "show".

Her head weighed a hundred thousand pounds, but she managed to hold it steady long enough to check out her reflection in the mirror. The girl looking back at her startled her for a minute before she realized she was staring at herself. She studied the blue eyes, almost disconcerting in their pop of color. Mostly because the pupils were like pinpoints in the midst of all that blue. The whites were bloodshot. Dark circles bruised the tender skin underneath.

The cheekbones were more prominent than she remembered, the jawline sharper. Pale lips moved, and she realized she was muttering something to herself, something important. But when she tried to listen, the lips stopped.

Who was this girl in the mirror? She should know her, but she felt like she was looking at a stranger. And it made her inexplicably sad.

Her hair was still pretty though. The bright copper color not quite as lively as it used to be, but still unusual. Of course, it was her hair that had gotten her into this mess. It made her stand out in a crowd, especially here in Mexico.

Before she'd been found by the *matron* and *patron*, she'd been earning some good money dancing in various strip clubs in the touristy part of town. The money had been enough to pay her part of the rent in the little house she'd rented with some of the other girls, and it was enough to keep her well supplied with her heroin habit.

But that pastime had soon gotten her fired and unable to hold up her end, she was kicked out into the streets almost immediately thereafter. No, it was more than a pastime now. It was a full-blown addiction. She hated it. Hated how it made her feel nothing. Hated how it had turned her away from everyone she'd loved. But she couldn't not do it. And not because of the sickness that would descend almost immediately now if she ran out. She feared the loss of her sanity if she stopped, for then she'd be able to hear the voices. The voices that were constantly hovering around in her head, just waiting to drive her insane.

Lifting her hand, she tried to rub the knots out of the ball of anxiety in the center of her chest.

They always came back — the voices, or demons as the *patron* called them, or whatever the hell they were. Ever since they'd found her when she was fifteen, they always came back.

She'd been in her little suburban school in northern California when it had happened the first time. In algebra class maybe? Someone or something had screamed, "Don't go!" right in her ear. Jumping out of her desk, she'd looked around for the person that had screamed, and wondered why no one else was reacting to what she had heard. Why the hell weren't they jumping up to help as she had? Why were they all just sitting there looking at her like she'd lost her mind?

It took them a while to convince her that she had.

Turning away from the memory of the girl with the haunted eyes, she started running water in the old bathtub. It was best to forget her. That innocent girl didn't exist in those eyes anymore, and never would again. She reached down to remove her shirt, and realized she didn't have one on. So she shimmied out of her skirt and G-string and left them lying on the floor.

Lowering herself into the lukewarm water, her mind wandered to her most recent "customer". He must have a lot of money to afford private performances, for he had been here a lot the last few weeks. She frowned as that tight feeling in her chest stirred inside of her again. No. That didn't feel right. The vibes she got from him when she was dancing almost felt as if she were torturing him instead of pleasuring him.

Was he here against his will too? It seemed plausible in her state of mind. He was in a lot of pain. She knew this even though she couldn't see him through the one-way mirror in the performance room. She also knew that it was always the same guy. She could feel him there, could feel the weight of his eyes on her as she danced. But not just watching. His emotions were so much more than she'd ever felt from anyone before. It was more than appreciation. More than lust. It was almost like he was...hungry. Starving...

An angry knock on the door shook her from her thoughts of the man, and she tried to hurry and finish, but her limbs didn't want to cooperate with what her anxious brain was telling them to do. Another angry knock was accompanied by a string of curse words spoken in Spanish.

"I'm coming!" Ryan shouted. At least she thought she had shouted.

Lifting herself out of the now chilly water, she grabbed the meager towel allowed to the girls and patted herself dry. Her skin, in direct contrast to the numbness she felt inside, was too sensitive for a vigorous rubdown. Behind the door hung a selection of clothing, each more ridiculous than the last, and all too revealing to wear anywhere but working the pole. Ryan grabbed the first thing she saw — a cut-off jersey shirt with orange stripes around the sleeves and a big number "10" on the front, along with a matching thong and knee socks with matching orange stripes along the elastic. White platform shoes completed the ensemble.

She was Sporty Spice today.

Ryan felt nothing as she turned to the stranger in the mirror and pulled her hair out of its messy updo, then fixed it into pigtails. All she needed was a lollypop to complete the fantasy, but they weren't allowed to have anything sweet here. They barely fed their girls at all. Some kind of grainy mush and water was offered to them twice a day if their stomachs could handle it, and that was it. But the drugs...the drugs were abundant. She guessed it was easier to keep them compliant that way.

As soon as she opened the door, the *matron* dug her bony fingers into Ryan's thin arm and threw her halfway across the room. Out of the corner of her eye, she saw her only friend,

Josefina, huddled in the corner with her head down. She was very still, trying her best not to bring attention to herself, and the other women were gone. Catching herself in the doorway, Ryan turned around and asked, "Where is everybody?"

The matron spun her back around. "No questions, *puta*. You know where to go." The door slammed in her face and she jumped. She willed herself to move before she was pushed around again, but eventually she realized she was alone in the dimly lit hall. Her head turned in slow motion and her eyes widened in dawning horror as she realized the *matron* hadn't come out of the cell with her, but was still in there with Jose.

Ryan approached the door and pressed her face against the window. Her blood froze in her veins at the scene playing out before her, and then the numbness faded and her emotions returned in a rush. The *matron* was standing over Jose, a leather belt in her hands as she prodded and then kicked the young girl with her foot. Jose huddled in the corner, trying to make herself as small a target as possible. Her eyes were wide and filled with unshed tears as she caught sight of Ryan.

She could feel Jose's fear like it was her own. Banging her hand on the glass, she tried to distract the woman from the child. "You bitch! Leave her the fuck alone!" She grabbed the handle and rattled the door. "Leave her alone!"

The belt rose and whistled through the air as it came down on Jose's tender flesh with a loud crack. Ryan flinched and Jose yelped, drawing her knees in closer and trying to protect her face and stomach. The belt came down again, catching her across the outside of her thigh. A large welt swelled up where she'd been hit, the brown skin turning white at first and then darkening to a purplish-red.

The *matron* lifted her arm to swing again, her eyes wild with bloodlust and the sick pleasure she got from beating those smaller and weaker than her.

"I'll fucking kill you! You hear me? I'll kill you!" Ryan fought with the rickety handle of the door but it was dead bolted with her key from the inside. She screamed with Jose as the belt cracked across her back, the thin slip she was wearing doing nothing to protect her.

A red haze of rage and pain came down over Ryan's eyes, blurring everything in her vision except for the bitch with the belt. Seething with hatred, she focused on the sick woman that got pleasure out of the pain of children. She never came after the adult women, only the young girls. But this was the first time she'd gone after Josefina.

Ryan nearly choked on her wrath as she watched her young friend being abused, her pain becoming Ryan's pain. "I'll fucking kill you," she snarled.

"Yes." The whispered reply was accompanied by a soft caress on her cheek, her shoulder, down her upper arm.

"Yes," Ryan consented, and the touch was gone as suddenly as it had appeared.

The *matron* raised her arm to strike again. She was covered in sweat both from the heat and her exertions and she was beginning to get tired, but the gleam in her eyes as she gazed down at her victim told Ryan that she wasn't planning on stopping anytime soon.

Ryan smiled as those crazy eyes flew wide. The *matron's* body suddenly seized, the belt falling from her hand as her other hand grasped at the material covering her chest.

A few seconds later, she fell dead to the floor with a loud thump as her skull cracked off of the cement floor, leaving a smear of blood on the cement. Jose raised swollen eyes to Ryan and smiled. Ryan smiled back.

Leaning over, Jose spit on the body lying next to her in disgust.

5

Christian heard the door open and close at the back of the room. Gritting his teeth, he managed to flop over onto his stomach. He lay there for a second, absorbing the pain that was shooting though his body. Pulling his legs underneath him, he struggled to his hands and knees as his muscles cramped and screamed in protest. His nerve endings were so sensitive, the slightest movement felt like flames licking across his skin, but he had to see. He had to see if it was the female, come to entice and torment him some more.

Lifting his head, he blinked the sweat out of his eyes and tried to control his breathing and work through the pain. It was her. She was back.

His fangs exploded from his gums at the sight of her sauntering towards him in what should have been a ridiculous getup. But on her, it was only incredibly sexy. She made her way slowly into the room in her white platform boots, looking slightly confused, and Christian noticed for the first time that no music was playing. The music always started as soon as she entered the room. How was she going to dance with no music? Because he *had* to see her dance, no matter the agony it caused him.

A horrific sound rent the air, startling him: A male's cry of pain and grief coming from another location in the building. The female paused only briefly when she heard it, and then picked up her pace until she was right in front of him on the other side of the strange glass. She knelt down until she was at eye level with him. Lifting one hand, she placed her palm on the glass between them and shut her eyes. This close, he saw her eyebrows were the same pastel orange as her hair.

"I can feel you," she said in a strange singsong voice. "I can feel your lust, and your pain. But I don't know why you hurt because I can't see you." She opened her eyes and looked right at him. "I can't hear you either. But I know you're there."

"Please," Christian hissed. He wasn't sure what he was asking for. For her to get him out? Or for her to run away before he brutally ripped open her throat and drained her dry? He'd never hurt anyone since he'd been turned, unless they'd threatened his maker or his friends. And in that case, they'd totally deserved it. How would he live with himself if he ever hurt this gentle female? It didn't matter what he was going through. Hurting her was not okay.

She turned her head slightly and nodded, like she was listening to something or someone he couldn't see. Christian glanced around and tried to quiet his rasping breaths so he could listen, but he couldn't pick out what she was hearing. He struck out at the glass in frustration. He was a fucking vampire! How could she hear something that he couldn't?

Suddenly she smiled. "Yes," she said.

Her long pigtails blew forward and back in a sudden gust of wind he couldn't feel from the other side of the barrier between them. It never occurred to him until later that there was nowhere for a breeze to have come from. There were no windows, and never once had he heard or felt an A/C unit kick on.

Her smile widened, showing straight, white teeth with the slightest gap between the two in the front. "Hang in there, soldier," she told him. "We'll get you out." Her features twisted in disgust. "They can't hold us here anymore." Then her eyes became worried, skittering around on the floor in front of her. "It's okay. I'll be okay. I'll deal with it."

Who the *fuck* was she talking to? She was the only one here beside him, but he had the uneasy feeling she wasn't talking to either of those two choices.

A loud "clank" sounded off to his left and the unbreakable glass in front of him lifted an inch off the floor and slammed back down. Then it started lifting again, and this time it kept going. Dropping his head back, Christian could see it rolling back over the metal top of the box he was in. It moved at a snail's pace, but it was moving, lifting off of the floor in front of him like a garage door. In no time at all, he'd be able to slide underneath of it.

Cold fear flashed through him, dousing the fires that were burning him. Not for himself, but for the female. No one would be able to save her once he was out. And he would kill her if he got to her, of that he had no doubt.

Bending to the side, she peered through the opening at the bottom of the wall. It was at about four inches and rising steadily. "Ah. There you are," she said as his hands came into view. "Don't be afraid."

How did she know he was afraid?

"Get away!" he rasped. "Get the fuck away from me!" When she didn't immediately obey him, he scuttled back away from the opening. The farther away from her he got, the more his body rebelled until he was coughing and gasping with the pain. "Please," he sputtered. "Get away. Hurry." The acid burned through his veins until he felt like his organs were going to incinerate.

The wall had risen to about eight inches now.

She reached under the glass. Her hand was slender and graceful. When she didn't feel him there, she bent over until she could see. "Why are you way back there? Come on. We're getting you out."

Why wasn't she running away screaming at the mere sight of him? He was panting through his open mouth, his long fangs fully exposed, and he could tell by the way his eyes felt that they were as bright as emergency flares. She had to see that he wasn't a normal man.

When he didn't move, she sat up with a jerk of impatience. As she did so, her ponytails swung back and forth again, and Christian caught the faintest whiff of her scent. He froze where he was, his fangs bared in a snarl. He took a deeper inhale. Gooseflesh broke out all over his body that had nothing to do with the temperature in the room.

Gods! He'd never smelled anything like the scent of the female in front of him. A low growl echoed off the walls and he jerked his head around searching for this new threat, until he realized it was coming from him.

Lord help him. He was well and truly fucked.

The wall continued to rise, and although he fought the blood lust with everything in him, it was no use. Moving too fast for her to track, he was underneath it and launching himself at the girl. She grunted as he landed hard on top of her, his weight knocking the breath from her lungs. One of his hands slid behind her head, protecting it from hitting the hard floor, and the other arm was beneath her waist with his hand sprawled across her bare ass. He held her tight to him and ground his hips into hers as that mouth-watering scent of hers rose up to surround him like a cloud.

He tried so hard to fight it. He really did. Whispering, "I'm so sorry," he reared back, preparing to strike.

Quick as a cobra, he went for the pounding pulse in her throat, but he wasn't fast enough. He'd barely nicked her skin when unseen hands gripped him by the shoulders and legs. They yanked him up and off of her and tossed him across the room. He landed hard on his back and slid into the far wall.

What. The. Fuck.

With a roar of frustration, Christian flipped his body forward and back up onto his feet. He ran towards her at vamp speed, only to be deterred again. This time, the hands didn't just toss him, but held him spread-eagle against the wall. No matter how hard he struggled, he couldn't free himself. Something between a scream of anger and a cry of heartbreak tore from his throat and echoed around the room.

Moving slowly, the female got to her feet. Her eyes never leaving him as she lifted one of those graceful hands and touched the side of her neck. Her fingers came away streaked with her blood. A few drops trickled down over her collarbone.

Christian's tongue touched the tip of one fang, then shot out to lick her blood from his lower lip. His eyes nearly rolled back in his head as the sweetest ambrosia he'd ever tasted tickled his taste buds just enough to tease him.

MINE.

She tasted like the finest liquor, the sweetest honey, the juiciest pear. But underneath all that, he could also taste why she was acting so strange. There was some type of opiate in her blood, along with something else, something he'd never tasted before. It wasn't just a normal speedball she was on. Exotic dancers were, after all, some of his favorite pastimes, and many got through their shifts with a little help. He knew the taste well, although he didn't much care for the aftereffects.

Her eyes grew larger with every second as they ran over his face, down his body to his muscles straining beneath his shirt, to the bulge in his jeans, and back up to his face. She took a few steps closer, blinking her eyes hard. She was finally seeing him. Really seeing him. Crossing her arms over her chest and hugging herself, she studied him much as he had been studying her all of this time.

Christian tracked her every tiny movement. He was running on pure instinct now, waiting for the opportunity to break free of his bonds and strike. His body warred between needing her blood and needing to be inside of her. Licking another drop of her blood from his lips, his cock pulsed painfully and a surge of strength shot through him, his need for her overcoming the agony he was in. Lunging forward, he managed to free one arm from the invisible hold. With a roar of triumph, he threw himself forward again.

The female jumped and stumbled backwards. Swallowing hard, she appeared to finally realize the danger she was in by staying there. Dropping her arms, she spun around on her heel and rushed from the room as Christian cried out after her in agony and need. She disappeared out the doorway and ran to the left. Less than a minute later, he was suddenly free to move.

He was on her trail in a flash, following her down the hallway to a door marked *"salida"*. He didn't stop when he reached it, but threw his body into and through the barrier separating him from his female.

Blinding hot sunshine blasted him all over, and Christian screamed as he backtracked as fast as he could. Even so, small fires had erupted on his face and arms just in the short time it took him to get back inside. Acting quickly, he yanked his shirt up over his head and used it to smother the flames, then pulled the burnt cotton back down again and collapsed against the wall.

Son of a bitch!

He threw his head back, smashing it into the plaster behind him. He was trapped. And his female was running around in nothing but a thong and a cropped up jersey shirt with her tits practically hanging out. Anything could happen to her out there. Wherever "there" happened to be. Anyone could get a hold of her. She could be raped. Murdered.

A surge of possessiveness hit him at the thought of any other male laying his hands on her, the feeling so strong it almost made him pass out.

MINE.

The thought didn't strike him as odd from where he was standing. She was the only other being in his world at the moment. And he was *hungry*.

Christian glanced towards the exit again. There was no way he could risk going back out there. Especially not in the condition he was in. He'd been starved for what...weeks? Months? He didn't even know. Kept in that fucking room and tortured with her semi-nude form, yet unable to get to her. To smell her. To feel her.

He hadn't gone this long without sex since Luukas had been taken and this strange affliction had overtaken him. He fucking hated it. Hated this need he had, hated using females like he did. Hated this obsessiveness with them that distracted from everything else that was going on in his life. Important things. Like doing his job as a Hunter. If it weren't for his fucking dick, he wouldn't be in this mess to begin with.

Sucking in a ragged breath, his mind veered back to the girl that was now roaming around a strange town in her stripper-wear. He'd have to go find her. As soon as the sun went down, he would go find her. Make sure she was okay, and wipe her memory of what she'd just seen. But before he did that, he would find someone else to feed on. Someone society wouldn't miss if he became a bit overzealous.

No sooner had that thought crossed his mind than he heard a keening cry coming from the opposite direction. Punching up off the floor, Christian was down the hall, down a rickety set of steps, and in front of an open doorway before he realized he'd meant to move. The fact that he was able to do so with barely any pain didn't register as he zeroed in on his next meal.

An overweight, brown-skinned man was sitting on his knees on the floor. He had a dead woman in his lap. She was nearly as large as he was. A quick glance around proved the rest of the room to be empty. Looking closer, he saw the floor was concrete with nothing but thin blankets thrown down to sleep on. What looked to be a small bathroom was in the back of the room. There were no windows except the one in the door, and bars covered the glass there. A deep breath carried the scents of multiple females, including the one he now knew well.

He wasn't in a room, he was in a cell. No wonder she'd escaped as soon as the opportunity had presented itself.

Stepping inside, he waited for the human to notice him. Underneath the sour smell of unwashed skin and the spicy stench of Mexican food, he could smell the blood that pulsed through his veins. It didn't smell near as good as the girl's, even with the drugs in her system, but it would serve his needs. He had to feed, to heal his skin and regain his strength somewhat before he headed out at sunset. There was no telling who or what he might run into.

The man on the floor finally noticed him standing there. His eyes crawled slowly up Christian's large form, from his thick-soled boots to his burned face, and on up to the long fangs, exposed in an aching snarl. "*Dios Mio!*" he muttered. In his shock, he dropped the dead woman onto the floor and crossed himself.

"I'm sincerely sorry about this," Christian told him, but then shrugged one shoulder. "But I'm also pretty fucking sure you hold girls here against their will, so yeah, I'm not really *that* sorry." Joining the man on the floor, he gripped him by the hair and yanked his head back. The man closed his eyes, mumbling what sounded like a prayer in Spanish. He didn't fight back. Didn't struggle to get free.

"I'll try not to kill you," Christian told him. Then he reared back and struck hard. He nearly retched at the first vile mouthful of blood but forced himself to keep drinking. With pure force of will he managed to keep it down. He needed this. He needed to regain his strength and hopefully a little self-control so he could find his female, before another guy like this one did.

6

Josiah rubbed his palm back and forth over the tight curls that covered the top of his head. His steps were short and stilted as he paced the length of Leeha's room in the little country house they'd escaped to.

Everywhere he turned, she was there. Her scent filled his nose. Her dressing gown was still lying on the armchair exactly where she'd left it. One of her sheer gowns — the white one, his favorite — was hanging on the closet door. It was covered in dried blood. Both her own and the blood of the two vampires she'd attempted to kill. Looking at it made him want to puke.

He knew he should pack it all up. Put her things away somewhere. Hell, he could make this into his room. He was the one in charge now. And his love was dead. Beheaded by that fucking werewolf right in front of his eyes.

He could still see her gorgeous, timeless face lying in the grass where it had landed next to his feet. Could still see her lifeless eyes staring up at him, the color and life in them faded to a dull brown. All of the nightmares gone.

Grief welled up inside of him, so hard and fast he dropped to his knees with the power of it. He rolled with it, knowing that was the only thing to do, letting the pain run its course. Josiah stayed on the floor even after he'd gotten his emotions under control again, his mind and body too numb to move.

Showing weakness like this would never do in front of others, but sometimes when he was alone it just snuck up on him. He had loved her utterly and completely for all that she had been. He would've done absolutely anything for her, but now she was gone. Truly gone. Forever. All thanks to those fucking vampires.

Especially that British son of bitch, Aiden.

He still didn't know why she'd been so obsessed with that one. He was nothing but a smartass and a pussy. At least her thing with Luukas he'd understood. Josiah hadn't liked it, but he'd understood it. Luukas was a formidable Master vampire. He controlled the entire continent and all of the colonies within. By his side, Leeha would have controlled it with him. And Josiah knew how power hungry his lady had been. There was nothing she liked better than being in control. Yet Luukas had turned out to be stronger than either of them could've guessed. Seven years of starvation and torture had not broken him, and he'd eventually escaped thanks to that worthless witch, Keira. Josiah had even heard that they were now mated.

Mated to the female who had used her magic to keep him powerless so Leeha could play her sick games. Go figure. Honestly he was surprised Luukas hadn't killed her the first chance he'd gotten.

But now Leeha would never get the chance to show the world just what she was capable of. All of that passion, all of that hunger, all of that beauty and life was just...gone. She could have been the most formidable queen their species had ever seen. And he would have been right there with her. Maybe he would've been on the sidelines, seen as unimportant by the masses, but he would've been there. All that mattered was that *he* would've known how important he was to her.

She'd needed him. She'd needed him to pull her back to earth when her passions had risen too high and clouded her judgment. She'd needed him to take out her frustrations on.

Alone, in her bedroom, she'd enjoyed proving her authority over him. And he'd enjoyed letting her. Though he'd never let her know as much, for then it wouldn't have been fun for her anymore.

If it were the last thing Josiah ever did, he would make them pay for taking her away from him. Every last one of those fucking vampires. And their pet dogs.

A hoarse sob broke free and echoed through the chilly room. He missed her. He missed her so much. He was nothing without her. Nothing! Who would ever understand him the way she had? Who would understand his needs? She had known exactly how to handle him without his having to tell her. It was like she could read his thoughts, knew all of his darkest desires. She'd known what he wanted before he had. No other female would be strong enough, or twisted enough, to feed his cravings so completely. What would he do now? Without her?

Josiah was so lost in his grief that he didn't notice the shadowy form flickering near the window. Its head jerked to the side, much like a bird studying a juicy worm, right before it plucked it from the dirt to feed to its young. Red eyes glowed with a psychotic fervor from within the hazy features, the color getting richer and clearer the longer they watched him grieve. The spectral woman reached out a hand towards him and smiled, then she began to fade.

By the time he lifted his head and pulled up the bottom of his shirt to wipe his eyes, she was gone.

7

Ryan shot into the side alley between the building she'd just left and the one next door. Her hair stuck to her forehead from the intense heat, and she pushed it out of her eyes.

It wasn't real. It wasn't real. It was a hallucination...or something.

Her eyes squinted against the sun, and she glanced back over her shoulder to check that the creature with the glowing eyes and pointed teeth wasn't following her. When all she saw was the empty alley, she went straight to the dumpster and threw back the lid. Rummaging around through the rotting food and plastic bags of old clothing, she found what she was looking for: a pair of shorts and some decent flat leather sandals that were fairly clean. Whenever new girls were brought in, their old clothes were thrown out. It was just another tactic to discourage them from trying to leave. The combination of the lack of clothes and the mind-altering drugs kept the escape attempts to a minimum.

Tossing her ridiculous shoes into the bin, she slid the shorts on over her thong and slid the sandals onto her feet. They were a little big, but they would work.

Closing the lid again, she had to stop for a moment. She ground her teeth together to keep them from chattering, and wrapped her arms around her middle so they wouldn't flail about. Her stomach cramped as bile rose in her throat, and she knew that aching bones, fever, and the rest of the flu-like symptoms would be following within a few hours. She needed to get herself somewhere safe before that happened.

Another sucky symptom of her withdrawals? The voices were back with a vengeance. They swirled around her, screaming things she couldn't understand, things that made no sense. Her head was already aching from the noise, and the hot Mexican sun was making her dizzy. Her stomach rolled and she bent over behind the bin, grateful that her hair was pulled back off her face.

She was almost glad she was feeling so shitty. At least it took her mind off what she thought she'd just seen. Because if her eyes were telling the truth, she'd just released some kind of monster from the room behind the glass.

It wasn't real. It wasn't real. It was just your mind playing tricks on you. He was just a guy. Like all the other guys that came to watch you.

Just a guy who had tried to attack her like some kind of...of... a vampire or something as soon as she'd let him out. She reached up and touched the small wounds on her throat again. No, she hadn't imagined that part.

She hoped Josefina had made it out okay. After the *matron* had fallen to the floor, Jose had dug the keys out of her pocket and unlocked the door. They'd debated looking for the other girls, but Jose had been against it. She'd said they'd figure it out for themselves when they were brought back to the room. Besides, they were total *perras*.

Bitches.

Holding hands, they'd crept down the hall and up the rickety stairs. Quickly and quietly, they'd stolen down the hall towards the exit. But when they'd gotten close to the performance room, Ryan had pulled her young friend to a halt. Jose had tried to get her to come along, but she couldn't move. Feelings of pain and need, anger and hopelessness had pressed down upon her. They were so heavy, her chest had physically ached.

It was him. And he was hurting.

Jose had been excited and scared during their escape, but also determined. Ryan deduced quickly that she would be fine on her own. She'd given her vague directions to her old apartment about six miles away. The girls there were dancers, like her, and although they'd kicked her out for being unable to pay her part of the rent, they weren't heartless. They would help her young friend. She was sure of it. So Jose had taken off, and Ryan had gone in to help the guy in the viewing room.

Her thoughts drifted back to the present, and Ryan headed in the opposite direction Jose had gone. She was in the rundown portion of *Zona Norte*, the red light district of Tijuana. The hot air carried the stink of fried chicken, sweaty people, and beer. Prostitutes littered the streets even in the middle of the day, their outfits ranging from innocent schoolgirl to evening dresses and heels and everything in between.

Ryan fit right in with her short shorts and sleazy shirt. But she wasn't looking for a trick right now, she was looking for a dealer. Maneuvering her way along the cracked sidewalk, she kept her head down, dodging the neighborhood locals and a few American tourists, mostly men, until she saw the person she was looking for: A young, thin guy leaning up against the wall near the side of a club. His skin was bronzed from the sun, and his dark hair was clipped short off his neck. He was dressed like all the other guys in the area in a tee shirt and black pants, but she could tell by the way his eyes went from person to person as they walked past that he was looking for potential customers.

Plus, she used to be a regular of his before her latest little adventure.

With a discreet look around, she struggled to appear normal. Gritting her teeth against the sickness in her stomach, she walked up to him. "Hey Greg, *como estas?*"

"Ryan!" His smile was all teeth and false cheerfulness. "Where have you been, *chica?*" he said in perfect English. "I haven't seen you in forever."

"Yeah, I, uh, ran into some friends." She tried to ignore the ever-increasing volume of her invisible companions, but it was hard. She could barely hear what he was saying over all the racket they were making. "So, whatcha got for me?" she asked.

With a furtive glance around, he smiled and gestured with his head for her to follow him around the side of the club. Once they got about halfway down the alley, he ducked into a doorway and she followed him.

"How much do you need?" he asked. She could already see him calculating his profit in his head as he pulled a foil packet out of his pocket. Opening it, he showed her the dark, sticky substance inside.

Ryan couldn't answer for a moment as her stomach cramped again. Although she wouldn't call Greg a friend, he'd been her normal dealer for quite a while now, and he'd always been good to her. He'd never tried to take advantage of her, never gave her bad dope, never asked her for sex or even for a blow job. And with her pale skin, blue eyes, and strange orange hair, she attracted a lot of attention from the men around here.

She flinched and closed her eyes, pain ricocheting around in her head as a particularly insistent voice tried to get her attention. It would help if they wouldn't speak all at once and she could understand what the hell they were saying. She opened her eyes to find him looking at her quizzically. "I'll take all you've got," she told him.

He laughed. "*Chica*, you can't afford the amount of tar I've got."

Swallowing hard, she pushed down her feelings of self-hatred for what she was about to do. "You're right. I can't. But I need it." Because she wasn't sticking around this piece of shit town, and it would take her time to find a new dealer wherever she ended up. Her vision blurred, from tears or from the stabbing headache she now had, she wasn't sure. "And you're going to give it to me."

Greg laughed again, a bit uncomfortably this time. He ran his eyes up and down her sleazy clothes. "I don't see any wads of cash hidden anywhere on you. And I'm not interested in having my dick sucked by a whore. So, how are you planning to pay for all of it?"

Her back stiffened and her eyes hardened at the insult. "Like this." Ryan spoke silently to the voices in her head, telling them what she needed them to do. A few made sounds of protest, but she didn't want to hear it.

Her dealer watched her. Amused. Waiting. Then suddenly his eyes popped open wide. The foil fell from his hand and he started to gag. One hand went to his throat as the other grasped the side of his head. Blood trickled from his nose and ears.

"I'm so sorry," she sobbed, her hurt at his uncouth comment quickly dissipating. But it was too late. His eyes were confused as he dropped down hard onto his knees in the street. Spittle leaked from the corner of his mouth as he tried to draw breath. Then, with one last spasm, his body relaxed and rolled onto his back as his arms fell to his sides.

Ryan quickly and efficiently cleaned him out of everything he had. She even found a lighter and a couple of clean needles. Simultaneously racked with guilt and complete denial that she'd just done that, she shoved everything into the pockets of her shorts and ran out of the alley as fast as she could without drawing attention to herself.

She didn't look back.

8

Nikulas watched from the comfort of his bed as Emma attempted to perform her hocus pocus on him. She stood at the foot of the bed, her eyes focused completely on his, but squinting a bit as she concentrated. She was trying to use her magic to make him immobile. So far, she hadn't been able to do it. Not since that one time when they'd gotten into that fight right after they'd had sex for the first time.

Speaking of sex...

Crossing his arms behind his head, he grinned at her, flashing his fangs. He couldn't help it. She looked so fucking cute with her face all scrunched up and her strawberry-blond waves pulled back on her head, leaving little wispy things curling around her face.

"Stop moving!" she fussed at him.

"I thought you were supposed to be taking care of that part?" he teased.

"Nikulas! I mean it. Stop distracting me."

Biting his bottom lip, he lowered one arm and slowly pushed the sheet farther down his torso, not stopping until every inch of his rock hard stomach was showing. He wasn't wearing anything underneath the sheet, and he slid his hand under the thin material. Cupping himself in his palm, he slid his hand up and down his swollen shaft as he watched her watch him do it. The scent of her desire grew strong in the air and he growled softly as his upper lip pulled back from his fangs.

"Nikulas!" Her tone wasn't quite so irritated this time as she tried to keep her eyes anywhere but on that sheet that barely covered him now.

He moved the sheet down a little more, until the head of his cock was showing. She caught the movement and her eyes dropped down to watch each new centimeter of skin as it was revealed. Then she closed them tight and raised her hands, palms out.

"Nik, stop. Please. I really want to practice this. I haven't managed to do it since that one time."

He stopped teasing her and stared with disappointed blue eyes. "You're lying," he told her.

"What?" Her eyes popped open to stare at him with disbelief.

"You're lying. You suck at it. Still. You'd much rather be in this bed with me."

"Nikulas..."

"Come here, Em," he ordered. "I want to fuck you until you're too senseless to wield any spells on me."

Her mouth dropped open, then closed, then opened again. Her eyes flew to his to see if he was joking.

He so wasn't.

His cock kicked and he tightened his hand around its wide girth. But he would much rather it be her tight little body squeezing it. Or maybe that lusciously smart mouth. "Emma, take off my shirt, and get your little ass in my bed. We can practice later. And leave the lights on," he demanded, knowing she would turn them off the first chance she got. She didn't like him to see her scars. Sometime in the next hundred years or so, he hoped he'd be able to convince her that they only made her all the more beautiful to him.

"Um..."

His body arched on the bed as he worked himself up. "Emma, I'm hungry." For more than her blood. "Now come here."

He could scent her rising desire and could hear her blood rushing through her veins, but she still tried one more time to talk him into letting her practice. "I just want to try..."

That was as far as she got. Launching himself from the bed, he grabbed her around the waist. She squealed as he lifted her up off the floor. Twisting around in midair, he was back on the bed with her squirming underneath him before she realized what had happened.

"Nikulas..." she breathed as he ground his hips against her thighs. His cock was hard and ready. He was always ready for his female. Her scent drove him wild, and he growled deep in his throat. Her heart pounded against his chest in response, but not in fear. Oh, no. His Emma was lifting her hips, rubbing herself against him.

She was naked under his shirt.

Moving down just a little, he teased her with the tip of his fang, scraping it lightly down the side of her throat as he slid one arm under her hips, holding her still while he rubbed her clit with the head of his cock.

Emma moaned and tilted her head away, giving him better access to the throbbing pulse there. At the same time, she spread her legs and arched her hips, asking him for what she needed without words.

Kissing his way up to her ear, he whispered, "I want to taste you." Her body shivered underneath him at his words, and another moan escaped her as her fingers squeezed his biceps.

Nik took that as a "yes".

Lifting his weight up and off of her, he sat up, bringing her with him. Grasping the bottom of the tee shirt she was wearing, he yanked it up and off. Her hands automatically went for the sheet to cover herself, but he pulled it out of her reach with a warning look and laid her back down on the bed. Tossing the offensive shirt across the room, he followed her down and took her mouth with his before she could protest the lack of any covering.

Distraction. That was the key. And how he loved to distract her.

Her arms wrapped around his neck, and he groaned at the feeling of being held by her. He'd never get tired of it. Whenever she touched him, it was like the first time. One hand slid under her leg and gripped the back of her thigh, lifting it and opening her to him. His mouth left hers as he made his way down the tender skin of her throat. Pausing at the scar by her collarbone, the first one she'd ever shown him, he kissed it reverently, and then continued his way down her luscious body to her small but perfect breasts. They filled his palms perfectly, the nipples puckering for his attention, and he was more than happy to oblige.

Baring his fangs, he scraped one hard nub and then sucked it into his mouth and flicked it with his tongue. When she arched up to him, he bit down. Emma cried out, and he suckled her, flicking with his tongue again and then sucking hard. Her sweet blood filled his mouth and he swallowed, still surprised by the effect it had on him, even after all this time. As her essence flowed throughout his body, his muscles strained with the power it wrought and his cock throbbed almost painfully between his legs at the intensity of their connection.

Ah, gods. The *taste* of her.

Licking the wounds closed he continued on his way, down her belly to the thatch of soft reddish-blond curls between her legs. Inhaling deeply, he breathed in the scent of her arousal, another animalistic growl escaping him as he did so. Pushing her legs farther apart, he savored her until she was lifting her hips and pressing them to his mouth with an urgency that rivaled his own. Her cries rose in the air and her hands tangled in his blonde hair. She held his head right where it was, like she would die if he dared to move it.

Opening his eyes, he watched her gorgeous body arch, straining upward as he drove her higher and higher, her excitement feeding his own, until he couldn't take it anymore. Lifting her hips to get a better angle, he pierced her swollen nub with his fangs, holding her against his mouth as her body jerked violently with her orgasm. Her head was thrown back, her thighs open wide, the taste of her blood and her woman's desire filling his mouth.

She was the most beautiful thing he'd ever seen.

Without waiting for her to calm, he reared up over her body and slammed into her, only to pull out and do it again. And again. Wrapping his arms around her tight, he held her to him as he picked up speed, burying himself over and over in her slick sheath. He held off as long as he could, but the tight warmth of her was his undoing, and he couldn't wait for long.

"Emma..." he grated out. He didn't need to finish what he was saying.

"Yes, Nik. Yes." Tilting her head to the side, she bared her throat, and this time he took advantage of her offer. He struck so fast he startled her, but then he felt her arms tighten around him as he began to feed in earnest. His heart pounded in his chest, aligning its rhythm with hers, his muscles strained, his balls tightened.

Not releasing her from his bite, Nik roared against her neck as his orgasm hit him like a freight train. Burying himself as deep as he could inside of her, he rode it out, his body shaking, her answering cries music to his ears.

When he could finally think straight again, he loosened his arms, licking and kissing her throat until the bleeding stopped. Turning her face to his, he kissed her softly on the mouth. "Are you okay?" He always worried that he was too rough with her, or took too much blood.

But she just gave him a lazy smile, her large hazel eyes blinking at him sleepily. "I'm okay."

He smiled back and kissed her again.

The bedroom door slammed into the opposite wall. "Nik! You need to come...Oh, sorry about that. I see you've already had a go."

Nikulas spun around on the bed, crouching over Emma and protecting her from this new threat. His lips were pulled back from his teeth in a vicious snarl as his hands fisted at his sides, and his blue eyes burned with possessiveness.

"Hey, Aiden," Emma greeted him irritably from where she'd burrowed under the blankets.

The damn Brit crossed his arms over his chest and leaned oh-so-casually against the doorframe. "Hallo, poppet," he said with a grin, completely ignoring the imminent threat to his life that was even now tensing to launch himself at his best friend. "I do hope I didn't interrupt."

"Uh, yes and no."

Nikulas was breathing hard, trying to reign in his instinct to kill the male who was still grinning like a lunatic at his female. His *undressed* female. Did the idiot not see how close he was to making Grace a widow? A hair-raising hiss escaped without his notice, and his teeth ached to sink into his friend's throat.

Just as his muscles tensed to leap across the room, Aiden deigned to notice him. "Put some clothes on, mate, will you? I don't need to see that. Truly. And then if you would be so kind as to meet me in the other room?" With a naughty wink at Emma, he left, pulling the door firmly shut behind him.

Nik leapt off of the bed. Striding over to the door, he turned the lock with a flourish. "I'm going to have to kill him," he stated to no one in particular as he ran his hands through his hair and tried to chill the hell out now that the "threat" was gone. Feminine laughter sounded behind him, and he turned to find Emma heading to the bathroom wrapped in the comforter.

"You know that lock won't stop him. I'm going to go get a shower," she told him as she blew him a kiss. "Why don't you go see what he wanted?"

"I'm going to go start packing his stuff is what I'm going to do," Nik told her. "It's high time he and Grace got their own place."

Emma stopped and pushed out her bottom lip, effectively gaining his attention. It made him want to bite it and kill whatever it was that was making her sad all at the same time.

"But I like Grace being here, and she doesn't know anyone else but us. And, if Grace leaves, she'll take Mojo with her."

"They can come visit whenever they want," he muttered distractedly.

Emma just tilted her head and looked at him.

Nik tried to stand firm with his decision, he really did, but it was no use. There was no arguing with that sad face. It broke his heart. He sighed in resignation. "Fine. They can stay."

"Yay!" Throwing her arms around him, she kissed him soundly. "Thank you." Then she ran off to the bathroom to start her shower.

Nik found a pair of sweats and pulled them on, then headed out to the living room of his apartment to kill his best friend. He found the pain in the ass on the chair by the window, thumbing through one of Emma's running magazines. Nik tore it from his hands and threw it on the coffee table.

Aiden quirked an eyebrow. "Don't stand there huffing and puffing over me, Nikulas. We both know you're not going to do anything. You love me. Why, it was just this morning that you were hovering over me like a momma hen, worrying that my demon was going to come out and play."

Accepting defeat, he plopped down onto the couch. The bastard was right, but Nik gave him one last glare. "I don't worry about your demon."

"Yes, you do. As do I. Now let's move on to something a bit more pleasant, shall we?"

"What's up?" Nik asked, leaning back against the cushions and crossing his long legs at the ankles. His rage receded as quickly as it had come on.

Scooting to the edge of his seat and leaning forward, Aiden rested his elbows on his knees and laced his fingers together. He opened his mouth to speak, hesitated, frowned, then straightened up and reached back into the hood of his hoodie. Pulling Mojo out, he placed the hedgehog on the coffee table where he huffed and puffed much like Nikulas had earlier.

"*Why* is that thing in your hood?" Nik asked for the tenth time that week.

"No bloody idea," Aiden answered. Then he shrugged. "He likes it in there. But he is quite prickly." Leaning forward again, he picked up the conversation where he'd left off. "So, Leeha's possessed vampires are running amok in the area. We need to do something about it."

"How do you know?"

Aiden just stared at him with steady grey eyes.

"Ah. I didn't realize you were that in tune with them."

"I'm not. But Waano is. And he can feel his kind whenever they're anywhere near. I used to not notice it until they were quite close, but I'm getting better at it."

"And they're in the area?"

"Yes. She had a group up by her mountain. She showed them to me right before she…" He didn't finish what he'd been about to say, but he didn't have to. He cleared his throat. "Anyway, they must have gotten bored. Or maybe they sense that she's gone now. They're running around, probably causing havoc and terror. But there is good news!"

Nik glanced up from watching Mojo. "What news is that?"

"Well, at least we know they're still alive and didn't expire immediately when she did."

"That is good," Nik agreed. They'd been worried about exactly that happening. Those vampires she'd possessed had all originally been created by Luukas, and if they died, he would weaken with every death. At least that's what they thought. But with all the voodoo she'd done to get the demons inside of them, who knew what would happen?

"Okay. Let me finish getting dressed and we can head up and get Luukas and go check out that van. We can tell him about it on the way and see what he wants to do."

"Sounds good, mate. C'mon Prickles," he told the hedgehog as he scooped him up from the table. "Time to go to your home till Grace gets back."

Mojo stared at him with forlorn black eyes.

"Don't look at me like that, you can't come with me. If we got into trouble and you fell out and I lost you somewhere, Grace would never forgive me."

Nik left him to argue with the hedgehog and went back into his room to see if he could catch Emma in the shower before he had to leave.

9

Christian stood in the room where he'd been held prisoner for so long. He felt slightly less homicidal since he'd fed, but not much. Unfortunately, the human hadn't survived his hunger. He'd dragged the body along with the woman's up the stairs and down the hall and placed them near the door. He'd give them a proper burial as soon as he could. No matter what they'd done in this life, or what circumstances had made them do it, they both deserved at least that much. After checking the rest of the building for any others, he'd found himself back in this room.

Running his hand down the stripper pole, he bided his time until the sun went down and he could leave. He didn't dare get any closer to the showing booth he'd been trapped in out of fear that the fucking glass wall would come slamming down again, capturing him like an animal. And no one was here to get him out of the box this time.

There was no clock on the wall to inform him of the time, and he'd dropped his cell phone when he'd been abducted. So he had to rely on his vampire instincts to tell him when sundown came, and they were telling him that he still had a few hours. So he stared at the box, and he waited.

A trail of sweat ran from his temple to his jaw, and he wiped it away with the bottom of his shirt, showing off rippling abs covered by light, copper colored skin. The air inside the building was thick and heavy and hard to breath, and he knew from the short excursion he'd taken outside that it wasn't much better out there. He had stripped down to nothing but his cotton tank and jeans, but he still felt overheated.

A hiss escaped from between his clenched teeth as he adjusted his swollen member away from the zipper of his pants. The fucking thing never went down now. He almost laughed thinking about his younger pre-vamp self. Back then, he would've thought having a never-ending hard on was awesome as fuck. Man, was that guy fucking stupid.

However, he felt strangely calm. Yeah, he was still uncomfortable as all hell, but he wasn't as hungry now, and somehow he knew the woody from hell was only temporary now because of the girl. He just needed to find her.

He hoped she was okay out there. And then he did laugh at himself. Why wouldn't she be? And really, what did he care? Other than the fact that she'd been dick teasing him for weeks…months?….with her slutty little outfits that never stayed on her long and her sexy dances simulating all the nasty things he wanted to do to her in bed.

Leaning against the pole and crossing his arms and ankles, his nostrils flared as he caught a whiff of her lingering scent, and he had to adjust himself again.

Sometimes he wished he could just tear the damn thing off. It had caused him nothing but grief for years now, ever since Luukas had disappeared. He'd never been this much of a horn dog before that had happened, and he often wondered: Why now? Why this insatiable lust for females now? When his friends and fellow Hunters needed him to be on top of his game?

Although, come to think of it, strange things had happened to all of them since Luukas had disappeared. If he believed in that stuff, he would think it was a fucking curse or some voodoo magic or something. Or maybe it was just a natural reaction to whatever was happening with their maker. After all, they were connected by blood. Maybe this was what happened when a master vampire was out of the picture.

Christian's eyes were again drawn to the box where he'd been caged like nothing more than an animal. Maybe if he'd been more worried about his Master and less concerned about his dick he wouldn't have gotten himself into this mess. His face burned when he thought about facing the others again. Nik, Aiden, Dante...and Shea. How was he going to explain to them what had happened?

Yeah, sorry guys. See, I took off from our meeting to go meet up with this blond that worked in that little strip club right there in Belltown so I could get a good fuck-n-feed in before we went to go meet up with Nik and Aiden to save Luukas, instead of prepping for the mission like I should have been.

And maybe if I hadn't been so worried about my dick, I would've noticed whomever it was who had snuck up on me in that alley. But it happened, and I've been stuck in a steel box behind a wall made of glass that's not really glass because I couldn't break it, and forced to watch this beautiful girl take off her clothes and dance for me. No, really. And the same chick finally released me, and then she just took off. Oh, and to top it all off, I lost my phone. Think I can get another one?

That would go over well. He'd be lucky if Shea ever spoke to him again, and Dante…yeah, he didn't even want to think about what that mean motherfucker would do to him when he saw him again. He was more afraid of him than Luukas, if they had, indeed, managed to get him back from that crazy bitch, Leeha, without Christian's help.

Shaking it off, Christian rolled his head around on his neck. He'd make it up to them. To all of them. He'd earn back their respect, if it was the last thing he did. They were his family. He owed it to them. And to himself.

10

Ryan's hands shook as she held the lighter under the foil packet, dissolving the tar inside until it was bubbling. A hypodermic needle was held between her teeth, ready to be used as soon as she was ready. Withdrawals had hit her quick this time.

A quick glance around told her no one else was in the back alley with her, and by the location of the sun, she figured it must be around dinnertime. The song that was playing inside the restaurant she was hiding behind sounded like sad carnival music, and she laughed weakly as tears ran unheeded down her face. It kinda suited the situation and how she felt at the moment.

Laying the foil on the dirty pavement, she grabbed the needle out of her mouth and stuck the pointy end in the liquid. She didn't have a filter. She should have a filter. But she had nothing to use. Slowly and carefully, she pulled back on the plunger and filled the barrel. Was it too much? Not enough? She'd have to take her chances.

A good vein was hard to find, but she finally found one in her leg she thought would work. The voices screamed around her, but she ignored them. Or tried to. They didn't want her to shoot up. They hated it when she did it, because she couldn't hear *them* anymore when she was high. Of course, that was the whole goddamned point. They were the reason she'd gotten into this shit to begin with, so they could just fuck off.

The shaking eased off as she jerkily pushed the plunger down. Leaning back against the wall, her body became light as a feather while sinking down into the pavement at the same time. She almost didn't remember to pull the needle out of her leg, but she managed, dropping it next to her as her eyes slid closed and blissful peace and quiet descended upon her.

The thought crossed her mind that maybe she should've found somewhere where she'd be safer before she did this, but she'd barely managed to stumble back here before fully succumbing to the sickness. A last tear slid down her cheek at how low she'd become, even as relief flowed through her.

Her stomach suddenly revolted out of nowhere and she barely leaned over just in time. There wasn't much in her stomach, but what was in there was ejected quite effectively. By the third time she got sick, her stomach muscles were so sore she could barely straighten up again.

It would be okay. She'd just sit here for a bit, and she'd move somewhere else before it got dark.

It would be okay.

11

Christian cracked the door open, then immediately recoiled from the light coming through the opening. But it was only streetlights, not sunshine. Pushing it open wide enough for him to get through, but not so far that casual passerbys would see the dead bodies lying within, he squeezed through the opening and closed the door firmly behind him. He stood just outside, getting his bearings as he looked around and tried to figure out where the hell he was.

A couple of guys stumbled into him as they passed by, their eyes on a pair of scantily clad girls leaning against a building on the other side of the street.

"Oh! *¡Perdóname!*" the shorter one exclaimed. His eyes widened comically as he looked up, up, up to Christian's face. Grabbing his friend by the arm, he yanked him along with him and down the street, not slowing down until they far away from Christian.

Interesting. Did he look that bad?

As he started down the crowded street, he figured that he must. People cleared a path for him, and by the fear in their eyes, he didn't think it was because he stood a good head taller than most of them, even the men.

Large palm trees swayed overhead on the night breeze, their trunks crammed into the tiny spaces between the clubs and restaurants. Red lights lit up the sidewalks, and girls much like the ones his human friends had been ogling held up the walls of the one and two story buildings in a solid line. The majority of the people were brown skinned and he caught more Spanish words here and there, usually along the lines of the few curse words he knew.

He stepped over a college age female passed out on the edge of the sidewalk, such as it was. At least he hoped she was passed out. Her friends stood to one side of her, laughing and carrying on, at least until they caught sight of him. Then they left her to her fate, backing away directly into the street as he passed. A taxi laid on its horn, swerving to miss them and just barely sideswiping another car as the driver shook his fist out the window. He didn't stop, but took off to where he was going, as did the car he'd hit.

Christian knew of only one country where the driving was that reckless. He must be in Mexico. A border town by the looks of it. Tijuana if he were forced to guess. How the hell had he gotten here? And how was he ever going to find his female in the midst of all of this chaos? She could be anywhere by now.

Taking a deep breath, he tried to catch her scent, but all he could smell was hot dogs and corn from the vendors that lined the street, and something that smelled like the stench of a wet, mangy dog. Or at least what he imagined a mangy dog would smell like.

One of the women caught his eye. Her hair was light and sort of reddish and she had large tits and long legs just like he liked. As he got closer, she eyed him up and down and smiled. But to his surprise, his cock only showed a very mild interest. In spite of the hair, she was just all wrong. Her skin was too dark, her eyes the wrong color, and though very pretty, she smelled like cumin. With an apologetic smile, he moved on.

More girls lined the street. And though his entire body was one large throbbing, painful hard on, his mind, and his cock, lusted after only one female. Considering she'd been the center of his dirty fantasies, and even dirtier reality, since he'd been taken, he wasn't really surprised. Once he'd had her, he'd be on to the next one, as usual.

He walked about another block before he stopped and looked around again. Maybe he'd gone the wrong way? Crossing the street, he headed back the other way. He'd walk up and down this street until the sun rose if he had to. Maybe when the people started clearing out a bit, he'd be able to catch a break as to which way she'd gone.

But he *would* find her.

12

Josiah sat at the small desk in the spare bedroom just down the hall from the master. A keyboard was on top of it, and on the wall in front of him were numerous feeds from the security cameras that Leeha had had installed in her many places of interest. But there was only one screen that he was interested in at the moment.

He typed in a combination of letters and numbers and hit the enter key again, but the damn thing still wouldn't give him access to rewind the security tape. He could watch the live feed, but he couldn't manipulate the tape. And he needed to be able to scroll through the tape, because what he was looking at right now was an empty room. An empty room with no vampire inside of it. And that meant Luukas' Hunter had escaped, and Josiah needed to find out how that had happened, and where he was now.

Throwing himself backwards in the chair, he stared at the screen. Password. Password. What the fuck was Leeha's password? He'd tried all of the obvious ones. Why the hell hadn't he paid more attention the few times he'd been in here with her?

Linking his hands behind his head, he swiveled in his chair... back and forth...back and forth...his forehead furrowed in thought. Leaning forward again, he typed in the name of Leeha's adoptive father and punched the "enter" key with the tip of his finger.

Bingo. He was in.

Quickly, he found the keys to back up the tape. Scenes flew past, all of an empty room. How long ago had he gotten out?

He slammed his finger down on the key that would stop the tape. Hitting play again, he watched the vampire lean up against the stripper pole. But where was the stripper? And why was he out of his "viewing room"? Backing it up a little more, he went past more scenes of an empty room, stopping when he saw movement. The vampire was running from the room. Hitting rewind one more time, he found what he'd been looking for.

The human slut was on her knees in front of the one-way mirror, and the fucking glass was opening, lifting up from the floor. But she was nowhere near the controls, and no one else was in the room. How was she opening it?

Grabbing the headphones off of the table, he stuck them on his head and turned the volume up. Her soft, lilting voice came through strong and clear, almost like he was in the room with them.

"Ah. There you are. Don't be afraid."

"Get away!" the vamp yelled at her.

What was his name? Christian?

"Get the fuck away from me...Please, hurry."

Poor guy sounded like he was in really rough shape. Josiah smiled at the thought.

"Why are you way back there? Come on. We're getting you out."

Josiah stopped the day, searching the picture on the screen. Who the hell is "we"? She was the only one there.

Backing the tape up a little more to see if maybe someone had come in with her and then left again, he confirmed that she was indeed the only person that had entered the room. Was she talking to herself? No. She was definitely talking to someone other than the vampire. Maybe the bitch had a few screws loose, or was hallucinating or something. Wouldn't surprise him, living a life like that.

He watched the tape over a few times, trying to figure out what the hell had happened. Not that it mattered much now. He sighed and leaned back in the chair again. He shouldn't be obsessing like this. Who cares if the stupid vampire had gotten out? He'd be sizzling like a fajita in the Mexican sun soon enough.

Except it did matter. It mattered because his love would not have wanted this to happen. Leeha had gone through a lot of stress and planning to get back at Luukas and the ones closest to him for exiling her. But her plan had failed, and instead of spending their immortal lives miserable and alone, they were all finding happiness. Finding the mates they were fated to have. What were the damn chances of that happening? Especially now?

And what had they done to repay her for that happiness? They'd killed her right in front of him. Took his maker. Took the only female who had ever understood him. And for that, he, Josiah, would see that they paid. All of them. Luukas and his witch, Keira. Nikulas and his Emma. And especially Aiden. Even that British pussy had found his mate, and with a fucking demon inside of him! Of course, she was a witch so she could deal with it. They were all witches...

Josiah suddenly jerked straight up. Son of a bitch.

They were all witches.

That was the loophole in the curse Keira had done! That's why Luukas and his bastards were finding their mates, making them even stronger than before. Somehow, Keira had snuck that in as a way to break the curse. It had to be! They just had to find their mates, who were all witches, of course. And surprise, surprise, they all *somehow* happened to be in the right place at the right time to find their vampire mates.

He watched the slut come in and kneel in front of the mirror again. Watched her nod and say yes, and then watched the mirror wall begin to rise. This time, he continued to watch after Christian had gotten out and attacked the girl. He hadn't bothered before, assuming he had killed her. But now that he thought about it, he didn't remember seeing her body in the later scenes. Josiah's eyes shot open wide as Christian was lifted off of the girl by an unseen force and flung across the room.

Well, well, well. Didn't that explain a lot?

"Gotcha, bitch."

Picking up the phone, he secured their private jet to fly to Mexico. Those two would not be having their happily ever after. As a matter of fact, they wouldn't be leaving that foul country.

The jet touched down at the Tijuana International Airport just after sundown. Josiah waited patiently in his plush leather seat until the plane came to a full stop. He sat still as a statue other than a small twitch under his left eye. That one small movement belied his otherwise calm demeanor, giving away the excitement that had been building inside of him since he'd seen the surveillance tape.

After weeks of doing nothing other than skulking up and down the halls of his home mourning the loss of Leeha, he finally had some direction. After weeks of floundering amidst the chaos that had accompanied her death, he was finally getting his feet under him. He had something to do. Had a plan of sorts taking shape in his head.

Better than that, he'd had the most amazing dream. Leeha had come to him, and she'd looked so evil and so beautiful.

She'd leaned down over him as he reclined in his seat, and one hand had reached up to caress his cheek while the other had stroked the length of his cock. Her long, red hair had fallen around his face. He could still smell it. She'd smiled at him, her head tilting to the side, and she'd said many things to him. She'd thanked him for avenging her. She'd told him he was correct, that he must kill them all. All who had turned on her. He was the only one she trusted, she'd said. The only one.

She'd told him she would come to him if he did this for her. She'd come to him and show him how grateful she was. And when he'd first opened his eyes, he'd seen her standing in the aisle in that sheer white gown he'd so loved. Only there was no blood marring the sheer material. She'd smiled at him with those luscious red lips. Then she'd kind of flickered, and she was gone.

He glanced across the seating area at the idiots who had accompanied him on this little adventure. Directly in front of him was Philip, his seat facing Josiah's on the other side of the small table between them. Philip had been working on the same Sudoku puzzle or some such shit since they'd left Canada, passing the time with his shaved head bent low and his brows screwed up in concentration. He hadn't said a word the entire flight.

Sitting beside Philip was Andy. Andy's chin was resting on his chest and his fingers were laced over his protruding belly. He appeared to be dozing, if the mucus-filled snores coming from him were any indication. Andy was quite a bit older than both Josiah and Philip, having been reborn as a vampire over a hundred years before. But he was a quiet soul, and seemed content to let others lead. With his slight build and average intelligence, he wouldn't have been Josiah's first choice to accompany him, or second choice, or even the twentieth for that matter, but he and Philip were all that he had.

Sleepy and Dopey over there. They were his backups if shit got real. Great. But as they were the only ones from Leeha's colony that hadn't run off once she was no longer there to feed their disgusting appetites, he didn't have any other choice.

A bell chimed twice from above and the lights flicked on, indicating it was safe to remove their seatbelts and move about the aircraft, but no one bothered to get up as they waited for one final announcement.

"Twelve minutes until full darkness. Please remain on the plane until then. Another announcement will be made."

The windows were all sealed to prevent any accidental vampire burnings, so they had to depend on their human pilot to let them know when it was safe to disembark. Josiah unbuckled his seatbelt and pulled his bag from the overhead. Sleepy and Dopey continued as they were.

Josiah wasn't expecting to be here very long. His mission was simple: Find the witch and the vampire, kill them both, and go home. Mission complete. He knew that Leeha would want him to do this. If she had found out about the loophole in the curse before she had been taken, she would be doing this exact same thing.

Once he got home, he would begin to make plans. He couldn't spend the rest of his immortal life wandering around like a ghost mourning the dead. Life would go on, at least for some.

13

Christian pushed his dark hair back off his forehead. Damp with sweat, it stuck straight up where he left it. It was so fucking hot, and there were still hours to go before the sun came up. He'd found her, finally, in an alley behind what could only be described as a "questionable" restaurant. Well, not her, exactly, but evidence of her. He knew she'd been here and that she'd been using. Her scent hung heavy in the air, and when he looked closer, he found a few strands of her distinctive hair stuck to the rough brick of the wall. A needle was lying on the pavement next to a small piece of foil. It also looked like she'd gotten sick. A wave of sadness went through him as he stared at the evidence of her addiction. He wondered why she did it, because somehow she didn't strike him as the type who was in it just for the high.

Walking in tight circles around the area where she'd been sitting, he searched for signs that would tell him which way she'd gone. It didn't take him but a few seconds to find her trail. He must've just missed her, and she couldn't have gone very far yet.

Picking up his pace but staying at human speed so as not to spook the locals, he set off after her. His head was down, his eyes sweeping back and forth across the alley searching for any visible signs of her having passed this way.

He didn't stop to think why he was obsessed with finding the woman who had become the star of his fantasies. Something was driving him on, some instinct, and it was trying to tell him that she was a game changer, but Christian wasn't listening to that voice inside. He just needed to find her. Once he found her and talked her into bed, which he had no doubt he would, she'd be out of his system and he could get his ass back to Seattle. His friends were probably out of their minds with worry. Maybe he should call them and let them know he was all right. Yeah, he'd find a phone and call them.

Just as soon as he found the woman.

His tongue touched his bottom lip. He could still taste her sweet blood. Could still feel her body underneath his, even though it had only been there for a split second. A deep sound that was something between a moan and a growl rumbled through his chest. His mind went off into fantasy world, imagining all of the ways he would make her scream his name when he found her. He wondered if she was a natural redhead? Her brows were the same color as her hair, but they could be dyed to match, right?

Turning a corner, he glanced up without really seeing anything, so absorbed was he in his musings about her hair. If he'd been paying attention, he would've noticed the lack of people on the street in front of him. Would've noticed the rundown condition of the buildings. And maybe he would've heard the rush of air behind him as a bat wrapped in barbed wire came flying at the back of his head.

But he didn't notice any of these things. He did, however, feel that barbed wire imbed itself into his skin as the weight of the bat cracked into his skull. Vampire or not, that was one hell of a hit. Enough to throw him off just long enough for his attacker to rip the bat out of his skull and take another swing. This one caught him along the temple and face, and he toppled over in slow motion, the drama of it all enough to make even the most seasoned wrestler jealous of his acting skills. Only he wasn't acting.

Christian hit the hot pavement hard, landing half on his side and half on his back. Blood ran into his eyes to mix with the black spots he was seeing.

What the fuck had just happened?

A pair of dirty feet encased in worn leather sandals appeared in his line of vision. A voice like a rusty bucket of nails sounded above him, and another answered. His mind screamed in denial as his silver bracelet was ripped from his wrist while another pair of impatient hands rifled through his pockets quickly and efficiently. When nothing more was found, the one doing the searching stood up and gave him a shove with a foot on his arm. Rapid Spanish between the two followed, too fast for Christian to keep up with.

Rolling to his side and placing one hand under his shoulder, he attempted to get his lame ass up off of the pavement. He needed to get his bracelet back.

He saw houses...well, more like shacks...lining the sidewalk he was laying next to. Maybe someone would help him. The sun would be coming up soon.

He opened his mouth to yell for help, and looked up just in time to see the bat come flying through the air at him one more time.

And then there was nothing.

14

Luukas watched the city lights fly past the window from the passenger side of the SUV as it headed out of Seattle. His fingertips thrummed a steady beat on his thigh. He was worried. And he didn't like being worried. Being worried made him distracted. And what was worse, he didn't know exactly what he was worrying about.

Usually it was Keira, his little witch. He worried about her a lot. Mostly that something would happen to her. Or that he would discover her alleged feelings for him were all part of the plan to bring him down. Or that she would leave him.

That was the worst one of all. He was kind of surprised she hadn't already. But he was also grateful, because if any of those happened, it would utterly destroy him. She was the only thing that kept him somewhat grounded. And strangely enough, she was the only one he completely trusted, even with all of his worrying and all that had happened between them.

Turning away from the window, he checked out his brother's profile. Nikulas certainly had his hands full these days. His older brother was on the verge of losing his mind half the time and his best friend was reluctantly possessed by a demon.

As if he felt his eyes on him, Nik's blue eyes glanced questioningly in his direction. "What's up, bro? You okay?" he asked. One hand ran through his blonde hair, pushing it back off his face. It was a nervous gesture Luukas knew well.

"I'm good," he reassured him. "Just feeling a little unsettled for some reason. I can't quite put my finger on it."

"It's because the demons are running amok," Aiden chimed in from the back seat as he flipped the page of the old Rolling Stone magazine he was reading for the hundredth time.

Luukas cranked his head around and scowled at him. "What do you mean?"

"The demons," Aiden repeated. He flipped another page.

"Aiden! Explain." Sometimes Luukas wondered why he bothered to pull this one out of the muck of the battlefield he'd found him in.

Marking his page, Aiden shut the magazine and laid it on the seat next to him. "The vampires you created, the ones that left your colony to run off with Leeha, she possessed them with demons."

"Yes, I know that," Luukas stated impatiently.

"Well, now that she's gone, they're running amok." He waved a hand in front of him. "All over the Pacific Northwest and Canada. That's probably why you're getting that feeling."

"And how do you know this?"

Aiden just looked at him, much as he had Nikulas.

"Ah. Yes." Turning back around in his seat, he directed his next question to Nikulas. "And you knew about this?"

"He just told me tonight."

"But why would it be affecting me like this?" he murmured, more to himself than anyone else.

"Can I ask you something, Luuk?" Nik stopped at a red light and flipped on the turn signal.

"I don't know, *can* you?"

Nik stared at him blankly for a moment at the old childhood joke, then he grinned. "I can, and I will." He got serious again. "Did you feel it? When Leeha was changing all of those vampires? Did you sense anything?"

Luukas tensed at the reminder of those years when he was chained up in Leeha's underground cell. Trying not to sound like the madman he was when he first came out of there, the madman who screamed to come out still, he only said, "I don't recall. I didn't notice much of anything then other than what was going on with me."

The light turned green and Nik hit the gas. "Yeah." He cleared his throat. "I'm sorry. I shouldn't have asked. I only went there because we've been trying to figure out how it would affect you if something happened to them."

"It's all right," he told his brother. "What's done is done." His cell vibrated in his pocket. Pulling it out, he found a text from Keira asking him what was wrong and he smiled. Assuring her that he was fine, he stuck it back in his pocket. Even just that short communication with her made him feel better.

"Oh! Hey, I found this last night." Aiden handed something over the top of the seat to Luukas.

"This is Christian's phone." He knew right away by the phone case. He held it up for Nikulas to see. "Where did you find this?"

Aiden picked up the magazine again. "Over in Belltown. Close to that little strip club. I assume he was on his way to shag one of the dancers there. He's been out of control with the females since you've been gone, by the way. When he gets back, I think an intervention may be in order."

Nik glanced at him through the rear view mirror. "Did you see anything else? Anything that could give us a clue where he is?"

"No. Nothing, mate. Just the phone. I'm surprised it was still there. It was kind of hidden half under a pile of rubbish though. I only found it because I record the tracking on it, so I knew where it last was before the battery died." Another page crackled as he turned it. "There are so many bad feelings between Dave and the band, and now they brought Sammy on board. Personally, I prefer the original Van

Halen. David Lee Roth was a brilliant front man, if a bit unmanageable."

"Dude, that was like, twenty years ago." Nik rolled his eyes.

"What? It hasn't been that long." He checked out the date on the front cover. "Well, maybe it has."

"We're here," Nik announced.

Dimming the headlights, Nik eased the vehicle onto the side of the road next to the empty lot and turned off the ignition. They sat for a few minutes, feeling the place out before they left the safety of the vehicle. Then Luukas leaned forward and peered out the front windshield. "I don't see anything untoward. Let's check it out."

Quietly, they opened the car doors, slid out, and eased them closed. They had no weapons on them. They didn't really need them for something like this. They could move faster than a bullet, and knives were child's play. Besides, weapons just brought about unnecessary questions from anyone who saw them. Their appearance alone was suspicious enough to humans. Without a word between them, they went their separate ways and checked out the perimeters of the lot. When no alerts were called out, they converged near the back of the van.

Aiden tried the back doors. They were unlocked. "Looks like whoever dumped this thing left in a bloody hurry." Climbing inside, he rummaged around while Nikulas stayed outside with Luukas and kept watch.

"It smells like somebody missed the pot in here."

"What?" Nik leaned around the door and stuck his head inside, then quickly pulled it back out. "Ugh. It stinks like piss in there."

"That's what I said," Aiden called from the front seat.

Luukas rolled his eyes. These two were beyond ridiculous when they were together. They'd always been like that. Ever since they'd found Aiden lying in that field with his insides on the outside.

He was very glad they were back together.

Aiden hopped out of the back of the van. At Luukas' inquiring look, he just shook his head. "Nothing. Not a scrap of any evidence. Not a receipt, a burned match, nothing."

Nik sighed deeply. "Well, at least we have the consolation of knowing that Dante obviously scared the piss out of them. Like, literally."

"Wouldn't expect anything less from the commander," Aiden grinned.

Luukas let them carry on while he thought about what they should do next. That bad feeling in his chest was escalating, and he unconsciously rubbed the spot.

Nikulas fake punched Aiden, laughing at his imitation of Dante, and glanced over at his brother. He immediately got serious. "You okay, Luuk?"

He nodded. "I'm good. Let's call our guy and get this van towed back to his garage. I want to go over it more thoroughly. Make sure we didn't miss anything."

"I'm on it." Nikulas already had his cell at his ear.

Luukas rubbed the back of his neck as his eyes darted around the lot. He still wasn't completely comfortable. Well, he wasn't comfortable anywhere really. Not even in his own home. But he was getting there. And searching for his Hunters was good for him. It took his mind off the past and put it back on what was important.

He just hoped he could find them.

15

Ryan struggled against the band of steel wrapped around her neck to no avail. The guy's arm wouldn't budge an inch no matter how hard she kicked and twisted and threw herself around. Changing tactics, she gave up trying to pull it away and swung one arm straight down. Her hand formed a claw as she reached between his legs and grabbed a hold of the most sensitive part of him. Digging her nails in, she twisted hard.

The bastard only got more erect.

"Do it again," he panted into her ear. Tightening his arm around her throat and placing his other hand on top of hers over his crotch, he forced her to tighten her grip. "You don't know how much I've missed this." A wave of such devastating sadness flooded through her, she stopped struggling from the shock of it. Her heart ached in her chest for this unknown man.

Around them, the wind picked up, but Ryan only caught fragments of what the voices were saying. It sounded like they were arguing. That was new. She still had too much dope in her system for them to come through clearly and she was glad. She didn't need the distraction of her fucked up head right now. The dope was distracting enough. She kept forgetting that she needed to be trying to get away.

Two other men stood off to the side. They didn't look like much, and they appeared to be only mildly interested in the violence that was happening right in front of them. She could see she wouldn't be getting any help there, but Ryan was pretty sure if she could get away from this young one, the others wouldn't give much of a chase.

The one holding her lifted his hand away from his balls, taking her hand around to the front of her with his, and placed them both between her legs instead. Moving her hand up and down, he made her touch herself while he gyrated into her ass. His other arm loosened just enough that he could shove his hand down her shirt to roughly squeeze her breast.

Ryan began to struggle anew. Why was this being allowed?

"Yeah, I like a female with some fight in her."

Forcing her down to the ground, he shoved her face into the grass. It tickled her nose and although she knew it was completely inappropriate given what was happening, she wanted to laugh.

"Where's your magic now, witch? Huh? Why aren't you throwing me off?" He pushed her face deeper into the grass by the back of the neck. "I think you like it."

Magic? What the hell was he talking about? She felt unusually calm for a girl that was about to die, but she couldn't really bring herself to care. She was floating a foot off the ground, only vaguely aware of the fact that he was now undoing his jeans. Then suddenly he stopped, collapsing on top of her and rolling them both over until she was on top, looking up at the night sky between the tree branches. One arm went around her waist and the other around her shoulders to hold her there. She felt something nick the side of her throat.

"Move and she is dead," he said.

The skin on her neck tingled where the man's warm breath hit the small wound he'd just made.

An animalistic growl sounded from somewhere to her left and she shifted her eyes that way. A man stood there. A different man. The other two were gone. No. Not a man. It was the creature she'd let out of the viewing room. His lips were lifted in a snarl, his pointy teeth were bared, and his beautiful eyes glowed from his face. They pierced through the darkness like flames of hell, never wavering from the man underneath her.

She smiled up at him. Man, did he look pissed. He should try some of her stuff. She had a little left if she could find where she dropped it. It would chill him right out. He'd be comfortably numb. Just like her.

"Release her," he gritted out. "NOW."

Suddenly she was on her feet fighting a major head rush. The guy who had waylaid her in the park still held her from behind, using her as a shield, but they were on their feet. She didn't remember standing up, but now that she was, she could see what was left of the bodies of the other two men. Her stomach lurched. She had to tear her eyes away from the gruesome sight.

"I don't think you understand, vampire." His teeth scraped her throat when he talked, and she felt something warm trickling down towards her collar bone. In front of her, the creature's nostrils flared, and his tongue touched the tips of his sharp teeth as his body leaned towards her.

"This female isn't what you think she is," the one holding her continued. "Besides, look at her. She's nothing but a junkie. She isn't worth it." His voice became hard. "Not that it matters in any case, because you're both going to die tonight. My queen, she demands it."

The creature from the strip club was prowling back in forth in front of them now like a caged animal, never taking his eyes from the man holding her. She wondered if he had paced like that when he'd watched her dance.

"She?" the creature asked. "You take orders from a female?" Those glowing lion's eyes shifted briefly to her before returning to the scum that held her. "I knew you were a bitch the moment I saw you beating up on a girl," he told him.

She felt something warm and wet lapping at her skin and she frowned. Was he licking her? A hand went back to her breast and squeezed. Ryan glanced up just in time to see the creature in front of her stop his pacing. A scream of rage tore from his throat as he leaped towards them, just as she felt something sharp pierce her skin and tear. She fell to the ground. And then everything went cold and black.

Christian had woken up inside a run down shack posing as someone's home, white hot spears of pain lancing through his skull and his own blood sticking the side of his face to the floor. Cracking open one eye, he exploded up off the floor, fangs bared and fists up.

But the skinny kid standing in the doorway with a bowl of soup for him to eat had not been a threat. His aching head and rolling stomach on the other hand...yeah, much more concerning. It had all come back to him in a flash: The bat wrapped in barbed wire, the human man that had wielded it. Him and another guy leaving him in the street. Passing out before he could drag himself somewhere safe from the sun that would be coming up soon.

And the only thing they'd managed to get off of him was the bracelet he'd worn for as long as he could remember. A bracelet made by his mother's people. The only thing he had left of her.

He needed it back, but first, he had to find the girl.

The night was hot and sticky, and the smell of urine and garbage hung thick in the air. It was no wonder that vampires kept to the colder climates, at least for the most part. Besides the shorter daylight hours most of the year, the cooler air tended to help keep the stronger scents at bay. With their enhanced senses, being somewhere as aromatic as this neighborhood could really kill your appetite.

Taking a right, Christian didn't really think much about where he was going. He was just following his instincts at this point. And those instincts were telling him he needed to hurry. He headed south, away from the red light district, running full out. To those on the sidewalks, he was nothing but a blur. Some did a double take, but by that time he was long gone, and they would continue on their way.

He ran past fancy two story stucco homes protected by wrought iron fences directly across the street from closed up strip centers. He ran past an Auto Zone and swung a left.

Man, those things were everywhere.

As he ran, his chest tightened and his breathing became harsh. Not because of the physical exertion, he could run for hours and barely break a sweat. But something was going on, something was calling him to this particular location. He really couldn't explain it.

Up ahead he could see a park with a playground, trees, the whole deal. And the closer he got to it, the more anxious he became. Slowing down, he scanned the area around him. Picnic tables and benches were scattered throughout the place, and he passed by a statue of some dead, upstanding Mexican citizen. He didn't stop to see who it was.

There weren't any people around. He didn't know if that was the norm for this time of night or not, but he was glad in any case. He had a feeling that whatever was about to go down here wasn't going to be pretty. And would certainly not be something the humans needed to see.

His eyes darted from side to side, but he still didn't see anything or anyone that could be causing this restless feeling inside of him. Of course, he was jazzed up from lack of sex and jonesing for another taste of the girl. That could be all it was.

And she was here. He could *feel* her.

Fighting the urge to rub his hands together in anticipation, he forced himself to pay attention to his surroundings. He'd already been blindsided once. A fountain on his right had some water sitting in its bowl, and he stopped to splash the blood off of his face after a careful look around. He dried his face off with the bottom of his shirt and attempted to suppress his needs for the moment and focus.

All of his senses on high alert, his thick-soled boots made no sound as he wandered off the path to walk amongst the cover of the trees. He'd only gone about twenty feet when he heard a woman cry out. Holding perfectly still, he listened. She cried out again and his head whipped around towards the sound. He'd know that sound anywhere. It was his female.

Staying low within the trees, he ran towards her voice. His passage was completely silent, not even a crackling leaf giving any indication that he was there. When he arrived where she was, the scene spread out before him left no room for thought as to what he would have to do.

Vampires surrounded his female. They were hurting her. And they were about to die.

Taking out the two bystanders, he was about to pull the other one off of her when he popped up off the ground with her. He barely heard what he was saying, the buzzing in his head was so loud. Christian said something back to him. The vampire mauled her breast. And Christian lost it.

A red haze slammed down over Christian's vision as he watched the dark-skinned vampire rip into the girl's throat. So red, the color of her freshly flowing blood blended with the color of her shirt, forming nothing more than a wet stain.

With a roar of agony, he tore the young vampire off of her and threw him off to the side. Catching the girl before she hit the ground, he gently laid her down on the grass. Her eyes were wide with shock as they stared up at him for a brief second, and then the haze of unconsciousness crept over them and her lids closed.

Christian was on his feet and giving chase to the bastard who had hurt her before her body had settled on the ground. Rounding the gazebo, he stopped, torn between killing the son of a bitch and helping the girl. His need for revenge warred with his instincts to stay with her as he watched the vampire run off, but he let him go. Then he hauled back his fist and punched one of the thick supports so hard his hand went completely through it. Crumpled stone drifted slowly to the ground at his feet. He didn't feel any better.

Returning to the girl, he knelt beside her and pulled his shirt up over his mouth and nose to try to block her blood scent somewhat. He was afraid to touch her. She was bleeding profusely from the side of her throat, and her scent was so strong his makeshift mask was no help whatsoever. His fangs ached and his throat burned as he tried to pull himself together. His body was strung so tight he felt like he would shatter if anyone touched him. He was so hungry. And he wanted her. Then he felt like a son of a bitch for even thinking those thoughts in the condition she was in. But her sweet blood was a draw he didn't know if he could resist.

Distinct fang punctures and large, ragged tears marked her fair skin, and the urge to replace those marks with his own bite was so strong he was reeling with it. He needed to get her to a doctor. He couldn't handle this by himself, not without hurting her more.

Ripping a strip off of the bottom of his shirt, he wadded it up and pressed it over the wound. Keeping one hand on the makeshift compress, he slid his other arm underneath her and gently pulled her up into a sitting position while leaning her against him for support. The fiery hair on the top of her head was soft on his jaw, and without thinking he buried his nose in it and inhaled deeply. The red haze faded from his vision as every muscle in his body responded, tightening up with need. Gods, she smelled so good. Now that he had her with him, he didn't want to give her up.

You can fix her.

The thought came out of nowhere. No. He shook his head at himself. No, he needed to take her to a doctor. There had to be an emergency clinic or something around here somewhere.

She would bleed out before then.

No, she'd be okay. He'd make sure she was okay until he got her to a doctor. If he fixed her he'd be creating a bond between them, and he never did that. He liked clean breaks with the females he was with, and never offered them his blood. To do so would link them to him for months, for it would take that long for the bond to wear off. Of course, he'd never had a female dying in his arms before.

Christian debated with himself, his vampire brain going over every pro and con he could possibly think of for what he was considering at a speed unreachable by humans. All of this took less than a few seconds from the time he knelt down beside her. He needed to make a decision, or she wasn't going to be around to fret about.

Take her to the doctor and let someone else fix her, or take matters into his own hands and do something worthwhile with this mystical blood of his. In the end, it was the thought of another man's hands on her that decided him. Lifting his wrist to his mouth, he sank his fangs into his own vein, opening up a decent size wound. The compress fell off her neck, but she wouldn't need it in a few seconds. He let her head fall back over his arm, and pressed his wrist to her lips. "Come on, *she'ashil*. Swallow for me. It'll help you." His life saving blood dripped into her mouth, but she was too out of it to respond. Biting his arm again, he re-opened the wound and tried again. This time, her mouth moved slightly as his life force hit her tongue. "That's it. Drink for me. That's it."

She started sucking on his arm now, moaning quietly though her eyes were still closed. Christian threw his head back as his fangs tightened, aching to sink them into her supple flesh, and his cock jerked in his jeans. He had to fight the compulsion to adjust her on his lap and slide into her tight warmth.

She took a strong pull, and a flash bomb went off inside of him, the force of it nearly knocking him over.

MINE.

He needed to distract himself, so he leaned over her to check out her throat. The bleeding had stopped and the skin was fusing back together little by little. Another few seconds and she'd be good as new.

He was so engrossed in watching his own healing powers that he didn't notice at first that her eyes had opened. By the time he did, she was struggling in his arms, pushing his wrist away with a cry of alarm.

"What are you doing?" she cried in English.

He let her go, allowing her to struggle to her feet. Frantically, she wiped at her mouth with the backs of her hands and then spit out what was left in her mouth.

Holding both hands up with his palms out in front of him, he tried to look as unthreatening as possible. He knew he must look a sight: A vampire in full blown feeding and fucking mode. He was actually surprised she hadn't run off screaming yet. But he couldn't help the way he responded to her, and that being what it was, she would've ended up seeing him like this again eventually. "It's okay. I won't hurt you. I swear it!" Lowering his hands he backed away a step. "Please, don't run. Please. I won't hurt you," he repeated.

"What were you doing to me?" she repeated. She was standing with her weight on the balls of her feet, her body half-turned away from him, tensed to take off at the slightest provocation.

"I was helping you," he told her. He kept his voice low and easy, like he was talking to a skittish animal. "My name is Christian. Christian Moore."

Her turquoise blue eyes swept over him from his head to his feet and back again.

"I'm..." What? What did he say?

I'm a vampire and I was giving you my blood to heal you after another vampire ripped your throat open.

Somehow he didn't think that was gonna go over very well.

16

Grace set her glass down on the end table next to her chair and listened to the two sisters gabbing away on the couch. They weren't talking about anything of consequence really, just throwing ideas around for some stuff they could do to keep busy now that they'd relocated to Seattle.

"I really, really, don't want to go back to accounting," Emma told her sister. "I don't know how I did that job for so long."

Besides the fact that accounting offices normally kept an 8am-5pm schedule, the girls had all transitioned to the nocturnal hours kept by their males, and there was no way, no how, any of them would let their females roam the streets of the city all day while they were confined inside until the sun went down. Their protective natures wouldn't allow it.

"You could start your own organizational company," Keira suggested. "Or be a virtual assistant. Like the ones celebrities hire to keep their lives organized. You've always been a damn freak about stuff like that."

Emma laughed. "I am not!"

"You are so! Nothing can ever be strewn about. Everything is either in a file or a box. Even on the computer. Remember when you completely re-organized my room when I was gone that one Saturday? It took me weeks to find my Playgirl magazines that I stole off of that one bitch cheerleader at school."

"Well, you shouldn't have had them anyway. Mom would've freaked out if she'd ever found them. I was just trying to hide them better for you."

"If it wasn't for those magazines, you'd have never seen a real penis until you met Nik."

Emma sputtered, the sip of tea she'd just taken flying from her mouth, somewhere between being offended and laughing her ass off.

Keira pulled her long dark hair around and started braiding it out of the way. "I'm just saying you'd be a good organizer is all. You'd just have to use virtual boxes instead of real ones."

The box!

"Oh, hey!" Grace interrupted. "I like, totally forgot! Be right back." Jumping up off her chair, she ran down to her apartment and came back less then five minutes later with the jewelry box she'd brought with her from Dalian. Plopping back down in the large chair, she handed it to

Emma. "I took this from the Suits that were working with the vampires in Dalian. The ones that took Mojo."

Emma turned it over in her hands, tracing the symbol etched into the lid with her fingertip before handing it to Keira to look at.

"Why would they have a jewelry box? What's so important about it?" Keira asked. Opening the lid, she peeked inside and then promptly closed it again when she saw that it was empty.

"I'm not sure exactly. But there's an etching of a dagoba in the bottom, under the red felt."

Keira opened the box again and lifted the material from the bottom. She studied the picture for a minute before showing it to Emma.

"What is this?" Emma asked. "A dagoba. What is that?"

Grace held her hand out for the box. "A dagoba is like a tall tombstone. There's a place in China called the Forest of the Dagobas of Shaolin Temple, among others. Each one is different and has a different design etched into it, depending on who the monk was that is buried there."

"Why would it be hidden in the bottom of a jewelry box?" Keira wondered.

Grace shrugged. "Maybe it's a clue?"

"For what?" Emma curled her legs up to the side of her and tugged on the long sleeves of her light, cotton shirt.

"I don't know," Grace told her. "But Brock seemed to know something about it. It was the fact that I had the box that made him realize they would be coming after me, both the humans I took it from and the vampires they were supposed to give it to. He never said anything else about it though. He was too busy canoodling with my best friend on the plane over, and before that we were running for our lives. It didn't really come up. I'd forgotten about it until just now."

"We need to call the Kincaid pack," Keira stated. "Em, will you call Cedric if I get you the number?"

Emma frowned at her sister. "Why do I need to call him?"

"He likes you. They all like you. You're very likable. And you weren't the one that helped torture their friend for seven long years."

Her voice was teasing, but Grace could see the pain in her eyes at the thought of what she had done to the man she loved. She didn't know how Keira lived with it. It had been no fault of her own, and if the tables were turned, Grace thought she would've done the same thing if she had a sister whose life was being threatened.

"All right. Fine." Emma held out her hand for the phone and waited for Keira to run to the office for the number. Taking the piece of paper, she punched in the number and tapped the screen to put it on speaker. After the fourth ring, Cedric picked up the phone.

"What th' hell dae ye want?" he answered in his heavy Scottish brogue. In spite of the harsh words, he sounded genuinely glad to hear from them.

"Um, Cedric?" Emma asked in confusion. "It's Emma."

"Emma! My wee lass. I'm sae sorry! I didna ken it was you."

She smiled. "Yeah, I figured that part out. So, I was calling to see if Brock was there? Grace has a box with her that she brought over from China, and she thinks Brock might know something about it. You're on speakerphone by the way. Keira and Grace are here too."

"Och. A roomful of witchery."

Grace could practically see him shudder, and she exchanged an amused grin with Keira. Werewolves did not like magic. It totally spooked them.

"It sae happens that the pup is here. I'll get him for ya."

The girls listened to some shuffling of the phone, and then Brock's deep timbre came across the line. "Grace?"

"Hey, Brock. Is Heather there too?"

"No, she's back at the hotel."

Shortly after arriving in Seattle, Heather had had an abrupt change of heart about the guy after finding out he was, in reality, a werewolf. But Brock had followed her, and a week later, Grace had gotten a call from her friend saying she'd decided to stay here after all. She'd spoken little to her ever since, and had seen her even less. When she did talk to her best friend, however, she'd sounded ridiculously happy.

"Oh, ok. I'll try to call her later or something." Keira waved the box at her and she got to the subject at hand. "So, do you remember that jewelry box? The wooden one with the strange symbol etched into the lid?"

"Shit! The box! I'd forgotten all about it." He became deadly serious. "Grace, you need to get rid of that thing."

"Um, well, I was kind of hoping you'd tell me what the hell it is first."

"I told you in the car before we left China. I don't know why they're after it."

"I think you do know, and unless you want me to call Heather right now and tell her I saw you hitting on another girl, you'll tell me the truth."

"Pfft. She'd never believe you."

"Want to test that out?" When he remained quiet, she said, "Okay...here I go...I'm calling..." They waited to see if he'd call her bluff.

There was a brief pause, and then they heard him take a deep breath and curse quietly. "Yeah, okay. But you need to promise you'll get rid of it. At the very least, hide it somewhere no where near where you are."

Keira spoke up then. "Brock, please just tell us what it is."

"All right, all right. I *think* the box is a clue. Or rather, the picture inside of the box. I'd been following those demon things for a while before I came across you and Aiden. At first I was just going to kill them on sight, but they were up to something, and I decided to try to find out what it was. They've got two more of those boxes already. I don't know if that's the last one or if there's more. But I definitely think they're clues. I just don't know to what."

Grace thought about what he'd said. "But what could they be searching for that would have anything to do with the dagobas?"

"I have no idea, Gracie. I'm sorry."

One side of her mouth twisted up at his use of Heather's nickname for her, but she left it alone for now. She still thought this guy was trouble.

Or maybe she was just being overprotective of her best friend.

"I wish I had more I could tell you," he continued. "But all I know is that I've seen people get slaughtered without a moment's regret so they could get their hands on those boxes. And the ones they killed? They were Shaolin monks. I assume they're the 'keepers' of these boxes, or clues, or whatever they are."

"Probably for good reason if demons are so determined to find whatever they're hiding."

"I agree. Now keep your part of our deal and get rid of that thing. Hide it. Burn it. Whatever."

"They know I have it. They'll come after me anyway."

The stony silence on the other end of the line wasn't reassuring.

"Well, thanks for the info Brock."

"If I think of anything else, I'll call you."

"Sounds good. Tell Heather she's ignored me long enough and she needs to come over. And bring pizza."

He laughed. "Will do. Talk to you later."

The line went dead. "Well, that told us absolutely nothing," Grace said as she set the phone down on the table. She looked up at Keira. "Sorry. I should've found out more from the men I stole it from."

But Keira just gave her a warm smile. "It's okay. We found out enough. We'll figure out the rest ourselves."

Emma looked back and forth between the other two women. "We need to tell the guys. They're gonna go bat shit crazy at the thought of those things coming after the box, but they need to know so they can take precautions."

Keira stood up and smoothed her hands down the front of her jeans. "We can take our own precautions."

"What do you mean?" Grace asked.

"I mean, that we may as well put this 'witchy' stuff of ours to good use. We can put a ward on the box. It will hide it from them if there's anything about it that's calling to the demons that will tell them where it is. And there's no need to worry Luukas or the others."

Emma sank back against the cushions. "I don't know, sis. I can't even make Nikulas immobile at will." Then she grinned. "However, as you know, I'm really good at making things move around on their own."

"And all I can do is heal myself. Oh, and Aiden when he's on his deathbed, apparently," Grace added.

"It's okay. You both still have magic. I'll do the spell. I just need you to link with me to strengthen it."

Grace looked at Emma, and then they both stood up too. "Okay then," she said. "What do we need?"

17

Ryan gawked at the creature in front of her. He was strangely beautiful with his glowing topaz eyes, harsh features, and straining muscles. Not to mention the fangs. He looked like something out of the fantasy comics her friends in junior high used to read, except he wasn't pale and ugly. He was handsome, and his skin was tanned.

But that didn't make him any less scary. Because the thing was, she knew he wasn't a hallucination this time. She was completely sober. And she knew she was sober because the voices were back, making it hard for her to concentrate on what he was saying. They buzzed around her head, speaking so fast she couldn't understand them.

What was he saying? His name. He was telling her his name. Christian...something?

"Shut! Up!" she screamed out loud. "I can't hear!" And to her surprise, this time they did. The voices completely stopped. Realizing she had just screamed out loud at nothing he could see or hear, she raised self-conscious eyes to his. "Not you," she clarified. "I was talking to...someone else." God, she really was crazy, wasn't she? Of course she was. Why the hell else would she hear voices?

Dark brows lowered over those bright eyes, dimming them a bit. Then he did something completely unexpected after her little display. He took a step closer to the crazy woman in front of him. "My name is Christian Moore. What's your name?"

She only hesitated a second. "Ryan." That was all he needed to know for now.

He smiled, although he still looked like he was in pain or something.

"Why are you following me?" she asked. Because he must be following her. How else would he have found her here?

"I don't know," he answered, and his honesty didn't make her feel any better. "I don't know," he repeated. "I should be well on my way home by now, but instead I found myself hunting you through the city."

"Well, it took you long enough to find me."

He startled, and she almost smiled a little at his taken aback expression. Then she did smile when he laughed out loud.

"Yeah, sorry about that. I would've been here sooner except that I ran into a similar situation." At her questioning look, he shrugged those big shoulders. "I got mugged." His hand rubbed his opposite wrist. "I got knocked over the head pretty good. Took a little nap." He glanced away. He seemed embarrassed to be telling her.

"How does someone like you get mugged?" Although she was no longer poised to run, she still hadn't relaxed completely. She noticed his hands were clenched at his sides and he was breathing hard, like he was having a hard time keeping himself still. Just because he had saved her from a similar, or worse, fate, didn't mean she trusted him.

"I, uh...I was distracted," he murmured. "And they had a bat."

It didn't really matter, actually. "So, you didn't answer my question," she said. "What were you doing to me? Just now?" She ran her eyes over his tense figure again. "What are you?" When he didn't respond right away, she continued, "I thought I was having some kind of a bad trip when you attacked me back at the club. But now I know I'm not. And yet there you stand. And your eyes are glowing. And you have...fangs."

He took a step closer and she took a step back. He stopped where he was. For long moments, he stared at her, his eyes intense upon her face. She had to give him credit. Most men would be zeroed in on her breasts, hanging out of her shirt as they were. But not this guy. This guy was searching her features like he was looking for the answers to the universe within them. But then again, he wasn't a normal man, was he?

"What are you?" she repeated, more insistent this time.

"You wouldn't believe me if I told you."

Her neck was sore and itching. She rubbed at it, and noticed that he closely followed every movement she made. When she pulled her hand away, his eyes stayed on her throat. His body seemed to lean towards her, yet he hadn't moved at all as far as she could tell.

Ryan narrowed her eyes. Nervously, she licked her lips, and his eyes immediately flicked from her throat over to her mouth. The vibes coming off of him were intense. She could feel what could only be described as hunger. But not a "I haven't eaten in a week" hunger. It was different. It pulsed off of him so strongly she was surprised she couldn't see it shimmering around him, like an aura.

What was even stranger than the feelings she was getting from him? Her body was answering that hunger with a longing all its own. Without the barrier of the drugs in her system, the connection she felt to him was amazing. She didn't understand it. Was it because they had spent so much time together the last few months? Intimately?

And it had been intimate, even though she'd never actually seen him until now. She'd felt him behind the glass. Every time. So much so, that the last time she'd danced for him, his craving for her had affected her so much that she'd stopped dancing and done something she'd never done before.

Imagining his hands on her, she'd touched herself until she came for his viewing pleasure. She'd never done anything like that for any of her "customers". Immediately after, she'd had to leave. The anguish coming from him in response had been too much, and she'd run from it.

And now here he was in front of her, and she could feel that hunger up close and personal, and a part of her wanted to throw herself into his arms and let him do what he wanted to do. But that was crazy, right? They were complete strangers in spite of both of them being stuck in that horrid place. That was the crazies talking.

"Please," she whispered. "Tell me who you are. Tell me what you were doing to me."

"I was saving you," he said.

"I don't understand..."

"That asshole hurt you. You were bleeding. You would've bled to death before I could get you to a doctor. I had to do it."

She sliced her hand through the air, cutting him off. She remembered the other one hurting her. That's not what she was worried about. "But what did you do? What did you give me?" She looked around, but only saw the other two bodies. "And where is he?"

He took a deep breath. His nostrils flared and he closed his eyes for a moment. When he spoke, his voice was strained. "I gave you my blood."

Ryan stared at him as her mind went blank, forgetting about the guy that had grabbed her. "You did what?"

He didn't take his gaze from her, didn't act uncomfortable, didn't mince his words. "I gave you my blood. It healed you."

"Why would your blood heal me?" she asked. She drank his blood? And she hadn't gagged?

He barely hesitated before he confessed, "Because I'm a vampire."

This time it was her turn to laugh out loud. He let her get it out. Watched her as she went from laughing to an awkward half laugh/half grimace, because she knew he was deadly serious.

He put his palms out again in a gesture of peace before she could react. "I won't hurt you. I won't. I just…You would've died."

She wasn't sure if he was trying to convince her or himself. A vampire? Was he serious? Ryan took in his tense features, those long teeth, the eyes…No. He was just as crazy as she was. That's all it was. It was nothing but fake teeth and contacts. But somehow she couldn't quite convince herself of that, because it *felt* like the truth.

How was that even possible?

And why the hell wasn't she running?

She shook her head. "That's not possible."

"Why not?"

"Because vampires don't exist." She sounded a lot surer of that fact than she felt.

He stepped closer, and this time she didn't back away. He took another step, and this one brought him within touching distance. Still she didn't run. Instead, she felt drawn to him.

Just like she had at the club when she'd put off her own escape to help him.

"I've been watching you dance for me for weeks," he said quietly. "Or has it been months? I've watched you strip for me. I've watched you come for me. My entire being aches for you, *she'ashil*."

Her heart was pounding and she had to wipe her sweaty palms on her shorts. She'd like to think it was just from the muggy night, but she knew it was more than that. She felt oddly clear-headed. A state of mind she tried to avoid at all costs these days, and not just because of the voices, if she were going to be completely honest with herself.

Slowly, he reached out and picked up the end of one of her pigtails. He let the strands sift through his fingers while he stared at her hair in amazement. "All the colors of a sunset," he murmured. "Beautiful."

Ryan stood undecided. She couldn't seem to choose whether to run away as fast as she could, or to close the distance between them and get closer to the fire burning within him. But would that fire soothe her, or burn her until she was nothing but ash?

"I just want to kiss you," he told her. "Please let me kiss you, Ryan."

"I..." She what? Her head was spinning, and she forced herself to focus. She didn't think it was such a great idea to let a vampire kiss her, that's what. God, was he really a vampire? Maybe the hunger she sensed from him was blood lust, rather than normal lust. Or maybe it was a little bit of both? She should step away. She should back away from him. Tell him no. Why couldn't she bring herself to tell him no? Was he doing some kind of weird mind tricks on her or something?

Lowering his head until his mouth was barely an inch from hers, he held himself there, giving her the chance to refuse him. But she couldn't refuse him, she just couldn't. Her blood was singing in her veins, her nipples were puckering under her shirt, and there was a deep, steady throbbing in her lower belly. She wanted him to kiss her more than she ever thought possible.

When she didn't say anything to dissuade him, he lowered his head the rest of the way. His eyes held hers until he was so close his face blurred in front of her and she closed hers. Softer than she thought was possible, his lips brushed against hers a heartbeat later. Once, twice, three times. Cupping her face in his hands, he increased the pressure just a little. His lips were soft and firm at the same time, and when he ran the tip of his tongue along her bottom lip, her legs began to shake and she gasped in surprise. He slid inside her mouth, the kiss becoming more insistent now. More urgent. A soft groan escaped him, and she answered with one of her own.

She felt his teeth scrape her lips, but she barely registered the minor pain, or the fact that his entire body had stiffened and he had stopped breathing. He tasted wonderful, and without thinking, she stepped into him until her body was pressed against his. He was hard and warm. Her hands travelled from his slim waist up to his chest. His hands left her face and his arms wrapped around her, lifting her up and pulling her in even closer as he kissed her with all the passion she felt in him. His hunger fed her own, and she responded to him in kind.

All thoughts of running were chased away by the overwhelming presence of this male so tenderly taking what he wanted.

Christian felt his entire body shudder in ecstasy at the taste of her blood. He'd been reckless as he kissed her, and hadn't been careful of his fangs. He hadn't meant to feed without asking her. For some reason, having her permission was very important to him. He didn't want to do anything where he'd have to pull a memory swipe like he did with the others. He didn't want to erase what had happened when she let him out of his cage. He wanted her to remember him.

Forcing himself to slow down, he eased off on the tight hold he had on her. The last thing he wanted to do was frighten her more than the mere sight of him already had. But gods, he hadn't realized just how severely he'd been craving her until she was here in his arms.

Why she was allowing him to kiss her, he had no idea. But he wasn't going to pass up the chance. No fucking way. The reality of her was, oh, so much better than watching her through the glass. And by some miracle, she was responding to him just as intensely as he was to her.

Her thin arms wrapped around his neck as he licked and sucked the drops of blood from her lips. He wanted to grab a handful of that glorious hair and yank her head to the side and expose the artery throbbing just underneath her pale skin. And at the same time, he couldn't bring himself to act so rough with her. But gods, he needed more of her.

Breaking off the kiss, he tucked his face between her head and shoulder and inhaled deeply. Her sweet scent invaded every cell of his body. His fangs and his cock ached with equal intensity. Groaning with the pain he was causing himself, but unwilling to let her go, he held her close and tried gain some control.

She tensed up in his arms. He was probably squeezing her too tight. "Christian, what's wrong?"

He heard the note of alarm in her voice and hurried to reassure her. "I just don't want to scare you."

"Should I be scared?" Pulling away just enough that she could look at him, she studied his face.

He couldn't lie to her. "Yes," he whispered.

Blue eyes flared in alarm. "Let me go."

But he only tightened his grip on her and shook his head. "I won't hurt you."

"You just told me I should be afraid of you! Now let me go!" She started to struggle against him.

"Ryan, stop. Stop moving," he pleaded. "I swear I won't hurt you. Please, I need you..."

She socked him with a hard shot to the kidney. Her small fist didn't really hurt, but it was enough of a shock that he loosened his grip on her, and she was able to wiggle her way out of his arms.

Backing away from him, she held her hands to either side of her head, covering her ears. Her face was all scrunched up as she backed away. In confusion? In pain?

Concern for her instantly cooled his ardor. "Ryan? What's wrong?" He took a step towards her and was immediately pushed back by the same unseen hands that had thrown him off of her at the club.

Tears ran down her cheeks as she shook her head. "I'm sorry," she sobbed. "I can't control it." Turning on her heel, she ran.

"Ryan!" He tried to follow her, but the hands held him back. A roar of anger rent the night air as he fought them with everything he had, but it was no use. The more he fought and raged, the stronger they became. They held him there long after he'd stopped fighting. Then suddenly, just before sunrise, they released him just in time for him to find shelter nearby in what looked to be a small, abandoned clothing factory.

As he buried his aching body beneath the bolts of cloth, he berated himself for making her run. Why the fuck didn't he just tell her what she wanted to hear like he did with all of the other females he hooked up with? But he couldn't lie to her. He didn't know why, he just couldn't. And now she was gone again. And that son of a bitch that bit her was out there somewhere, and he'd had her blood too. That meant he could hunt her. It meant he could feel her if she was anywhere near him now, just like Christian could.

The only thing that kept him from taking his chances with the Mexican sun was the fact that he knew the other vampire was holed up for the day somewhere also.

As he felt the call of Ryan's blood getting farther and farther away from him, he turned his mind to the vampire who had attacked her. Mostly just to distract himself from his raging hard on, cramping muscles, and the acidity poisoning his veins.

He assumed that the one who had almost killed her was just some local vamp who'd happened to run across her wandering around high as a kite and all by herself.

But no, that couldn't be right. The young vamp's words came back to him, right before he'd bit her. He'd said they were both going to die because she demanded it. Who the fuck was "she"? And out of all the people in the world, why would he, or she, or whoever want to kill a vampire being held in Mexico and the stripper who had helped him escape?

When it finally came to him, he felt completely stupid for not thinking of it right away. Of course! It was Leeha. That bitch was the reason he was here, and this young guy who was doing her dirty work was probably just one of her little bitches. Christian thought back to all the vampires that had followed her when she left Luukas' colony to start her own, but no, this guy was not one of Luukas'. He was sure of it. She must've found him somewhere, or created him or whatever.

It didn't matter. What did matter, was that he found him before the little shit found Ryan. He wondered if the two that had attacked him earlier were working with this guy too? But after some thought, he decided that was probably not the case. The two that had assaulted him were human, for one. And, they were locals. Everything pointed to just a case of wrong place, wrong time. The ones that had found Ryan in the park were all vampires. Unfortunately, Christian hadn't taken the time to place his two helpers before ripping them into pieces. The Mexican authorities were going to have quite a heyday when the bodies were discovered the next morning, at least if they were found before the sun came up and the bodies burned to ash. And his prints were all over that crime scene. Probably some boot prints too.

Ah well, it wasn't the first time he'd clashed with the *federales*. Although it had been quite a few years since his last run in. Around two hundred, or thereabouts, actually. And they weren't police back then, they were ranchers. And they didn't appreciate a half-breed Navajo Indian coming around looking for work.

But same thing.

Christian shook off thoughts of his past. The only good thing that had come out of his human life was Luukas finding him when he had. If it hadn't been for him, he wouldn't be here right now hiding under a swatch of silky purple material with pink flowers and obsessing about a girl who was probably more fucked up than he was.

He had to find her again. And he would. As soon as the sun went down he'd set out after her. Hopefully, she hadn't gone far. But somehow, he didn't think that would be the case. More likely she'd find some dope somewhere and hole up for the day.

He would find her, and he'd apologize profusely for scaring her. Maybe he'd feed again before he saw her, even though just the thought of another's blood was enough to make him heave. But if he could manage it, maybe it would stave off his hunger for her enough that he'd be able to keep it under control and look a little more human when he saw her again.

Until then, he'd try to get some rest. He was so fucking tired, in spite of how jazzed up the female had him. He hadn't slept in so long his eyes felt dry and gritty and his brain was just bouncing around aimlessly from thought to thought.

Ignoring his throbbing groin and spasming muscles, he settled in and closed his eyes.

18

Ryan ran as fast as she could away from the creature she'd just kissed. She didn't want to watch what was happening to him right now. She couldn't. The last time the voices had gone after someone like that, they'd died. Of course, the bitch who'd been hurting Josefina? She'd deserved it. Her dealer...Ryan stumbled and almost fell but caught herself just in time.

Oh god, what if it was her doing it? Was it really her that had killed them? What if it was her that had thrown Christian around back at the club?

Was she crazy? Or was she some kind of freak?

She's always assumed she was a paranoid schizophrenic. When the voices had started talking to her, she'd thought they were just that: Voices in her head that weren't really there. She'd been so sure that she was crazy.

She'd tried to keep it hidden from her family for as long as she could, and she'd actually managed to do so for years. But by the time she'd turned seventeen, it had gotten to be too much, and even her little brother had started watching her with a strange look in his eyes. So she'd run away from home. Because she'd known that if she'd stayed, her parents would've dragged her to the doctor. She knew they loved her, and would only be trying to help, but their concern would've gotten her thrown into a psychiatric hospital. And there she would've stayed for the rest of her life. So she'd run away. And she'd been running ever since.

That was six years ago. She'd been running for a year before she'd discovered the diminishing effects of heroin on the voices, and her life had changed drastically in that moment. Unlike many of the past years, she remembered that moment clear as if it had happened just yesterday.

The red pill or the blue pill, Ryan?

The red pill meant living with the voices, not sleeping, not eating, wandering the streets talking to herself. The blue pill meant an entirely different life. The blue pill, the drugs, meant the voices were dimmed, meant she could act somewhat normal, but she had to become a person that she didn't like to be able to have a constant supply.

Exhausted, starving, and suicidal, she'd chosen the blue pill.

The first time she'd used had been with another homeless girl she'd met. She had left California by that time, and traveled as far as she could get on foot to put some distance between herself and her family. She'd made it all the way across the border, and shortly thereafter she'd met a girl around her age. They'd started hanging out together for safety. It had been a good arrangement while it lasted. They both suffered with mental disorders, and they'd understood each other. Whenever one went off the wall, the other would watch over them until they got through it.

One day, her friend had shown up in the food line at the shelter with a big, goofy smile on her face. Grabbing Ryan by the arm, she'd pulled her out of line and taken her back to their sleeping spot close to the highway. Giggling, she'd pulled a small bag and a syringe out of her pocket. She'd asked Ryan if she wanted to go away for a while.

Ryan stared at the drugs. She knew what it was. She also knew it was a dark path to go down. But by this time, she had been so desperate for an escape from her own mind, any escape, that she'd stuck her arm out and practically begged her to turn her on to it.

That first rush was something she'd never forget. As soon as the drug had hit her bloodstream, her mind had gotten fuzzy, her body had relaxed, and the fucking voices had dwindled away. It was wonderful. Tears had run unabashedly down her cheeks at the relief she'd felt to be all alone in her head for the first time in years.

She'd spent that day curled up on her sleeping bag, dozing and enjoying the every day noises of the city. But she fast discovered that it was only temporary. As soon as the dope wore off, the voices came back with a vengeance. Her pounding head had woken her up, the voices screaming at her for what she'd done. Tears had started anew as she shook her friend awake and asked for more, but she didn't have any more.

Stumbling around the homeless camp, she'd begged and pleaded for someone, anyone, to tell her where to get more of this wonderful stuff.

Back then, she'd done things she wasn't proud of. Things she didn't like to think about. But after living with strangers screaming in her head for years, she'd done what she'd needed to do to shut them up and save what was left of her sanity.

Until the day she'd gone to a new dealer's apartment to "trade" for some tar, or black heroin, and she'd woken up in a prostitution ring in Tijuana. She'd been sold by the dealer — a large supply of drugs in exchange for a pretty little white girl.

Except the joke was on her new "owners". The voices wouldn't let anyone touch her even if they were willing to take a chance with a crazy *gringa*. Her new managers quickly found out this white chick was no good for them unless they kept her supplied, for without the drugs, the voices took over. After the third day of finding her curled up in a corner arguing with no one they could see, they shot her up just to shut her up and threw her out to work the pole.

Now dance? That she could do. And she did. As long as she had dope and music to dance to, she didn't care where she was. Until the day the *matron* had gone too far with Josefina.

And now she was back on the streets, the voices were screaming at her, and she didn't have any more dope to shut them up, so she ran. She ran as fast as she could, down this street, and down that one, running aimlessly without looking back until she got to a familiar part of town.

She was running so hard that she didn't notice she'd run into the street. She didn't hear the car come around the corner. And she certainly didn't see it when it appeared suddenly in front of her because of the tears filling her eyes. Not until it was too late.

Brakes squealed as she hit the hood and went flying up into the windshield. Glass shattered and fell as she slid back down to land with a grunt back on the pavement. A man stood over her, looking around and yelling in Spanish, then he bent down and spoke soothing words to her. Sirens sounded in the distance, and Ryan tried to get up. She didn't want to go to the hospital. She couldn't! If they took her to the hospital, she'd never leave. She'd be stuck in a padded room with only the voices to keep her company forever. But the man, trying to be helpful, held her where she was and insisted she not move so she didn't injure herself further.

The sirens were louder now, so loud he couldn't hear her telling him that she was fine, that she needed to go. The next thing she knew, there were more people around her. Hands were touching her, taking her vitals, feeling her limbs for broken bones. No one listened to her as they stuck a neck brace on her and strapped her onto a gurney, and then she was in the back of an ambulance and they were on their way.

19

Josiah headed back to the jet. But he wasn't leaving. Oh no. Not yet. He just needed a safe place to hole up for the day so he could think.

Fucking morons. Why did he even bring them? Useless, the both of them. Taken out by one measly Hunter before they'd even realized he was there. Josiah had had no choice but to retreat from the scene. For now. If he hadn't, that Hunter would've added him to the pile of bodies before he'd finished draining the witch. He needed to regroup, rethink how he was going to do this. It was just him now. He was going to have to come up with a new plan.

At least her mortal wound kept the Hunter busy for a while so he was able to get out of there. If there was one thing you could count on with Luukas' vamps, they were all a bunch of fucking bleeding hearts.

He tried to think of how Leeha would handle this, but that was no help at all. Leeha was powerful, a force of nature, and much older than him in vampire years. At least, she had been. He had nowhere near the tricks that she did. If she were here, she'd meet them somewhere alone. She'd seduce the male while she sucked the witch's soul into her hypnotic red eyes, forcing her into the nightmares that existed there. Her favorite way to kill humans.

What powers did he have? A whole shitload of nothing. He'd been her plaything, nothing more. She hadn't taught him anything. He'd have to figure this out for himself.

Maybe he should head home. Gather up the vampires that were running loose in the area. Try to talk to them. She'd released the demons and possessed the vampires, and then kept them on standby while she amused them with humans for food and sex. Well, they weren't amused anymore, they were bored. They needed a purpose. And he would give them one.

As he approached the jet on the runway, he snagged a young male employee and brought him on board with him. He needed to feed and pass the time until nightfall, and this pretty boy was just the thing.

20

Ryan blinked her eyes against the setting sun, gradually coming awake. As she glanced around at the sparse furnishings in the room, nothing looked familiar. She didn't know where she was. Her heart began to pound and she began to sweat. But then it all came back to her in a flash: Dark hair. Glowing yellow eyes. A delicious taste in her mouth. Blood. Sultry kisses. Running, running as fast as she could. The shock and pain of the car hitting her. The medical personnel as they swarmed around her bed, hooking her up to wires, taking her pulse, and taking her for x-rays. They'd hooked her up to an IV, and that was where the memories ended.

She was in a hospital bed. There was a large window to her right, and the blinds were only partially closed. The walls were beige with the bottom halves painted a dark brown. One picture hung next to the window, some bright, flowery thing. A small T.V. hung in the corner.

Flashing hot and cold, she went to lift her arm to push the sheets down that covered her and discovered she was restrained to the bed with leather cuffs around her wrists. Panic alarms rang in her head. No! No! Dammit! The chains clanked loudly as she fought against the restraints, and a nurse came rushing in.

"Shhhh..." she soothed. "It's okay," she told her in broken English. "Those are only for your own safety."

Ryan turned wide, panic-stricken eyes on her. "Please, you have to let me go. I have to get out of here."

"That's not going to happen today, miss. I'm sorry. You were brought in late last night. You were hurt. Do you remember?"

Throwing herself back against the bed so hard her IV pole rattled, Ryan didn't bother answering her. As the nurse fussed around the bed, checking her lines and pushing buttons on the machine that was watching her vitals, Ryan stared at the ceiling. She was acting like a toddler, but she couldn't help it.

What was she going to do now? How would she get out of here? They would call her family. They would have her committed. She'd never see the outside world again.

Except, she didn't have any kind of ID on her. They wouldn't know who she was if she didn't tell them. Ryan's mind flew over all of the possibilities of what she could say when they asked. She could just claim she didn't remember anything. Not what happened, or who she was, or anything. She may still end up in a mental facility for the rest of her life, but at least this way she wouldn't burden her family. They probably thought she was dead by now, and it was better that way.

She turned to the nurse. "Tell me again how I got here?"

"You were brought in last night. You were hit by a car. Don't you remember?"

Ryan frowned and shook her head. "No. No, I don't."

"Can you tell me what your name is?"

She returned her inquisitive look with a blank stare. "Um..." Wrinkling her forehead, she tried to look distressed.

The nurse patted her arm. "It's okay. You rest. There were no major head injuries, but you have some fractures in your left leg and quite a lot of bruising, both inside and out. The doctor will be in to see you a little later."

"Um, okay. But is there any way I can get out of these?" Raising her arms as much as she could, she showed her the cuffs and tried to appear calm.

Shaking her head, the nurse gave her a sympathetic smile. "No, not yet. I'm sorry. You were quite violent when you arrived. Not until you're cleared by the psych doctor."

"But you said I was in an accident. I must've been upset..."

"No. I'm sorry. But since you're awake now, I can remove this. If you promise to behave." She pointed to a bag hanging from the bed, and Ryan realized she was also hooked up to a catheter.

"Yeah. Please. That would be great."

The nurse quickly and efficiently removed the tube. "Just call me if you need the bedpan." Tucking the sheet around her, she gave Ryan a wide smile. "I'll see you in a little while. Try to get some rest." And with that, she walked purposely from the room.

Ryan sank down into the bed. She could've at least left the remote control within her reach so she could watch T.V. Turning her head to the left, she saw a phone sitting on the table next to her bed. But she couldn't reach that either, and even if she could, she had no one to call. So she settled for staring at the obnoxious painting on the wall and tried not to think about what a mess her life was.

It was quiet in her room. Unusually so. She glanced up at the IV drip. It was just saline. Nothing there that would cause the voices to ease off. They were probably just in shock from the accident, gearing up to return full force as soon as she let her guard down.

Seconds ticked by, gradually turning into minutes, which dragged into hours. No one came to check on her. No one came to ask her if she needed anything, or if she remembered who she was yet. The window darkened as the sun set, and still, no one came.

The peace and quiet was actually really nice. There were no voices. No withdrawals either. Had they given her something?

Ryan burrowed into the bed and tried to enjoy it by not thinking about anything in particular. However, try as she might, she couldn't shake the brilliant topaz eyes that seemed to be everywhere in the room. Yet as soon as she looked their way, they disappeared. The thought of never seeing them again made her strangely sad.

Exhausted, she closed her eyes and tried to do as the nurse told her. There was no sense in freaking out about her situation. She'd just have to take it day by day.

"Are you planning on laying around in here all night? Or would you like to come with me?"

Ryan's eyes shot open wide. Christian, the guy from the club, the *vampire*...it was still so weird to think that...was standing next to her bed eyeing up her restraints. He looked different. His features, although still striking, were softer somehow. And his eyes weren't glowing. At least not like they had been the night before. His skin was slightly flushed too. "How did you get in here?" she asked.

He gave her a grin that showed off creases in the sides of his cheeks, and she forgot how to breathe when he reached over and brushed her hair back away from her face with gentle fingers. "I walked. It's not like you have guards." He pulled his hand away, but not before running one fingertip down her cheek, tracing her cheekbone. "Sorry it took me so long to get here, *she'ashil*. There was something I had to get back first, or I would've been here earlier." Holding up his arm, he showed her a silver cuff bracelet with turquoise stones embedded in the band.

She blinked at him like an idiot, still unable to fathom he was actually there, then she glanced towards the window again.

It was barely an hour after sundown.

"So, what do you say? Wanna get out of here?"

She wasted no more time with questions. "Yes! Please," she added. Lifting the arm closest to him, she waited for him to unbuckle her cuff.

"There's just one condition," he said.

Her eyes flew back to his face in unspoken question and her arm fell back to the bed.

"You have to stay with me," he said. "No more running."

She chewed on that for a few seconds. "For how long?" she asked.

"Just for now. There's a crazy vamp out there that's out to get us, remember? We can renegotiate after we get you out of here and make sure you're out of any immediate danger."

"Okay," she said.

"Okay?"

She nodded and held up her arm to him again. "What about you? He's after you too."

Unbuckling the cuff around her wrist, he walked to the other side of the bed to undo the other one. "Don't worry about me. I'll be fine." When the other cuff was undone, he pulled out her IV line with practiced hands and dug through the drawer to find a band-aid, which he taped to her arm. "Where are your clothes?"

Glancing down at the attractive hospital gown she was wearing, she said, "I don't know. I can go like this. I just want to get out of here before someone comes in."

He strolled over to the bathroom and came back out with a plastic bag. "You need something to wear besides that ugly thing. Here you go." Tossing the bag on the bed, he went to the door and checked the hall before quietly closing it. "Go ahead and get dressed," he told her. "I'll keep watch." He kept his back to her to give her a little privacy.

She wasted no time but jumped right off the bed; belatedly remembering the nurse saying her left leg was fractured. But she was standing on it and there was no pain. Shifting her weight from side to side, she tested the strength of the bones, but it seemed fine.

"What's wrong?"

Glancing up, she saw Christian watching her over his shoulder. "Um, the nurse said my leg was broken. Well, fractured. But it feels fine."

"It's probably healed by now."

"How is that possible?"

"Vampire blood," he told her with a self-satisfied look. "But be careful on it, just in case." And then he turned back around.

Holding the gown up out of the way, she stepped into her shorts, then pulled it over her head and tossed it onto the bed. It's not like he hadn't seen her naked before. Well, almost naked anyway. In any case, she'd lost her modesty a long time ago. Grabbing her cut-off shirt, she'd gotten one arm in a sleeve when she heard a sharp intake of breath. She froze in panic, worried that someone was about to barge in and force her back into the cuffs again.

But the only one looking at her was Christian. His eyes were roving over her breasts at a leisurely pace, like they had all the time in the world, even as his posture told her a completely different story. She didn't move, completely entranced by the desperate hunger she saw there. No one had ever looked at her like that before. Not ever. Not even when she was working the pole.

His upper lip curled back from his teeth, two of which were growing longer right before her eyes. Anger and something else she couldn't name emanated from him. It shot out from him and straight into her until she couldn't tell his emotions from her own. Those haunting eyes of his grew lighter and brighter as they stared at her, until they glowed yellow like a large cat of prey.

Shaking herself out of the trance he put her in, she continued getting dressed. Moving cautiously now, she pulled her shirt the rest of the way on. When her head popped out of the hole in the neckline, he had turned back to the door again. She searched the bag for her hair ties, but they weren't in there. Oh, well. Calming her hair down as well as she could with her hands, she twisted it up and tied the mass into a knot of sorts on the back of her head. Sliding her sandals on, she said a bit unsteadily, "Ready."

Christian glanced over his shoulder and opened the door. His emotions were less intense now that she was dressed, and his canines were hidden again. Checking the hall again, he waved her forward. "Come on."

When she reached him, he held her in front of him and looked her over, then tucked a stray piece of hair into her makeshift bun. Lowering his nose to the top of her head, he inhaled and then exhaled with a soft groan. His behavior should've weirded her out, but it didn't. Not at all. She wondered for a moment if he was going to kiss her again, but with a last longing look, he turned away. "Okay." He cleared his throat and tried again. "Let's go. Just stay calm. Remember, they can't keep you here. Not while I'm around."

She took his hand, and he glanced down in surprise. A scowl marred his smooth brow, but then he tightened his fingers around hers. Taking the lead, he led her from the room. Ryan's heart was pounding a mile a minute, and he must have heard it, for he gave her fingers a reassuring squeeze. But he didn't seem nervous at all. He just strolled down the hall like he didn't have a care in the world. And it worked. They only saw one staff member this late, and they were walking in the opposite direction. Before she knew it, they were out the front doors and on the sidewalk outside the hospital.

"Just keep walking," he murmured to her, and she nodded.

Once they got about two blocks away and no alarm was raised, she found she could breathe again. Taking a deep, cleansing breath, she asked, "Where are we going now?"

"Uh, not sure. I haven't thought that far ahead yet. A hotel? Somewhere quiet?" Glancing over at her where she walked beside him, he ran his eyes over her face. "We have some talking to do, you and I."

Her pulse sped up again at the thought of being alone in a hotel room with him, and he stopped walking, turning to face her. Ryan stared up at him, mesmerized by those amazing eyes. She felt a little like the rabbit cornered by the lion.

"You don't have to be scared. I swear to the gods I won't hurt you."

She could only nod.

He sighed. "Come on." Taking the lead again, he led her away.

A few blocks later, they found a small motel. "Wait here," he told her, and left her outside the front door while he went in to secure a room. She wasn't sure how he was going to do that, and honestly, she didn't think that she really wanted to know. Two minutes later, he came walking back out with a key and took her hand again.

"Did you hurt them?" She didn't mean to ask that out loud. It had just come out somehow.

He frowned down at her. "No. Of course not. I just helped him realize that it would be to his benefit to rent us a room. He won't remember anything in a minute. Just that he rented a room to a well dressed gentleman and his wife." Climbing to the second floor, he led her to room 204. "Here we go."

She hesitated only briefly before entering the room. He closed and locked the door behind them, then went around checking the blinds and turning on the small air conditioning unit. It kicked on with a knocking sound, and within minutes surprisingly cool air was blowing into the room.

Ryan rubbed her arms.

"Is that too cold?" he asked, but she shook her head.

"So, you can mess with people's heads? Is that what you did back there?"

Shoving his hands into his front pockets, he took her measure from across the room. Probably wondering how much truth she'd be able to handle. Then he shrugged. "I can change memories, or erase them all together. A human will know what's going on when I'm standing in front of them, but as soon as I leave their sight, they only remember what I want them to."

"Do you do this a lot?"

"I do it when I need to."

"Have you done it to me?"

"No," he said after a pause.

He was telling the truth. She could feel it.

"Ryan, can I ask you something?"

She gave him a sarcastic smile. "That's why we're here, isn't it? To talk?" Turning away, she pretended to check out the room. She knew why they were really here. And even though she should be worried, or offended at the very least, she wasn't. If she was going to be honest with herself, she hadn't stopped thinking about him since he'd kissed her. She had her back to him now, so she closed her eyes and let the things she felt rush through her.

She wished his arms were around her right now, his hard body pressed to hers.

She was suddenly very aware of her breasts and the delicious heaviness low in her belly. What would it feel like, she wondered, to have him ease that ache?

A deep growl from behind her skated across her sensitized skin, and when she opened her eyes, Christian was standing in front of her. She hadn't heard him move.

His eyes roamed over her face and his hands buried themselves in her hair. "Would I live up to your crappy expectations of a typical man if I kissed you right now?"

Excitement and a tiny thread of fear shot through her at the thought of this beautiful creature wanting her. But the fact that he was dangerous only increased her attraction to him. She had no idea why she reacted the way she did to him, and right now she didn't really care. "Yes. But I'd like you to do it anyway."

She saw the muscles in his cheeks as he clenched his jaw, and then he was lowering his mouth to hers. This was no tender exploration like the last time. Oh no. This kiss was all dominant male. Although he'd wanted her permission before he kissed her, he took her lips in a way that led her to believe he knew he hadn't really needed to ask. And the fact that he had endeared him to her even more.

Ryan moaned as he thrust his tongue inside, devouring her like the predator he was. Her hands found their way to his biceps, and the muscles flexed where she touched him. She gripped his arms, hanging on tight, because if she didn't she was afraid her legs would give out and she'd crumple to the floor in a puddle of feelings.

One of his hands left her hair and travelled down her back, then slid around to squeeze the side of her hip. From there it moved down to cup her backside. Her skin burned everywhere he touched, even through her clothes.

His other arm wrapped around her shoulders and he pulled her up and into him until she was on the very tips of her toes. She felt his hard length against her belly, and her body responded with a rush of moisture between her legs.

He growled again as he broke off the kiss. Pulling away just enough that he could look at her with apprehension filled eyes, he asked, "I don't scare you?"

Her own eyes roved over his taut features, his strange, beautiful irises, down to the tips of his fangs she could see peeking out of his parted mouth. "I think you're beautiful," she told him honestly.

He inhaled sharply and clenched his jaw again as he studied her. Trying to determine if she were telling the truth? A look of determination came over his face, like he'd made a decision. Turning around and taking her with him, he carefully laid her out on the bed. He followed her down, trailing kisses from her jaw to her throat, over her fluttering heart and lower, to nuzzle underneath her swollen breasts that were begging for his attention. She arched her back, encouraging him without saying a word.

Pushing her shirt up, he bared her breasts to his hungry gaze. And even though he'd seen them many times before, he caught his breath and stared in awe as if this were the first time. Her nipples tingled under his hot gaze, and she threaded her hands through his dark hair and pulled his mouth down to one tight bud. He sucked it into his mouth eagerly, and she cried out at the scratch of his fangs grazing her tender skin.

Then without warning, she felt a sharp sting as he bit her. But the sting was instantly replaced with the most amazing feeling as he started to suckle her, gently at first, and then with greater insistence. Appreciative moans accompanied every pull. Licking her wounds closed, he did the same to her other breast. Ryan writhed beneath him, then opened her legs wider and raised her hips, rubbing herself against his hard ridge until he thrust against her with a hoarse groan.

"Gods, I want you," he whispered. Her nipple stiffened even more at the feel of his warm breath against her wet skin. "I don't want to stop." His voice was husky and strained.

"Then don't," she told him.

Eyes too bright for a human flared impossibly brighter, and his body suddenly went rock still, the muscles in his arms bulging with the strain of holding himself above her. Running her hands over those muscles, she tilted her hips up towards him. "Christian?" Her voice sounded breathless even to her own ears.

Those eyes bore into hers for a moment longer, and then he seemed to make another decision. Lowering his head, he took her nipple in his mouth and flicked it with his tongue, then moved lower still to spread slow warm kisses and little sharp bites across her stomach.

When he reached her shorts, he yanked them off impatiently. His shirt quickly followed, and she swallowed hard at the sight of those powerful shoulders and rippling abs. She waited for him to remove his pants, but he didn't. Instead, he came back to her and picked up where he'd left off. Burying his nose in the soft reddish curls between her legs, he inhaled deeply, his low growl vibrating against her sensitive skin on the exhale.

He pushed her thighs even wider apart and she felt a flash of nervousness. She'd never felt so exposed in front of a male before, not even when she was dancing. But her nervousness was quickly forgotten when she felt the first wet touch of his tongue. Pleasure seared through her and she cried out as her body bucked upwards of its own accord. His arms slid under her thighs and his hands tightened down on her hips, holding her still. He settled in, separating her folds with his mouth and finding that sensitive spot.

Ryan's eyes rolled back in her head and she forgot everything but the sensations he was pulling out of her.

She'd lied before. She didn't want to die of an overdose. If she had to go, she wanted to go while doing this with him.

21

Christian rolled his hips into the mattress, seeking relief for the rock hard erection that was popping out of the top of his waistband. He wanted to be inside of her. *Needed* to be inside of her. But he also wanted to be right where he was. The taste of her sex was nearly as good as the taste of her blood, and he was in no hurry to leave this spot.

Besides, he wasn't going to have sex with her. Not all the way. This fucking dick of his was not going to rule his life. Not anymore. Never again. He didn't care what kind of shape he was in. He'd rather be unable to do his job because he was racked with pain, than unable to do it because he was getting led around by the wrong head.

Resisting her completely though? Yeah, he'd have to work on that.

Because even though his brain was telling him to back away from the bed and the gorgeous female on it, the rest of him wanted nothing more than to hear her scream his name as she came against his mouth. And came from his fingers as he sucked her pretty nipples. And then his mouth again...

Her fingers slid through his short hair and gripped tight, holding him against her, and his hands dug into her hips in response. Adjusting her position so he could see her better, he looked up her hot little body.

Ah, gods.

She was lifting her hips in spite of his tight grip, moving herself against him, her body undulating like she was working the stripper pole. Only this time, she was dancing a private dance only for him.

He laved her, sucked her, flicked his tongue against that sweet little bud. He committed to memory every little sound she made, every time she said his name, every response of her body. Expertly, he worked her higher and higher until her thighs were quivering against the sides of his face. She suddenly tensed, then her entire body jerked as his name tore from her lips.

His balls tightened and his hips bucked against the bed as he strained to reach his own orgasm, but it wouldn't happen. With a grunt of frustration, he brought her down gently and then turned his face and kissed her on the inside of her soft thigh.

"Oh, my god." She ran her fingers through his hair, gently now, and he closed his eyes and fought the fire burning through his veins.

Do it. She's right there. Naked and ready for you. Just do it! What the fuck is the matter with you?

No. No! He wouldn't do it. He needed to get a grip on this shit. The weeks in that little room had proven to him that he wouldn't die if he didn't get laid, even though there were times he'd wished he would. He just needed to learn to control it. That was all. Yeah. He'd learn to control it.

"Christian? Is something wrong? Did I do something wrong?"

Ah, fuck. "No! Gods, no." Crawling up the bed to lay next to her, he cupped her cheek in his hand and brought her face around so she would look at him. "You're beautiful and amazing. And you drive me completely wild for you."

Her brows lowered in confusion. "Then why are you stopping?"

"I just..." What? What was he going to tell her?

Sorry babe, it's not you, it's me.

"I just..." *Just think of something! Anything!*

But before he managed to say anything else, she rolled towards him and lifted up onto one elbow. He fell onto his back and her fiery hair fell across his bare chest. He moaned as the soft strands teased his hypersensitive skin. She traced the skin under his eye with one finger, then ran it across his cheekbone, and down his jaw and over to his mouth.

His lip pulled back, exposing his fangs. She glanced up and he closed his eyes, not wanting her to see how she was torturing him with just that small touch. But then they popped open again as he felt her pressing against the tip of his fang with her finger. She pushed until a drop of blood appeared on the tip.

Christian's body felt like it was made of burning steel. He couldn't move if he wanted to, but could only lie there and let her torture him with her soft exploration. Keeping his arms at his sides, his fists gripped the comforter as he let her satisfy her curiosity.

Her finger left his fang and she used it to rub her blood across his bottom lip. His nostrils flared as he caught the scent, and his tongue immediately found where she had touched his lip. At the first taste of her his entire body seized, and he had to fight like hell to keep from flipping her under him and sinking his teeth viciously into her throat.

A bead of sweat trickled down his temple in spite of the A/C, and he closed his eyes again and tried to think of something, anything, that would get his mind off of what she was doing. But the only thing that came to mind was the way her body had moved when he'd made her come. He wanted to see her do that again.

Something warm and wet touched his collarbone, then moved down to his smooth pecs. By the time he realized what she was doing, her little tongue was teasing his nipple. Something between a hiss and a moan tore from his throat as he watched her from beneath hooded lids, and she took that as encouragement. Running one hand down his stomach while she continued to kiss and lick at his chest, she found the button of his jeans. His cock kicked up as she pulled open his jeans and set him free.

He needed to stop her before she drove him completely insane. And he was just about to, but then her small hand wrapped around him and he lost all thought. He could feel her eyes on him as she slid her hand up and down his shaft. He was so cranked up, her fingers wouldn't reach all the way around. Coming back up to the head, she gave it a tentative squeeze.

Ah, gods!

Before he could reach down and pull her hand away, she had scooted down the bed to kneel between his legs. At the first tentative touch of her lips, his back arched up off the bed as his fists slammed down to grip the blanket again.

Holy. Fucking. Shit.

Her name burst from his lips as her mouth engulfed him as far as she could. Her hand stayed wrapped around the bottom half, and she started up a pumping rhythm that was just the right speed. Every time she pulled back, her tongue would flick around his head, and then she'd take him in again. The hot wetness of her mouth and firm grip of her hand was the perfect combination.

The heat in his blood all rushed to his groin as she worked him as expertly as he'd worked her. His legs stiffened and his abs tightened as he rocked his hips up and down and in and out of her sweet mouth. His balls tightened up and the head got all hot. He was so close to coming. He was right. Fucking. There.

But no matter how hard he strained towards it, he couldn't bring himself to go over the edge. Tears escaped his closed eyes even though he was squeezing them tight. He needed to stop her. She was killing him. He opened his eyes and his mouth to tell her to stop...

Sliding her hand up his stomach and across his chest as she sucked him off, she bent her hand back and exposed her wrist to him. Christian's eyes latched onto the blue veins pulsing beneath her translucent skin. With an animalistic growl, he grabbed her hand in his and sank his fangs so far into her he nearly hit bone. Her blood hit his throat just as her teeth scraped up the sides of his cock, and then bit him just underneath the swollen head.

With a roar, he came violently in her mouth, and she took it all. Every last drop. And then she licked him a bit more, just to be sure.

When his heart started up again, he pulled out his fangs and sealed her wounds. Reaching down, he grabbed her under the arms and pulled her up to lie across his body. He held her gently as he caught his breath and came back to his senses, rubbing the soft skin on her back over and over.

Holy. Fucking. Shit.

22

"Ryan? What's wrong? What's the matter?"

They'd been lying in bed, enjoying the feel of being skin to skin. But the more time that went by, the more Christian sensed that something was wrong.

She shook her head and refused to look at him. "I'd like to take a shower. I smell like a damn hospital."

"You smell wonderful," he argued. "But a shower sounds great. Maybe I'll join you?"

"Um, well, I was kind of hoping to have some time," she started to say.

Kissing her on the forehead, he cut her off. "How about if I go find us some clean clothes while you do that. I can get cleaned up when I get back."

She smiled up at him gratefully. "Okay. Thank you."

Rolling off the bed, he grabbed his jeans and slid them on. He wasn't sure what was going on with her, but he didn't want to bully her into telling him. He wanted her to tell him on her own. Once he was dressed, he took her face in his hands and waited until she met his eyes. "Do NOT leave this room or unlock that door for anyone. Understand? I won't be far. I think I saw a place just down the street that had clothing."

"Okay," she said.

He narrowed his eyes. "I mean it, Ryan. Not for anyone. And don't even think about running. I will find you, no matter where you go. Please," he added.

"I promise," she told him. And he believed her. But he'd hurry, just in case.

"I'll be right back." With one last kiss on her cupid-bow lips, he locked her in the room and took off at vamp speed to the little store he'd seen on their way here.

He was so distracted with thoughts of his female that it took him a while to realize how amazing he felt. Like, really fucking amazing. Normally, he'd already be jonesing for another female. But not now. Even though he'd only orgasmed once, and only had a small amount of her blood, he was completely satiated. Amazing.

Arriving at the store right before they closed, he picked out some new clothes for himself and some drawstring shorts and a tee shirt for Ryan that would bring out the blue in her eyes. He even grabbed her some underthings and a new pair of sandals that looked a lot more comfortable than the ripped up flaps of leather she was wearing now. Taking his stuff to the counter, he let her ring up his purchases and then "suggested" to the clerk that he'd already paid. With a smile of thanks, he took his bag and left.

The smell of a nearby restaurant reminded him that humans needed to eat, and he made one last stop for a to-go order. Racing back up to the hotel, he let himself in with the key. Ryan was still in the shower.

Laying the food on the dresser and the bag of clothes on the bed, he walked over to the door. His hearing being what it was, he could hear every distinct drop of water. He could also hear that she was crying and was trying to do it quietly so he wouldn't hear her.

His heart dropped in his chest. Knocking on the door to announce his presence, he let himself in. "Ryan. What's wrong? Why are you crying?" Leaning against the wall just outside the shower, he watched her through the white curtain. "Ryan, please talk to me."

Her hands were pressed over her ears as she sobbed. She whispered something about, "They're back."

Taking off his boots and quickly stripping out of his clothes, he stepped in behind her. Her gorgeous hair was plastered to her thin back, and he was glad he'd gotten her some food. She needed to eat more. He covered her hands with his and gently pulled them away from her ears. Turning her around to face him, he asked her, "Who's back?" He noticed that she watched his mouth when he spoke.

She raised swollen, teary eyes to his. "The voices." Then she laughed, but not in a happy way. "I guess I should've warned you." Closing her eyes, she cringed away from him.

"Warned me about what?" She didn't answer, so he got her attention by tipping her face up to his with a finger under her chin, then he repeated what he'd said. "Warned me about what, *she'ashil*?"

"That I'm crazy. Schizophrenic," she clarified. Her voice was quiet in spite of the loudness she must be hearing to warrant her covering her ears. "I think. I hear them all the time, and right now they're screaming at me."

"What are they saying?"

"I don't know." She sobbed anew. "They all talk at once, and I don't know what they're saying."

"Well, tell them to shut the fuck up."

She half laughed, half cried, her eyes on his lips as she tried to read what he was saying. "What?"

"Like you did at the park. Remember? That *is* who were telling to shut up, wasn't it?"

She looked at him like he was either the smartest man she'd ever met, or just as insane as she was. Then she screamed, "Shut up! Just shut up! Leave me alone!"

He waited, watching as her tears gradually slowed and then stopped all together. "Well?" he asked. "Did it work?"

"Yes," she whispered, like she was afraid of getting their attention again. "Yes, I think it did."

"Good!" He smiled. "Now we can talk."

Frowning up at him, she asked, "Why aren't you running away from the crazy bitch in your shower?"

"Why aren't you running from the scary vampire in yours?" he retaliated.

"But that's different," she insisted.

"How so?"

"You may be a vampire, but at least you're sane. If you were running around talking to people that only existed in your head, maybe I wouldn't be so eager to stick around."

"Really? Not even for my mind-blowing kisses?" And to prove his point, he leaned down and took her mouth with his until she was moaning and leaning into him, her full breasts pressed against his bare chest. His cock rose to full attention and he could feel her heart pounding. What was he saying? Oh, yeah. "Besides," he murmured against her lips. "I don't think they're all in your head."

It took her a moment to catch up. She pulled away just slightly. "What do you mean?"

Christian ran his fingers over what was left of a lingering bruise on her shoulder. He was very glad he hadn't seen her when she'd first arrived at the hospital. Seeing her all banged up like that would've killed him. Just imagining it was bad enough.

"Christian? What do you mean you don't think they're all in my head? Can you hear them?"

She looked so hopeful, he hated to tell her. "No, I can't hear them. But I've felt them."

"What do you mean?"

Finding the small bottle of shampoo the hotel provided, he poured some into his palm and then spread it through her long hair. As he washed, he talked. "Do you remember anything from the day you let me out of that room at the club?"

"Sort of. I was kind of out of it."

"You were high as a kite," he corrected without accusation. And then a thought occurred to him, and it all started to make sense. "Is that why you do it? The heroin? Does it help with the voices?"

She'd closed her eyes as he'd rubbed her scalp, and though she didn't answer him, a single tear slipped from underneath her lowered lashes. That was enough of an answer for him. Guiding her head back until her hair was under the water, he rinsed the shampoo from the long strands. When he was finished, he unwrapped the bar of soap and grabbed a washcloth from outside the shower.

He kept his voice low and soothing as he washed the tear stains from her face. "When you let me out of that room, I'd been in there for weeks. I was starving, and completely jazzed up from watching you dance every day. You can't imagine the torture that was for me."

"Because you're a vampire?"

"Yeah, kind of. And when you let me out, I was so scared that I wasn't going to be able to control myself. I was so thirsty. I hadn't fed in all that time." He decided to leave out the sex-starved part. She didn't need to know that about him. "I was afraid I would kill you. That's why I kept telling you to get away from me."

She stood still and let him wash her while she listened. "You came after me."

"I tried, but something—or *some things*—threw me off of you. And thank the gods they did, or I really don't know what might have happened."

She seemed to consider that for a minute. Taking the washcloth from his hand, she took over her bath as he washed his hair. Leaning forward, he rinsed the spiky strands of his grown out crew cut and opened his eyes to find her staring at the curtain with a bemused expression on her face.

"What is it?" he asked.

"You really think that something threw you off of me? Like, you felt it?"

"I did. And it happened again when you ran away from me at the park. I could feel the hands on me, holding me there so I couldn't chase after you. I don't think you're crazy, I think you're hearing the voices of some sort of...entities the rest of us can't hear or see."

"Like ghosts?"

"Yeah, something like that." Finishing up, he shut off the water and handed her a towel, then grabbed one for himself. "One thing's for sure, they're very protective of you."

"Then why are they trying to land me in an asylum?"

One half of his mouth lifted up in a smile. "I sincerely doubt that's their main objective. They're probably just communicating the only way they know how."

She was quiet as she dried off and wrapped the towel around herself. He left her to her thoughts and went out to the main room to get her clean clothes. Dropping his towel, he slipped on his new jeans and then walked barefoot and shirtless back to the bathroom to show her what he'd gotten her. "I hope they're the right size. I just kind of guestimated."

Her eyes wandered down his naked torso and the strong scent of her arousal rose in the air around them. His cock instantly responded, but he'd be a bastard and a half to jump on her again already. She needed to eat, and rest. She looked exhausted. He held the bag closer to her and she reached out and took it from him.

"I'm sure they'll be fine. Thank you."

"There's some food out here for you too when you're done."

"Okay."

He wanted to stand right where he was and watch her drop that towel, but he didn't dare. Instead he cleared his throat awkwardly and went back to the other room. Ryan joined him a few minutes later. The clothes he'd gotten for her fit well. Waving his hand towards the food he'd laid out on the small table, he said, "Sit. Eat."

"Thank you for the clothes," she told him as she practically ran over to the food. "You guestimated well."

"You're very welcome." He watched her dig into the rice, and his chest filled with a self-satisfied pride that he was able to provide for her. But as he watched her scarf down the food, the unpleasant thought occurred to him that she probably hadn't eaten in a while. "When was the last time you had a decent meal?"

She was quiet a moment as she chewed. "Honestly? I don't really know. A year? They only gave us some kind of mush at the club."

"And drugs. They gave you drugs."

She stopped chewing and peeked up at him before averting her eyes. "Yeah." Sticking her fork into the food, she took another big bite.

"To keep you complacent."

It wasn't a question, he was actually kind of talking to himself, but she answered anyway. "That, and to keep me from acting like a total nut job in front of the customers."

Christian moved behind her and started running his fingers through her hair, separating the strands and finger-combing the knots out. He wished he'd thought to grab a brush or a comb for her. "You know it wasn't just heroin they were giving you, right?"

"How do you know?" she asked. "And I can do that. I just wanted to eat first."

"I love your hair," he told her. "And I like to play with it. I've wondered how it would feel for a long time." Plus, he just liked feeling a connection with her. Something he didn't want to look at too closely right now. "But if it bothers you, I can stop."

She stilled, and then shook her head, and he resumed playing with the heavy mass while he answered her first question, "I got a taste of your blood when you let me out. I could taste the cocktail they were giving you." His voice dropped. "I am really sorry if I frightened you, Ryan. Great way to repay your kindness, huh?"

She shrugged it off and picked up the can of soda he'd gotten for her.

Clearing his throat, he went on, "I've tasted all kinds of heroin before, and your blood definitely had something else in it. And it wasn't your usual add-in. It was almost like a combination of heroin, coke, and ecstasy or something." He paused. "Do you know what it was? It kind of worries me that they were shooting you up with who knows what."

She stopped with the soda can tilted halfway to her mouth and turned in her chair to look up at him. He sat down on the edge of the bed so she didn't have to crank her neck back like that.

"Why do you care?" she asked. She didn't sound angry or uncomfortable, just genuinely curious. "Like, really. Why does it matter? So I danced for you a few times. We were both stuck in that shithole. I did what I had to do, and so did you. I can even understand why you tracked me down like you did. I dick-teased you for weeks, and you wanted to have sex with me. Well, now you have...sort of...and that's out of your system. So what's the deal? Why do you care?"

"There's another vampire after you..." he began.

"That's not the reason," she told him. "If that was the reason, you could just lock me up in a church or a salt circle or wherever was safe and go after him yourself. Instead, you're here making sure I eat and combing out my hair for me. Even my fucked up head isn't scaring you away. What's the deal, Christian?"

What was the deal? He heaved a heavy sigh as his shoulders slumped forward in defeat. "Damned if I know," he finally admitted. "All I know is I want to be near you. I want to help you. Is that okay?"

She studied him for a long moment, and in her turquoise blue eyes, so like the stones that reminded him of his heritage, he thought he saw a brief flare of something akin to hope, but it was gone so fast he couldn't be sure.

"Yeah, that's okay." And then she turned around and started eating again.

23

Shea paced the small room she'd been stuck in for the past weeks, then went over and flopped down sideways onto the bed. The raven, Cruthú, was with her as usual. The silly bird had been her only company for the majority of the time she'd been here. Jesse had been scarce since their last conversation, when he'd informed her that she couldn't leave and left her huddled in the corner. She could count the number of times she'd seen her captor on one hand since then. He came by every few days to check on her and escort her to the underground spring to bathe if she wished. He always stepped just outside of the room while she did so, and then took her back to his room. Once assured that she didn't need anything else, he would stride off down the tunnel. He never stayed with her. Didn't he ever sleep?

Something stabbed at her diamond stud earring and she frowned at the bird. "Stop it. I know it's all sparkly and pretty and hard to resist, but you're gonna swallow it. And that can't be good for you."

Cruthú squawked in disagreement, but started playing with her hair instead. She liked to run the long strands through her beak, and Shea had to admit that she didn't mind it. However, she was seriously about to start wrecking the place if she had to sit here one more minute. She was bored out of her skull. Jesse hadn't been down here in days.

And she was getting thirsty.

Cruthú suddenly released her hair and flew over to perch on the edge of the dresser closest to the door. Cocking her silky black head, she watched the door with one beady eye. Shea joined her and pressed her ear to the door. She could hear the steady tread of Jesse's boots coming down the passageway. Her mouth began to water and her fangs shot down as his scent preceded him. Gods, he smelled so good. Retreating to the bed, she perched on the edge and rubbed her face, trying to get it under control before he entered the room.

His footsteps, so far away just a second ago, suddenly sounded just outside the room. Shea and Cruthú both held their breath as the knob turned and a cloaked figure entered the room, shutting the door firmly behind him. But unlike the silly bird, who flapped and squawked happily until he presented his arm for her to perch on, Shea's heart pounded for a reason other than excitement.

"Hello, my friend," he told Cruthú as she hopped up his arm to rub her head against his jaw. "I've missed you too. Thank you for keeping Shea company." Flapping her wings, she scolded him for leaving her for so long nonetheless, or at least that's what it sounded like to Shea. Apologizing profusely, he rubbed her under her feathers and ducked his head until she was under his hood with him. He spoke quietly to her, soothing her and thanking her some more until she settled.

Once she was finished scolding and loving on him, she ruffled her feathers and settled on his shoulder.

Shea watched him with the raven, and she wondered vaguely what it would be like to get such a welcome from him. Then she scowled and shook the ridiculous idea from her head.

He still hadn't greeted her as he coaxed Cruthú onto the dresser again and swept his cloak from his shoulders to hang by the door. A slight breeze made its way to her, carrying a strong gust of the smell of his blood, mingled with the masculine scent that was his and his alone. Her shoulders tensed and she looked away, unwilling to let him see how much she craved him. She was just thirsty, that was all. She'd ask him to bring her some blood today, then she'd be fine.

Besides, she couldn't feed from him even if she wanted to. Every nerve ending in her body would scream in protest if she dared. He was male, and therefore off limits to her.

Distracted by her thirst, she hadn't noticed that he still hadn't turned to face her and was, in fact, still staring at his cloak hanging by the door. His dark head was bent, and his powerful arms hung at his sides, his hands clenched into fists. When she did finally notice, she told herself that she didn't care if something was bothering him or not. Or if he even spoke to her or not. She just wanted to get the hell out of here.

But she did need that blood. "Jesse?"

He stiffened at the sound of her voice. Yet he didn't turn around or acknowledge her in any other way.

Annoyed at being ignored, she swiftly decided she didn't care. If he was going to keep her here, she needed to feed. "I'd like to take you up on that offer you made when I first got here."

Finally, he lifted his head and turned to look at her. His striking face gave nothing away. "What offer is that?"

Tucking her hands between her knees to keep them still, she said, "You said you could get me some bagged blood." He didn't confirm or deny her request. "Can you get me some? Today?"

With a nod, he turned and left the room.

What the hell was that all about? Shea rose from the bed and resumed her pacing. He couldn't be upset with her, she'd barely seen him since he'd locked her in here. Before she had time to worry about it farther, he was back, two bags of blood in each hand.

"Is this enough? I wasn't sure how much to get."

"Don't you feed the vampires here?" she asked. "The ones that work for Leeha?"

"Not personally, no. So I don't know what they're allotted. But I don't want you to be uncomfortable, so if you need more, please don't be afraid to ask." Setting the bags on the small table, he backed away.

Shea thanked him, and grabbed up one of the bags. Ripping it open, she tilted it up to her mouth, uncaring that he was watching. With his wonderful scent filling the room, the taste of the plastic infused blood was all wrong, and she nearly gagged. Gods, how the hell did Nik drink this stuff on a regular basis? She managed to get down one bag, but couldn't bring herself to open another even though she probably could've used it. "That stuff is horrible," she mumbled.

"Do you prefer a different kind?" he asked. "We have all blood types. I didn't know if it would matter..."

"No, this is fine," she assured him. His golden eyes bored through her, and she had to look away.

"Would you like to go outside?" he asked out of the blue.

Shea's pulse sped up at the thought. If she could get outside, she could escape! He couldn't have a spell around the entire area to keep her in. She tried to keep the excitement out of her voice. "I would love to go outside."

With a nod, he stepped back and indicated for her to precede him. "Come, Cruthú."

The raven was even more excited than Shea, flying around in a circle before landing on his shoulder. When she reached the doorway, he stepped in front of her and waited until she looked up at him.

"Do not try to run. Because I will catch you, and I'll have to touch you to get you back in here. And I won't let you out again."

Shea ground her jaw together. She didn't doubt that he would do just that. The bastard.

"Shea?"

"All right," she gritted out. "I won't try to run." She could feel him probing around in her head, but he must have believed her, for he let her pass. Stepping aside, he indicated for her to go ahead of him.

They had walked for quite some time when he said, "I'm not a bastard."

Shea stumbled over a non-existent object on the dirt floor of the passageway. So he'd heard that too, huh? She didn't want to argue. She was trying to pay attention to where they were going. They walked quickly, navigating the tunnels that led up and out of the mountain that Leeha had made into her home. Old-fashioned torches lit their way, and Shea remembered thinking when she was first brought here that she was being taken right to the depths of hell. Now she felt like she was rising from those depths. And she didn't want to go back.

"I just..."

"Yeah, yeah, I know," she interrupted bitterly. "You can't let me leave."

They walked on in silence for the rest of the way except for when he told her which way to turn. Shea had no idea how he ever found his room in this maze. She was completely lost. If she ever tried to escape on her own, she'd fail miserably.

"Take a right up here, and then a quick left. That passage will take us outside."

Her steps sped up at the thought of being able to gaze upon the stars and feel the cool breeze on her heated skin. Hell, she'd be perfectly happy if it was raining.

"Remember what I said, Shea."

She didn't bother to answer him. Up ahead, she could see the opening. Cruthú, who'd been riding happily on his shoulder until now, gave her wings a flap, and then flew past Shea through the tunnel. Laughing, Shea ran after her, and they both exploded out into the night with Jesse right on their heels. It was drizzling lightly outside, but she didn't even care. Running into the trees, she followed the raven to a grove of pines and cottonwoods. Cruthú wove in and out of the branches, then circled back towards Shea and Jesse.

Shea stopped and watched her fly, a wide smile on her face. Forgetting her ire at him for a moment, she turned to Jesse to share her joy. But instead of watching the raven, his eyes were glued to her face. Her smile faltered at the intensity she saw there. They dropped to her lips, and he came closer to her. Her breath caught in her chest, and she forgot everything for a moment. Just as he lowered his head towards hers, she stumbled back out of his reach. "No! Don't touch me!" She lowered her voice, saying more calmly, "You can't touch me."

The muscles flexed in his jaw as he tracked her movements. After a tense moment, he broke off the contact and turned away, but still kept her in his line of vision. "Shea, please don't hate me."

"Let me go, and I won't," she bartered.

He dropped his head back. The rain washed over his face and Shea wondered if he was asking the heavens for patience or just watching his bird. After a moment, he sighed deeply and came to stand in front of her. "I wish I could explain it to you, but I don't know how. I only know that something is telling me to keep you with me. And I trust my instincts."

"But I don't want to be here," she asserted. "Do your instincts tell you to keep females against their will?"

"I saved you. At least let me figure out what this is all about."

"What it's all about? What could it be about? Other than you don't want to hurt me."

"No," he agreed.

"You don't need me for anything. You can't even touch me, so I know that's not why you're keeping me here."

His eyes when they lifted to hers reflected all of the conflicting emotions going on inside of him, and Shea had to take a step back. He was always so guarded. He never revealed his emotions, inside or out. Why was he opening up to her now? And why was she responding to the need he was showing her?

She shook her head. "You can't even touch me," she repeated.

"But I want to. Desperately."

At his blunt words, she realized she wanted that too, and a deep ache opened up in her chest because it could never happen. With him, or anyone. "Please let me go," she whispered. "I swear I won't tell anyone anything. I'll just say I was locked up here and I escaped. Please, Jesse."

He stared at her for a long time. Every word he couldn't say on his agonized features. But there was nothing for it. He wasn't a good male. And even if he was, she could never be with him.

"Let me go."

He looked away, and when he looked back, that emotional wall was back up. Whistling to Cruthú, he turned and walked purposely away.

Shea stood there, waiting for him to indicate that she was to follow him. He didn't. And he didn't look back. She watched him disappear back into the mountain tunnel.

She was free.

So, why did it hurt so much?

24

Ryan woke up first. Lying on her back, she blinked her heavy eyelids as she stared up at the water stained ceiling. She didn't immediately recognize the tiles up there and the anxiety she'd felt at the hospital returned. For a long minute she was scared witless. As she tried to rack her brain, a quiet snore next to her had her nearly leaping with a scream from the bed. At least until she saw who it belonged to.

Immediately, she relaxed. And then her pulse picked up for an entirely different reason as she remembered his mouth and hands on her the night before.

He looked peaceful as he slept, but underneath that illusion of slumber, she could feel a sense of him being aware. Like he could never truly rest, but was always in a semi-awake state. She wondered if he always slept like that, or if it was because that other vampire was after them.

For the monster he was supposed to be if every vampire movie ever made was to be believed, he'd been nothing but protective and kind to her. And yeah, a bit stalker-ish. But maybe that's just the way these creatures are. In any case, though she appreciated his offer of help, she'd come to the conclusion right before she'd fallen asleep that she was a problem he didn't need to take on. She didn't need to be a burden on him. She could take care of herself.

Sliding out of the bed, she padded barefoot to the bathroom and closed the door quietly behind her. After she'd taken care of her most pressing needs, she went over to the sink to wash her face. A new toothbrush, toothpaste, and a hairbrush sat there. His thoughtfulness made her almost…angry, and she didn't know why. Telling herself she was being stupid, she cleaned her teeth and then set to work on the mass of orange tangles that were sticking out all over her head. Plaiting it into two long braids, she made hairbands by ripping off pieces of the cut-off jersey shirt she'd been wearing when they arrived. Throwing the remains of the shirt in the garbage, she splashed some cold water on her face.

During all of this, she kept her mind purposefully blank. She didn't want to think about the events that had brought her to this point in time, and she didn't want to think about where she was going from here. And she especially didn't want to think about the beautiful male in the next room and how she would miss him, even though she barely knew him. But he deserved something better than looking after a hot mess like her.

Leaving the bathroom as quietly as she could, she slipped on her new sandals and tiptoed to the table. The sun was still on its downward descent. If she could get out the door without waking him, she'd be able to get a good head start. And if he knew what was good for him, he wouldn't follow her this time. Because it certainly wasn't her and her baggage.

A pen and a small notepad lay next to the remains of her dinner, compliments of the motel, and she contemplated leaving a note for Christian. But what would she say? *Thanks for the food and the orgasm, but I have to go find my next fix now before the sickness hits. Maybe I'll see you in a strip joint somewhere sometime. Kisses!*

A small, derisive noise escaped her. Yeah, it would probably be better to just go. Turning towards the door, she quietly unlocked the deadbolt. Her hand was on the latch when a breeze rustled her clothes and hair and suddenly there was six feet plus of wide-awake and completely alert vampire leaning casually against the door next to her, holding it closed.

"Where are you going, Ryan?"

Lowering her eyes and keeping her hand on the door handle, she didn't bother to answer. There wasn't any need.

"I don't want you to leave," he said. Ducking his head, he tried to get her to look at him. But she couldn't. If she looked at him, she'd want to stay. And if she stayed, she wouldn't have anything to help when the voices came back. She wouldn't have anything when the sickness came from the withdrawals. And he'd be stuck here with a shell of a woman vomiting all over his bathroom and screaming at things that weren't there. And that wasn't fair to him. They were practically strangers. As soon as the going got tough, he'd be out of here like any normal person, or vampire, or whatever, and then she'd be stuck here by herself and too sick to find a dealer. The neighbors would hear her, the cops would be called, and she'd be right back in the hospital. And this time there'd be no escaping.

"*She'ashil*, I want you to stay with me." He stepped away from the door, giving her the choice, but she could feel the anxiety pouring out of him. "I'm asking you. Please. Don't leave. Stay with me."

"Why?" she whispered.

Carefully removing her hand from the latch, he turned her around to face him and tilted her face up with one hand cupping her jaw until she had to look at him. "Why not?" he asked. "Do you have somewhere better to be?"

She opened her mouth to name the list of places she had to be, but what came out instead was, "What does that mean? *She'ashil*?"

He brushed her bangs out of her eyes. "It means something like 'sweetheart' in Navajo."

Navajo Indian? "You're American Indian," she said needlessly. Well, that explained the naturally tanned skin and black hair. Maybe the eyes were a vampire thing.

"Yeah, sort of." At her look of confusion, he explained, "I'm a half breed. Half Navajo, half white."

"Oh." Stepping away from him, she made to say her goodbyes. "I really need to go. Um. Thank you. For the food and clothes…for everything."

He laced his fingers behind his neck and looked to the ceiling for answers. As she put her hand on the latch again, he dropped his arms to his sides. "Why are you leaving me? Did I do something? Say something?"

There was such a tone of desperation in his voice that she paused with the door barely cracked. A thin sliver of weak daylight shot through the opening as the sun made its last hoorah before sinking below the horizon. Pausing, she looked over her shoulder at him in confusion. She honestly couldn't imagine what would make him want her here. "*Why* do you want me to stay?"

He didn't seem to know how to answer that. Wrapping his arms around his lean waist like he was trying to hold in his emotions, he paced back and forth a few times before stopping abruptly and saying, "I honestly don't know. I just know that the thought of you leaving…the thought of you not being near me…" He couldn't finish the thought. "And the sun is still up. I couldn't follow you. I can't…" He paced again. "I don't know what's going on. I'm not usually like this with females. I'm the complete opposite of clingy."

So, he felt it too. She didn't understand what it was between them either. But she still needed to leave. "Christian, I'm sorry. But I have to go."

"*Why?*" The word was torn from his throat.

Ryan sighed. Might as well lay it on him. He'd be disgusted when she was through. He wouldn't want anything to do with her. But that was good. He deserved better. For a vampire, he was an all right guy. "Because if I stayed here and let myself get sick, I'll wish I was dead. Because I need to go find a dealer before that sickness hits. Because I can't go a day without shooting up. Because I can't deal with the voices screaming at me until I can't hear anything but them. And when I find that dealer?" Her voice broke, but she pressed on. "I'll do whatever I need to do to get my dope. I'll suck his dick if the voices let me. I'll let him jerk off while he watches me play with myself. Sometimes I do even worse things. And if they won't let me get close to him, I'll imagine his heart squeezing in his chest until it stops beating. Then I'll take what I need off of a dead man, and I won't look back." Her voice caught on a sob. "Because I'm not a good person. I'm a whore, and I'm a druggie. I'm disgusting. That's why."

He was quiet as she stood before him with her soul laid bare. She refused to look at him. She didn't want to see the look on his face now that he knew the truth of who she was.

"Go."

She sobbed in earnest this time, until she realized it wasn't Christian who had said that.

"Stay."

"Oh, god." They were back. Ryan started to laugh, the maniacal sound loud in the quiet of the room. She laughed and laughed as the tears ran down her face. Tears for herself.

Tears for her family. Tears for this great guy she'd just met. Tears for the life she'd never be able to have.

Strong hands gripped her shoulders and pulled her into a hard, warm chest. She let him hold her. He was telling her goodbye, she was sure of it. And she let him, because she needed this moment of comfort before she walked out that door and went back to her fucked up excuse for a life. She pressed her ear to his chest and let the solid beat of his heart drown out the voices.

"Ryan...*she'ashil*...shhhh. It's okay, honey. It's okay."

"How can you stand to touch me?" she mumbled into his shirt.

His chest rose and fell on a breath. "I'm no one to judge you. And you're not disgusting. Don't ever think that about yourself."

"It's true..."

"No," he insisted. "It's not."

She disagreed, but she wasn't going to continue to argue with him.

"However, now that you have that off your chest, I still want you to stay with me."

His deep voice rumbled under her ear, and she pulled away to look up at him in disbelief. How could he still want her to stay? Unless, he knew a way to get her some stuff...

"And no. I'm not enabling your habit."

"But I have to have it." She hated the neediness in her voice.

"No, you don't. I can help you." He smiled down at her and wiped the moisture from her cheeks. "Trust me. I can help you. But you have to stop running away from me."

A trembling surge of hope dried the last of her tears. She was afraid to believe him.

But if she wanted any kind of a life, did she have any other choice?

25

Christian reached out and re-locked the deadbolt. Backing towards the bed, he sat on the edge and pulled her onto his lap. He needed to sit because he was so weak with relief that she was still here with him, his legs were about to give out.

He didn't understand what it was about this female that was making him react this way. All he knew was that his heart had stopped completely when he'd opened his eyes to see her at the door, about to walk out into the sun where he wouldn't be able to get to her. He couldn't take another day waiting out the daylight while she was out there alone and in danger.

They sat in silence for a long time while he stroked her back and played with her braids. In spite of the interest his cock was displaying with her lush little ass nestled up against it, he was surprised by how at peace he felt. There was no agonizing cramping and burning. No mindless need for sex or blood. And although he could feel the lust for her building inside of him, it was a normal kind of hunger a male would feel for his female.

His female.

He continued to stroke her back as he tried to calm her.

Mine.

He scowled. It was unexpected how possessive he was over her.

Glancing at the clock, he saw it was nearly full dark, so he picked up the phone next to the bed. Ryan went to get up off of his lap, but he growled with displeasure and held her there until she settled in again with a contented sigh.

Punching in the number he knew by heart, he held the phone up to his ear and listened while it rang.

It was time to go home. And he was taking this female with him.

26

Luukas was jotting down notes as to what still needed to be done to find his Hunters when the phone rang on his desk. Picking up the receiver, he said hello just as Nikulas and Aiden walked into the apartment with their mates and greeted his Keira.

"Luukas," he growled, distracted by the sight of his mate's smile.

The line crackled, and then he heard, "Luuk?? Is that you? Thank the gods they got you back."

Standing up so fast he had to grip the edge of his desk, he said, "Christian?"

"Yeah, it's me."

Luukas tapped on the glass wall of his office, then put him on speakerphone while the other two guys hurried into the office and stood by anxiously.

"Christian, where are you?"

Nikulas and Aiden exchanged disbelieving looks.

"Closest I can guess, Tijuana." There was a pause, and then he confirmed. "Yeah, I'm in Tijuana."

"As in Mexico?" Nik asked. "The land of sun and fun?"

Christian's chuckle came over the line. "Hey, Nik. How are you, man?"

Luukas got back to business. "Are Shea and Dante with you?"

"No. No. It's just me. I woke up here locked in a room by myself. If they're here, I haven't seen them."

"Are you injured?" Aiden asked.

"No, I'm good."

Luukas nodded once at his brother, and Nik whipped out his cell phone. "I'm sending a plane. Nikulas is on the phone now. Hold on and I'll get you the details." As they waited for Nik to arrange things, a thought occurred to him. "Are you free? Will you be able to get to the airport?"

"Yeah. No problem. And there will be two of us coming back on that plane."

They heard a swift intake of breath, and Christian saying offside, "Yes, you are. We'll talk about it when I get off the phone."

"Another vampire?" Luukas asked.

"No. A human female." He paused. "She's...she needs help. And she helped me escape."

Nik and Aiden exchanged another round of looks. "Well, this is quite the surprise," Aiden said offside to Nik.

"You ain't kidding," Nik murmured. He waved his cell in the air. "We're all set."

Luukas shushed them with a look. "Not a problem. Bring the woman. We just want you home safe." Waving Nik over, he indicated for him to give Christian the flight info.

"Hey, man. It's Nik. So we have one of our jets hitting the Tijuana national airport in a few hours. Here's the info."

"Go ahead," Christian told him.

As Nik gave him the flight information, Luukas sat back down in his chair. He was anxious to find out where his Hunter had been, and if he had any information that would help them find Shea and Dante. But it could wait until he got home. In the meantime, he would put his plans on hold. They needed to check in with the local businesses he owned anyway.

In the kitchen, Keira laughed at something her sister said. Her laugh was throaty and sexy, and it immediately caught Luukas' attention. His entire body instantly hardened, and he had to suppress the urge to stalk out of the office and haul her off to their bedroom. Everything about her turned him on. From her sparkling hazel eyes and curvy little figure to the way she had absolutely no fear of him. Of course, she had no need to fear him. She could suck his powers from him almost instantly if she so chose, as she had proven when they'd first met over seven years before. And although he still had the occasional relapse into his head from those years, they were fewer and far between now. He still tied her to the bed more often than not, though these days it was usually more for her pleasure rather than to ease his fears of her leaving him.

Every day she was with him, her love healed him a little more.

But the magic still stressed him out. Actually, it more than stressed him out. There were times, when she and the other witches were practicing, that he could feel himself being sucked back to that dark place, no matter how he tried to fight it. Luckily, Keira could usually sense when he was falling down that hole, and she would call a halt to their practicing and come to him. She was the only one that could pull him back from that abyss, strange as that sounded, as she was the one who'd put him there.

His witch.

His angel.

Nikulas hung up the phone. "Okay, he doesn't have a cell phone, but I told him to call us from the plane once he and his female were on board. They'll fly through the day and be here at dusk tomorrow. Aid and I will go pick them up at the airport."

"I'll go too," Luukas said. He knew Nik still worried about him, and that was why he hadn't been included. But it still irked him. He was their creator for gods' sake.

Nikulas tried to act casual, and failed miserably. "Sure! Of course. I assumed you would be."

Aiden clapped his hands and rubbed his palms together. "One down, two to go! I have a good feeling about this, mates."

"And hopefully, once everyone is back," Nik said. "We can figure out how to lift Keira's curse from the others."

"Sounds like Christian already took care of that problem." Aiden grinned. "He's completely whipped already. I can hear it in his voice. Maybe we won't have to hold that intervention after all. Quite a change from his usual shag 'em and shuck 'em lifestyle he's been living. It's going to be right fun winding him up about it."

"Does there happen to be a hedgehog in your hood?" Nik asked innocently.

Aiden scowled at his best friend. "Sod off, Nik. It's not the same."

"Uh, yeah. It kinda is."

"Don't listen to him, Prickles. He's just jealous that he has no one that likes to hang out with him."

"All right, you two," Luukas cut them off before they really got going. "Let's get back to work. We still have two Hunters that are missing and business to run and borders to check."

"Right," Aiden said.

"Sorry. You're right," Nik apologized.

With a last longing glance at Keira out of the clear glass that separated him from his mate, Luukas sighed and picked up his pen.

27

Ryan shot up off of Christian's lap. She sucks him off and now he thinks he can just dictate her life? How dare he make plans without consulting her first! Did he really just assume that she would do whatever he said? "Where exactly do you think you're taking me?" Her voice was shaking.

Christian leaned forward and rested his elbows on his knees. He looked so calm. Why was she the only one freaking out here?

"We're going to Seattle. To my home. My friends have a private jet on the way here."

Holy shit. "Your friends own a private jet?" She was momentarily shocked out of her anger.

He nodded.

"Who the hell are you?" she breathed. "I mean, a vampire. I know. I have the bites to prove it." His eyes flicked down to her breasts. When they moved back up to her face, they were bright and intense.

Ryan caught her breath as her body reacted to that look she was already coming to know well. It took her a few seconds to remember what she'd been saying. Crossing her arms over her chest to still the tingling he'd created there with nothing but his hungry gaze, she said, "I think I deserve a little more information about what I'm getting myself into before you just haul me off by the hair and throw me into your cave."

Christian threw back his head and laughed. The sound was so free, so pure and masculine, that Ryan found herself smiling in response. She couldn't help it.

When he was able to speak, he at least had the decency to apologize for his behavior. "You're right. I'm sorry. I should've talked to you about it before I called. But I can't stay here. My home, and my colony, is in Seattle. Besides, it's way too bright down here for me. Odds are good that if I stayed here I'd end up with one hell of a sunburn. And by sunburn, I mean you'd be finding a pile of ash."

"What makes you think I would even want to go with you? I don't even know you." She was being belligerent, she knew. But she needed to make a point here. Even though she hadn't left yet, and yeah, they'd sort of slept together, she hadn't agreed to travel across the continent with him. No matter what he seemed to think. "I haven't made up my mind about anything yet."

He rubbed his strong jaw as he stared at her. She could practically see the gears in his head grinding away as he tried to think of a way to convince her to come with him. But after a few seconds, he sighed, and his arm fell back down to rest on his leg.

"I have to go home. And I want you to come with me, *she'ashil.*" He looked around, seeming to search for answers he couldn't find. "I can't explain these things I'm feeling. I just know that it feels right to have you with me. And I want you with me. Please," he added with a sexy little smile. "Unless, of course, there's something important keeping you here?" He cocked one heavy eyebrow in question, the sarcasm in his voice not escaping her.

She had to admit he had a point. There was absolutely nothing for her here. Just more of the same shit, different day. Days spent nodding off on the streets with the sun beating down on her, and nights taking her clothes off for a bunch of pervs to earn the money to get more dope. Or if she were really unlucky, she'd end up stumbling back into a human trafficking ring. Only this time, they might kill her for not spreading her legs for their customers, rather than just letting her dance.

Swallowing hard, she knew her life was about to take another major turn. If she stayed with him, it meant detoxing and living with the voices. But it also meant being with him, and maybe actually having a life she wasn't ashamed of. If she walked away now, she would be free to use all she wanted. And she would probably end up dead in the street sometime in the near future from an overdose or worse. Somehow that didn't hold the appeal that it had just a few days ago.

The red pill or the blue pill?

He'd said he could help her. And for some weird reason, she believed him. What was even stranger was that even though she'd only really known him for a few days, being in his arms felt like...home. The answer was very clear, if only she'd admit it.

"You don't even know me." She could feel herself caving, and made one last pathetic stand.

"I do know you, Ryan." He placed a hand on the center of his chest. "I know you here."

She hugged herself tight, trying to stop the words that she could feel bubbling up and out her traitorous mouth. "All right."

A look of cautious hope spread across his handsome features. "All right?"

She nodded. "I'll come with you. I'll stay with you. For now," she emphasized.

He was in front of her before she'd seen him leave the bed, but he didn't give her time to be freaked out by how fast he could move. Wrapping her in his muscular arms, he lifted her clear off the floor and pressed a kiss to the corner of her mouth. "Thank you, *she'ashil*. You won't regret this. I promise you." Setting her down, he took her face in his large hands and made her look at him. "Don't be frightened. I know we don't know each other very well, but I'll help you.

And no one will harm you. We'll find a way for you to deal with the voices that doesn't involve drowning them out with opiates. And when you've got that under control, I'll even help you get to wherever you're headed to next and make sure you have enough money to make a healthy new start. Deal?"

"Deal," she agreed, ignoring the stab of pain at the thought of leaving him. "But, um, would you mind putting that down on paper? And signing it?"

Throwing his head back, he burst into laughter again.

28

Josiah stalked through the front door of his temporary home. He was still seething about how fast everything had gotten out of his control. About how much he'd botched up such a simple fucking mission. All he'd had to do was kill one Hunter and his slut of a human girlfriend. It should have been a simple thing for the three of them to accomplish.

But instead, the only two loyal vamps he'd had were dead. And instead of staying and fighting he'd turned tail and hightailed it the hell out of there. He'd had no choice. If he had stayed, he would've ended up just like them. He'd only been reborn about ten years ago. He didn't have the power to fight one such as that Hunter on his own. He'd done the right thing.

So why did he feel like such a little bitch?

Not bothering to close the front door behind him, he headed straight back to Leeha's room and threw himself on the bed. Rolling over onto his back, he stared up at the ceiling tiles. He needed to think. He needed to regroup. Grabbing one of the pillows, he pulled it to his chest and hugged it tight.

Leeha's scent rose from the soft cotton pillowcase and his gut wrenched tight. Gods, he missed her. She was a crazy bitch, but she was ruthless and sexy as all hell, and he had been hers to command. Both in bed and out.

But with her death, he'd been thrown to the winds, tossing and turning in a cyclone of emotions. Not knowing which way was up, or which way to turn. He wanted to do right by her. But how could he do that when he couldn't even handle one of Luukas' vamps? Never mind killing all of them along with their pain in the ass mates. Gods knew what kind of spells those fucking witches would be throwing at him while he took care of their males.

He wondered if the bitch in Mexico was still alive. She'd been surprisingly easy to catch, or maybe not so surprising with all the dope she'd been on, and made excellent vampire bait. The Hunter had been doing what he did best, and had tracked her through the city straight to Josiah's little trap.

Josiah knew the reputation those vamps closest to Luukas had, but he was still stunned at the speed and strength it had taken for that Hunter to rip apart his two cohorts before he'd even noticed that he was there. He'd nearly pissed himself when those glowing amber eyes filled with fury had locked onto him like a tiger about to pounce. He'd never seen such possessiveness over a human. So he'd bet on the fact that the son of a bitch would try to save the girl, giving him the chance to escape. And luckily, he'd been right. But he hadn't left without leaving a little insurance that the vampire would stay with her. If he wanted her to live, that is.

Jacking upright, he tossed the pillow aside and began to pace. He needed to shake this off. So he'd failed this time. Now he knew better what to expect with those bastards. He'd just need to plan better. Be better prepared.

Much as he didn't want to, he needed to call in the demons. And hope they didn't kill him on sight.

"I swear to you, my love. I will rip Luukas and his fucking pack apart for what they did to you. I will. I'll avenge you, and you'll be able to rest in peace."

Josiah came to a stop in front of Leeha's dressing table, and he stared into the mirror there. But it wasn't his own reflection he was seeing. He was remembering how she'd sit there at the end of every night, removing her jewels and brushing her luxurious dark red hair before pinning it up on top of her head. He'd loved to watch her performing this ritual. His fangs would shoot down at the sight of the back of her delicate neck, and he would imagine what it would be like to sink his teeth through that translucent skin into the blue veins beneath. But she would never allow that. She enjoyed torturing him.

Palming the front of his jeans, he rubbed the hardening length with the heel of his hand. The zipper dug into his flesh, and his head fell backwards, his eyes rolling back in his head. He tugged the zipper down and fisted himself.

Running up and down his length slowly, he used his other hand to cup his balls and squeezed until the pain mingled with the pleasure.

Loneliness crept up on him, in spite of the nasty things he'd just done with the young human male on the plane. His hands stilled. With a sob, he released himself. He stood there with his rapidly deflating cock hanging out of his pants, his spirit defeated. Closing his eyes, he entertained the thought of walking outside and lying spread-eagle on the grass to greet the sun. At least then he could be with her again.

His longing was so deep that if he closed his eyes, he could imagine that he could smell her unique scent. Could hear the whisper of her gown. Could feel the touch of her hand on his naked flesh. He groaned as he imagined her stroking him, and his cock leapt to attention again.

Suddenly, he was forced to his knees. His eyes popped open as he felt a hand on either side of his skull tilting his head back. He blinked, a sound of disbelief escaping him as he stared into red eyes alight with horrors he hadn't seen before.

Unseen hands lifted her gown and held it floating in the air above his head, exposing her sex to his mouth. Leeha smiled at him as she shoved his face roughly into her crotch. His tongue sought her clit eagerly, and he moaned at the essence that he thought he would never again taste. Fisting himself once again, he eagerly jacked off until her voice stopped him.

"Release that sorry excuse of manhood." Her voice echoed through his mind, and he wondered if she was actually saying the words aloud or just speaking directly inside of his head. "You do not deserve any pleasure, Josiah. You are weak. You have displeased me."

When he didn't immediately obey her, his hand was forcibly ripped away. But it was too late. He ejaculated as his hand made that last trip upwards. It spurted out of him, splashing all over her shapely legs.

Her fingers tangled tightly in his hair and she forcibly rubbed herself against his mouth until she experienced her own pleasure. When she was finished, she shoved him away from her. He stared up at her in awe as she sneered down at him. "You can't even obey my slightest command, can you? You are worthless, Josiah." Her form flickered before him.

"No! No! Don't go! Please don't leave me again, Leeha!"

"Then you must make it worth the effort for me to stay." Her voice was naught but a whisper now.

And she was gone.

29

Christian took Ryan's hand as they taxied down the runway, stilling its fidgeting. She was anxious. He could feel it. And it wasn't just her clammy palm that was giving her away.

He studied her face. She was paler than normal, and a light sheen of sweat covered her skin. "Are you all right?"

She gave him a small smile that was more of a wince. "Not really."

"What's wrong?"

"Nothing, I'm fine."

He thought he knew what it was, but he wanted to know how bad she was getting. "*She'ashil*, I can't help you if you won't tell me when it's getting bad."

She was quiet for a moment, and then she gave his hand a squeeze and released it. Unbuckling her seatbelt, she rose from the plush leather seat. "I'll be right back." Then she practically ran to the restroom at the back of the jet.

Christian watched her go, a deep frown marring his features. A second later, he unbuckled his own seatbelt and followed her. Standing outside the door, he could hear her dry heaving.

Fuck. The withdrawals were hitting her. He didn't think there was anything in her body to evacuate. She hadn't eaten since the night before, and she hadn't had very much then. Just some rice and a tortilla. She'd said she couldn't handle anymore.

He waited until her stomach calmed down, then knocked softly on the door with one knuckle. "Are you okay?"

Her voice sounded rough when she answered him. "Just leave me alone."

Yeah, he couldn't do that. "Ryan..."

"Go away, Christian. Please!" The last word was cut off as he heard her trying to get sick again. He had to fight the impulse to kick the door in and save her from her body's revolt against itself.

Instead, he knocked softly again when she was finished. "Come on, open the door. I know you're feeling like you wanna die right about now, but I can help if you'll let me." He waited a few beats and then knocked one more time. "Ryan? Please let me help you, honey."

A few seconds passed by with no response. He was rethinking that whole kicking in the door thing again when he heard the latch slide clear and the little sign said "vacant". Cracking the door open, he peeked in at her. She was crumpled on the floor next to the commode. Opening it as much as he could without hitting her, he slid inside. Luckily, the bathrooms on the jet were a bit larger than normal commercial planes.

Grabbing some paper towels, he wet them with cold water and crouched down next to her. She was hugging the toilet, sweating and shivering at the same time. Every once in a while she would flinch like she'd just gotten a sharp pain, or like someone was yelling in her ear.

"I hate that you're seeing me like this," she whispered. Then she glared at him out of the corner of her eyes. "Why are you doing this to me?"

He wiped her face with the wet towel. "I can help if you'll let me."

"You keep saying that."

"Because it's true." Reaching up, he re-wet the towel. "My blood can make you feel better," he said matter-of-factly.

She stared at him like he was crazy.

"Remember how it healed you in the park after that asshole bit you?"

"You think because you can cure a little bite that you can make this shit I'm feeling now go away?" She pushed his arm away when he tried to wipe her forehead again. "Stop it."

Christian let her push him away. "Ryan, he tore out your carotid artery. It wasn't just a 'little bite'. You would've been dead in minutes if I hadn't been there."

"That doesn't sound like such a bad thing right about now," she grumbled into the toilet. Her frail body heaved, but there was nothing in her stomach. When she was done, she collapsed back against the wall. "Oh god. My body hurts." She turned to him in desperation. "Don't you have just a little tar? Some oxy? Anything? Something to take the edge off? I could just wean myself off of it instead of going cold turkey like this." She nodded her head over and over. "Please, Christian. It hurts."

Though it was killing him to see her suffering, he didn't go along with it. No matter how she begged and pleaded, he remained steadfast and just let her get it all out. There was no way in hell he would enable her addiction, even if he had access to anything at the moment, which he didn't.

Then she started crying.

Christian felt helpless. He wanted to help her, and he could, if she would quit being so damn stubborn and admit that she couldn't get through this on her own. She was going through all this needlessly. But he didn't want to just shove his bleeding wrist at her like he had last time. Last time had been an emergency of the life or death kind. This time he wanted her to take of him of her own free will. "*She'ashil*, let me help you."

Rubbing at her face with shaky hands, she eyeballed him warily. "What would you have to do?"

She looked exhausted. Her arms and thighs were all red where she'd been scratching at them since they boarded. And her cheeks looked pale and hollow. Why hadn't he noticed how quickly she was sinking? "If you drink from me, you'll feel better. I promise."

"Like, drink your blood?" she asked, her voice a bit shrill.

He nodded solemnly.

And she was back at it over the toilet again, shaking her head "no" even as she heaved. "I can't," she groaned.

He didn't understand. She'd done it before. And he'd heard a vampire's blood tasted amazing. "You did it before."

She sat back again, closing her eyes. "I didn't know I was doing it. And when I did, I pushed you away and spit it out if you recall." Her body shivered and her legs began to spasm. She pulled them into her chest, moaned with pain, and released them. Only to pull them in again.

Christian was losing patience. She was suffering for no fucking reason, and it was tearing him up inside. He was right fucking here, and he could *help* her. Lifting his wrist to his mouth, he released his fangs and made a good size gash. Holding it out to her, he tried to keep the anger from his voice. "Ryan, please. Take from me. I hate seeing you like this. It'll help, I promise."

She started to shake her head.

"Ryan!"

Her eyes popped open and she zeroed in on the wrist he held in front of her. Blood dripped down his forearm.

"Take it," he ordered.

"I don't think I can," she whispered.

The wound was starting to heal itself. "Ryan, don't make me sit on you and force you to drink. Because much as I don't want to, I'm about to do just that."

Bruised, swollen eyes filled with revulsion flew to his face. He held them with his own determined gaze. "Oh yes, I will. If it will stop your suffering. I will."

Another round of the shakes rattled her bones and made her teeth chatter. When they diminished and she settled, she closed her eyes and rested her head back against the wall.

"Okay," she said so quietly he would never have heard her if he were human.

Re-opening the gash he'd made, he quickly held it to her mouth. "Don't look if it'll help."

Even with her eyes closed, she looked like she was about to vomit again as she parted her mouth just a little. But when his blood touched her lips and trickled into her mouth, those beautiful blue eyes shot open in shock.

He gave her a small smile. "Not too bad, huh?"

Her little pink tongue flicked out and licked his wrist, and then he had to readjust the way he was sitting as she grabbed his arm with both hands and latched on. Her eyes closed again on a moan as she sucked on his wrist, but it was a different kind of sound this time. It was the sound of relief as her body eased up on her.

Each pull she made on his vein shot straight up his arm and down to his groin, until his erection was pushing painfully against its imprisonment. He discreetly adjusted himself, but it didn't help much. Bracing one tense arm on the wall above her head, he let her take what she needed and attempted to keep his own needs under some kind of control.

It wasn't an easy thing.

He watched her closely, taking stock of the effect his blood was having on her symptoms. Almost immediately, her color got better and the shivering stopped. As she drank more, her rigid muscles relaxed and her strength returned, if the hold she had on his arm was any indication.

A few seconds later, he noticed a new scent in the air just as she bit him hard, reopening the wound on her own. Christian gasped and his cock kicked up almost violently. Pressing his free hand against the hard ridge in his jeans, he tried to calm the monster, but only succeeded in making it worse. "*She'ashil*," he groaned. His fangs shot down and his legs shifted restlessly as she fed.

He'd never offered his blood to anyone before, except to his father. Well, he would've offered it to him, but he'd been too late. By the time he'd gone back home reborn as a vampire, his father was gone. Taken by the very disease that his race had brought to the continent. But that was different. He'd never offered this intimacy to a female until now.

One of Ryan's hands left his arm and reached for him blindly. Any and all thoughts of other people immediately exited his brain as he grabbed her hand with his own. Leaning forward, she followed his wrist even as she tried to stop drinking. With one last hit from him, she released his arm a bit reluctantly.

"Holy shit," she breathed. "I'm sorry. I should've stopped sooner. Are you all right?"

He licked the wound to heal it completely, and then cupped her face with his palm and pressed his forehead against hers. Breathing hard, he kissed her on the head and backed off. "Better?"

"Better. Thank you." Her eyes were alight with a life he hadn't seen before.

Releasing his hand, she got to her feet and stood at the sink to splash cold water on her face as he watched her from his spot on the floor. Christian stood up as she was rinsing her mouth. Though he enjoyed the view of her sweet little ass and shapely legs from his spot on the floor, he didn't want to spend the rest of the flight in the bathroom.

As soon as she shut the water off and dried her face and hands, he ushered her out the door and back into the main cabin of the jet. Guiding her to her seat, he pushed away her seeking hands and buckled her in as she protested. "Christian? What are you doing?"

"You need to be safe," he told her as he pulled the strap tight across her hips. "We could hit turbulence." When she was secure, he dropped to his knees in front of her. She'd never looked more beautiful to him. The reds and oranges and blonds of her hair framed her delicate face perfectly where small curls had escaped from her braids. And her eyes, accented by perfect brows the same color as her hair, had never shone such a turquoise blue. Her cheeks were flushed, her lips pink, and she just looked so...alive.

His eyes dropped down to her heaving chest, and he could see her nipples straining against her shirt, even through her bra. Breathing just as hard as she was, he brought his eyes back up to her mouth. Her lips parted and she leaned towards him as she pulled him in by the front of his tee shirt. He moaned as her lips touched his, softly at first, then with increasing pressure. She opened for him and his tongue swept in to take possession. Though she'd started it, the tables quickly turned as he took control and ravished her mouth as he wanted to ravish her body.

Breaking off the kiss, she said, "Christian. Please, touch me." Then she gripped the bottom of her shirt and yanked it up and over her head, tossing it into his seat. Her bra followed right behind it.

His lips lifted off of his fangs and a low growl rumbled through him at the sight of those breasts with their large, dusky nipples. Running her hands over them, she lifted one towards his mouth and he took her offering eagerly. His tongue swept over the rigid bud before he pulled it into his mouth. As the scent of her desire again rose up and surrounded him, he moaned against her soft skin. She started to pant as he suckled one and then the other, but he didn't bite her. Not yet.

Kissing his way up across her collarbone, he gently bit her neck. Not through the skin, but just enough to make her gasp. "Are you certain you feel up to this?" he asked.

"I feel amazing," she assured him.

Her words had him rolling his hips between her legs, but the damned seat was in the way. Leaning back, he picked up one small foot and then the other and removed her sandals, then he tugged her shorts and underwear off until she was sitting there gripping the armrests with nothing but the seatbelt covering her. Running his eyes over her sexy little body, he moved one braid off of her breast. Then he gripped her knees and pressed her legs further apart, exposing her completely to his hungry gaze. Her sex was swollen and wet, her nipples were hard, and her lips were parted as she watched him looking at her.

He made short work of his tee shirt, but that was as far as he got. He couldn't wait any longer to touch her. Sitting back on his heels, he spread her legs even wider apart. One thumb slid into her damp folds, separating them and finding that hard little bud.

"Gods," he breathed. "You're so wet for me."

Running his tongue along his bottom lip, he could practically taste her. He found the button on the armrest and pressed it, leaning her seat back. With his free hand laid flat between her gorgeous tits, he held her still as his thumb made small circles on that tight bundle of nerves. Every few seconds, he'd slide it down to her opening, press just enough to tease her, and then bring it back to her clit.

The sounds she made had his blood roaring in his ears as he explored her in the most intimate way possible until she was breathing hard and saying his name. He pressed his thumb against her opening again. Her hips jacked up to meet him, and it slid a little further into her tight sheath.

"You're so fucking tight," he gritted out. Sliding just the tip of his thumb in and out a few times, he leaned forward and hit her clit with his tongue.

Suddenly, her body stiffened and she released with a hoarse cry as her hands pushed his head against her. She didn't need to hold him there, he wasn't going anywhere anytime soon.

He brought her to climax twice more.

Ripping open his jeans, his cock sprung out, ready and eager. He just wanted to feel her, just a little. With one last lick, he rose up and slid between her folds her with a hard thrust. He didn't penetrate her, just slid his cock through her wet heat. Her body arched up and she cried out, but any concerns he had that he'd hurt her were diminished as she began to move her hips back and forth, encouraging him to keep going.

He wanted to take his time, but his body took over. His hands went back to her hips and he moved fast against her, unable to stop. It didn't take long for his own orgasm to rise up, hovering on the edge.

"Touch me, *she'ashil*," he commanded.

Her small hand reached between them and gripped him tight. Holding her hand there with his own, he pumped faster and faster.

Throwing his head back with a hoarse cry, his entire body jerked as he came all over her stomach, hot jets shooting all the way up to cover her breasts.

When he was finally finished, he collapsed on top of her. Tucking his face between her jaw and her shoulder, he tried to catch his breath.

"Christian."

"Hmmm?" He could barely breathe yet, never mind speak.

She tilted her head to the side. He could see delicate blue veins and her beating pulse. "Are you thirsty?"

Instantly, his fangs ached to pierce the delicate layer of skin that separated him from the sweet, sweet blood that was running directly underneath it.

"I'm okay."

He felt her deflate underneath him with his refusal, and hurried to clarify. "I want to feed from you. Gods, you have no fucking idea. But I don't want to hurt you."

"I'll be fine," she said. "I want you to do it. I want to know what it feels like to have you at my throat."

Who the hell was this woman? He'd fed from humans before, of course, but he never did it without a little convincing from his mind to theirs. And he would always erase that part from their memories, if not the entire encounter.

"Christian, I want you to feed from me, like this."

Her artery pulsed under his gaze. With a moan of surrender, he leaned down over her and took her up on her offer.

She flinched just a bit as his fangs sliced into her. But when he started to drink, she moaned and began to move her hips beneath him as her fingers dug into his sides.

Her blood hit him like a freight train; his muscles tightening and straining as it shot down to his stomach and spread throughout his body. His cock instantly sprung to life again. Sliding one hand underneath her ass, he lifted her to meet him as he began to thrust against her.

He hoped this was a very long flight.

30

China

The demon known as Mammot stood off to the side of the courtyard and impassively surveyed the slaughter happening within as his cohorts lost patience with interrogating the humans and decided to have an early dinner instead. That was the downside of possessing the bodies of these young vampires. The blood lust was almost impossible to resist as soon as skin was broken. The slightest scratch sent them into a feeding frenzy. But he didn't stop them. They needed the nourishment after the beating they'd taken by those fucking werewolves.

A section of a limb landed with a thud at his feet, warm blood spraying from the severed artery to speckle his pant legs. Kicking it back into the pile of bodies, he took a step back and linked his hands behind his back.

He actually preferred to go by the name "Steven" now, the name given to this vampire he'd recently inhabited. It was much less likely to draw attention than "Mammot".

Sweeping his gaze across the chaos, he searched for signs that any of the humans still had some life in them, but unsurprisingly, there was none. The monks had proven to be everything they'd always claimed to be — steadfast, loyal, and steeped in their ridiculous beliefs that there was somewhere better to move on to from this world. They'd "risen above". Literally. Mind over matter and all that.

He hoped those beliefs had brought them some comfort as their bodies were torn asunder and the blood had been drained from the pieces by hungry mouths filled with razor sharp fangs.

But now they were dead and he was no closer to finding the rest of the clues that would lead them to the only blood that was worth lusting over. The blood that had been drained from their demon forms as their souls had been banished to that fucking altar a thousand years ago. The blood that they needed to find very soon if there was any hope at all of having it in time to reverse the spell completely, giving them back their original demonic forms and allowing them to rule this world as the supreme beings they were once again.

Sending out a mental ten-minute warning to the others, he decided on his next move. There were five clues contained in five separate handmade wooden boxes, and he'd already found two of them. There were two more that were still hidden.

The girl that was with Waano had the third one. Steven was sure Waano knew that she had it, and was protecting her. Therefore, she wouldn't be easy to get to, but it was a challenge that Steven was more than ready for. Waano had had his chance to rule. It was time for someone new to take over the demons of hell, someone who would let them be demons. Waano had been perfectly content to rot from existence chained to that altar, and he hadn't cared that he was condemning the rest of them with him. But he would.

Steven was really looking forward to that particular confrontation, but first they had to find the other two boxes.

They didn't have much time.

31

Ryan had a death grip on his hand as they disembarked from the jet. On the runway, a black SUV with tinted windows sat waiting for them. The passenger side door opened and a tall male with dirty blonde hair climbed out. His blue eyes lighted on the female at his side and ran over her slender form from head to toe. Happy as he was to see Nikulas, Christian found himself pulling her behind him as they reached the bottom of the stairs.

Nik turned his megawatt smile to him. "I see we have similar taste."

Christian frowned, not knowing what he was talking about, and Nikulas didn't bother to explain. He just strode forward to meet them and grabbed Christian up in a bear hug. Christian pounded him on the back without letting go of the girl at his side. When his feet were again on the ground, he made introductions. "Nik, this is Ryan. She helped me escape. Ryan, this is Nikulas."

"Hellooo..." The "o" ended on an expulsion of breath as Nik grabbed her up and hugged her also, though with a little less exuberance so as not to hurt her.

A low growl of displeasure rumbled through Christian's chest, but before he could act on it, Nikulas set her down again. With a hand on each of her shoulders, he told her sincerely, "Thank you for what you did."

"It was nothing. Really, I..." her explanation was cut short as two more males got out of the vehicle. One was just slightly smaller than Nikulas and was wearing running pants and a zip-up hoodie with the hood pulled up. The other walked around the vehicle with a quiet dominance he wore like a second skin. He was wearing all black, his dark hair was a little longer than it had been the last time he'd seen him, and his eyes were haunted with things that Christian couldn't even begin to imagine.

He'd never been so happy to see anyone in his life. Giving Ryan's hand a reassuring squeeze, he left her with Nik and approached the male that was now leaning casually against the SUV with his arms crossed over his broad chest, away from the group. He smacked Aiden on the shoulder in greeting as he passed. Pausing less than two feet away, he studied the male who had saved his life all of those years ago. Though he returned his scrutiny with a steady gaze, Christian could see horrific shadows of the past seven years swimming around in the grey depths.

"Luukas? Fuck, man. I thought I'd never see you again." He wanted to hug him like he had the others, but something in the Master vampire's stance told him it wouldn't be well received.

Luukas ran his eyes over him and then dropped his arms. Gripping Christian's shoulder in one large palm, he indicated his concern while making him keep his distance at the same time. "Are you all right?" he asked.

"I should be asking that of you," Christian answered.

Luukas gave him a small smile. "Let's get you both home and then we'll talk."

Christian nodded. As soon as Luukas walked away, he turned back to the others as they approached the SUV and caught Nik's eye, a large question in his own.

"We'll catch you up later," Nik told him quietly, exchanging looks with Aiden. "But he's better than he was."

Clapping him on the back of the shoulder, Aiden said, "Come on, mate."

Indicating for Ryan to walk in front of him, they waited for Aiden to get in the back. She hesitated when it was her turn to get in next to him.

"What is it, *she'ashil?*" he asked her.

Not taking her eyes from Aiden, she shook her head slightly. "I don't know. There's just something about him."

"Aiden? He's harmless, I promise. Want me to sit by him?"

But she shook her head again. "No. It's okay." She gave him a small smile. "Sorry."

"It's okay." Taking her elbow, he helped her inside. Nik raised his eyebrow in a silent question while Ryan was distracted with her seatbelt, but Christian indicated everything was fine so Nik turned back around and got busy with his own belt.

The drive through Seattle was quiet other than some minor small talk. Then Nik spoke up, "So, I should warn you. It's not just us at home anymore."

"What do you mean?" Christian asked. "Did Dante and Shea show up too?"

"No, no...I wish. I meant there're females there now. Our females."

Christian wasn't sure he'd heard that right. "*Your* females? As in, *your* females?"

That smile flashed back at him. "Yeah. My girl is Emma. She looks a little like your Ryan. Same nose. Same skin. Similar build. Smaller tits." He instantly looked mortified. "No offense," he told Ryan, then continued what he was saying. "Same bright hair, although yours is a bit more intense," he spoke directly to Ryan again. "But not any prettier."

"Um. Thank you?" she responded.

"Emma's sister, Keira, is with Luukas," Nik continued. "She looks nothing like her sister except for her eyes."

Christian felt like he was in an episode of Punk'd. He was so sure they were messing with him that he turned around and checked the seat behind him for Ashton Kutcher. Facing forward again when he saw nothing but an empty seat, he looked around Ryan to Aiden. "What about you? You're unusually quiet over there."

Aiden cocked an eyebrow. "Me?"

"Yeah, you. Any life changing events happen to you while I was gone?"

"Mmm....Not really."

"Aiden! Seriously?" This from Nik in the front seat.

"What? My life hasn't changed. It's exactly as it always has been."

"It so isn't!" Nik cranked his entire upper half around and told Christian, "He has a female too, a pet hedgehog that likes to hang out in his hood, and Leeha fucking possessed him with a fucking demon named Waano. And it's still inside of him."

Christian felt his jaw drop to the floor. He couldn't help it. "You have a pet hedgehog that hangs out in your hood?" he asked Aiden. "Doesn't it stick you?"

"He is a bit prickly, yes. I have to wear a heavy shirt underneath when we hang out."

"Are you kidding me?" Nik yelled. "He HAS a fucking DEMON inside of him! Did you not hear that part?"

"I heard it," Christian said.

"But...you...I..." Nik stuttered. "Oh, fuck it." Turning around, he faced the road and left them to their hedgehog conversation.

Christian turned back to Aiden. "So, what is it about your hood that he likes so much do you think? Is he there now?"

"No, I leave him at home when we go out anywhere. If I lost him, Grace would never forgive me."

"Oh for gods' sake," Nik mumbled.

Ryan looked back and forth between Christian and Aiden before settling on Aiden. "You're really possessed by a demon?"

"Thank you!" Nik exclaimed. "Finally, someone with some sense."

"All right, Nik?" Aiden asked. "You seem a bit more anxious than usual today." Aside to Ryan and Christian, he said, "He really worries too much."

"You. Have. A. Demon..."

"Everyone. Enough." Luukas' deep voice cut through the chaos inside the vehicle. His knuckles were white where they gripped the steering wheel, and his jaw was clenched. The three Hunters immediately shut their traps.

The rest of the trip to downtown Seattle was made in silence.

32

Ryan was grateful to get out of the vehicle and put some distance between herself and the three large males. All of the emotions that were flying around the small space and not being talked about were too much for her at the moment.

There was something dark and almost crazed in Luukas. Something that felt like he was at the edge of a drop-off and may go over at any moment.

And Aiden was right about Nikulas; he worried about everyone too much. If he were human, his blood pressure would be through the roof.

And Christian was the worst of all. Now that they'd shared blood, she could feel everything he was feeling so intensely it was hard to tell his emotions from her own. And right now he was feeling happy, anxious, and furious all at the same time. The happy and anxious she got, but she had no idea who he was furious with, or why.

Aiden was the only one that was actually as chill as he appeared. She got nothing from him other than an occasional rumbling within him that he quickly suppressed. But it was enough that she could hear that thing in there. Although, she hadn't known what it was until they'd told her. Otherwise he was like a toy boat floating on a calm pond. She could also sense that he possessed an unusually quick mind underneath all of the seeming nonchalance. But anyone would be able to see it if they bothered to look beneath the happy-go-lucky facade he put out there.

Christian took her hand again as they walked into the elevator. His fury was escalating, and his touching her only made it worse for her, but she didn't want to give up the security of his hand. She watched him staring at Luukas, and could feel his emotions flickering between anger, guilt, and sorrow.

The master vampire appeared unaware of being under such intense scrutiny, however. He stood with his eyes front and center on the closed elevator doors. But then she saw his fists clench and unclench at his sides. Maybe he wasn't as oblivious as he appeared.

As soon as the doors opened, Luukas strode out and headed straight to the only apartment door there. It opened before he reached it and a stunning woman with dark hair and a perfect hourglass figure ran out into the hall and jumped into his arms. His sense of relief was so profound, the calm stillness that surged through him was visible to all as he held her. "I missed you, witch," he murmured in her hair.

"I missed you, too," she answered right before he kissed her in the middle of the hall. Their love was tangible, Ryan didn't think you needed to be sensitive to it like her to feel it.

"Em! Where are you, woman?" Nikulas bellowed as he walked around his brother and Keira and into the apartment. Aiden followed close behind.

"In the kitchen!" a female voice answered.

Ryan could hear pots banging around and noticed for the first time that there was a heavenly scent coming from the open doorway. Her stomach growled loudly in response and Christian looked down at her with a frown as he closed the door behind them, giving Luukas and Keira their privacy. She frowned back. "I'm fine. I'm just a little hungry."

They followed the others through the modern apartment and into the kitchen. There they found two more women. One had thick, long, auburn hair and skin like peaches and cream. Moss green eyes smiled up at Aiden.

"Hallo, luv," he greeted her. "Where's Prickles?"

She hugged him and pointed with her chin. "In the bedroom snuggling with your shirt."

"You're letting him ruin another of my shirts?"

"He misses you too, you know," she answered with a smile and turned back to the pot she was stirring.

Nikulas came towards them then, pulling — she presumed — Emma behind him. Ryan couldn't help but stare as the woman came closer. He was right. They did look similar. Weirdly similar, as a matter of fact. Emma smiled brightly when she reached Ryan, who was standing a bit awkwardly just inside the kitchen with Christian at her side.

Nik made the introductions. "Emma, my love, this is Christian. And this is Ryan. She helped him escape...uh..." He wrinkled up his forehead, but then waved it off as unimportant. "Wherever he was in Mexico."

Although Nikulas didn't say as much, Ryan frowned at the silent implication he made that anyone who was paying attention would have noticed. And Emma was definitely paying attention.

Shaking Christian's hand warmly, she expressed her happiness that he'd made it home safe. Then she turned to Ryan. "Welcome to our home. I think you're going to fit right in here."

"Thank you," Ryan answered. "But I don't know that I'll be staying."

"Mm hmm. Okay." Emma gave her another bright smile. "What's your last name, Ryan?"

"Um. It's Moss."

"What?" Keira and Luukas had finally joined them, and Keira came around to stand by Emma. "What did you just say?"

Ryan drew back, afraid she'd said something wrong, but she felt nothing threatening from any of the people in the large kitchen. "I said my last name is Moss."

"No kidding," Keira breathed. "Gracie, did you hear that?" she called over her shoulder without taking her eyes from Ryan. She looked between her and Emma and back again, a sudden comprehension on her face.

"Hear what?" Grace asked as she joined them while the guys hauled Christian away and took a seat at the counter to talk amongst themselves. She stuck her hand out at Ryan. "Hi! I'm Grace."

Ryan took her hand in hers. "Ryan Moss."

Grace's green eyes widened in shock. "No shit?"

The front door opened. All four vampire males were off their chairs and lined up in front of the entrance to the kitchen before it had closed again. A feral hiss from one of them made goose bumps lift up on Ryan's skin, and she was very glad that she wasn't the one that had just walked through that door.

"It's me," a female voice said.

Christian was the first to come out of his defensive stance. "Shea?" he asked incredulously.

The women in the kitchen attempted to peer around the guys' broad shoulders as footsteps came down the foyer. A stunning female with long, dark hair and cattish green eyes walked into the room. She was wearing dusty jeans, thick-soled boots, and a man's tee shirt. Ryan saw the tips of her fangs when she spoke. She suddenly felt hot all over, and it took her a moment to recognize what she was feeling.

Jealousy. Jealousy that Christian was the one that knew who it was. What was this woman to him?

"Christian!" She ran up to him like she was going to hug him, but stopped just out of his reach. "I went looking for you and Dante! I was grabbed right off the street! Where the hell were you?"

"Same scenario," he told her. "Shea, I'm so sorry. Are you all right? Where were you?"

"I'm okay. I got away. Luukas? Oh my gods..." Shea took a step towards him, but then seemed to rethink that decision and remained where she was. "And Aiden?" Her hand covered her mouth and she seemed to be fighting back tears. "Oh thank the gods you're okay. I was told...no one knew if you'd survived."

He grinned at her. "I'm all right. It'll take more than a little demon possession to get rid of me."

"So, you're not...?"

"Oh, no. He's in there," he answered her unspoken question. "But apparently not by his choice. He doesn't come out to play much."

Shea wiped her eyes. "I'm so glad you're still with us. Even if there's a little more to you now."

Luukas reached out a hand to her, but she stayed out of reach of his touch and didn't come forward to meet him. He let his hand drop. "Shea. Where have you been?"

Ryan noticed that neither of the other guys made a move towards her. And the women were still barricaded in the kitchen.

"We went searching for you," Aiden said. "But you were just bloody gone. We dug through the rubble, all that was left of the mountain when Luukas was finished with it, but we didn't catch a scent of you anywhere."

"We kept digging anyway," Nik picked up where Aiden left off. "You weren't there. What happened?"

Shea held up her hands. The palms showed signs of recently healed cuts. "I *was* there."

"Not possible," Aiden told her emphatically. "We searched…"

"I was way down there, somewhere in the bowels of hell underneath all of those underground tunnels."

"But we dug all the way to the altar room. All of the tunnels leading there were caved in!" Nikulas' horrified expression matched Aiden's.

"Not all of them." Shea eyes softened as she looked between the three males. "It's okay, guys. I'm here now. And I appreciate that you went looking for me."

"Three times!" Aiden stressed, holding up three fingers for emphasis. "We went there three times in the last few weeks.

And we were about to go again when Christian finally took enough time from his holiday in Mexico to ring us."

"Fuck off, Aiden." Christian grinned and gave him a playful shove.

Ryan stood in the background with the other women, wondering why there was no hugging going on. Pats on the back. Something. Instead they all just stood there staring at the female vampire.

Her beautiful green eyes finally landed on the four of them still in the kitchen. "Who is this?" she asked. "What's going on?"

Luukas stepped in and took over then. "Come here, Keira." He waited for her to join him before making the introductions. But as soon as she stepped forward, Shea bared her fangs and hissed at her, her torso leaning forward on her hips as her hands fisted at her sides.

Keira, Ryan was surprised to see, showed no fear towards the threat, but gazed at her steadily from Luukas' side. The hair on Ryan's arms suddenly rose straight up as the air around her became infused with magic.

"Keira. No." At Luukas' command, the air around her calmed down. Stepping in front of his mate, he bared his own fangs at his Hunter in a spine-chilling snarl. "Shea, restrain yourself," he growled. "Keira is MINE."

Her eyes were wild as she tore them from the woman and focused on him. "How can you protect her?" she hissed in fury. "She's the reason that bitch was able to hold you! She's the one that kept you there! She *tortured* you! Oh yes, I heard all about it," she told him. Then she turned to Christian. "You're his Guardian! Why are you just standing there?"

"Shea, you need to calm down," Christian told her.

But she ignored him, turning back to Luukas. "You should've killed her the moment you had the chance. And if you can't do it, then I will."

Before anyone had the chance to move, Luukas had crossed the space separating them and had Shea by the throat. Her body jerked spastically in the air, her eyes rolled back in her head, and her keening cry mixed with his bellow of anger. He shook her like a ragdoll. Once. Twice.

"Put her down!" Christian yelled as he and the other males surrounded the two of them. "Luukas! You can't touch her! Put her down!" When he didn't seem to hear him, he joined Nikulas and Aiden as they physically tried to get him to release her. But it was like trying to pry open the jaws of a steel trap to get it to release its prey.

It was Keira that finally saved the female. "Put her down, vampire. She won't hurt me." His eyes flickered over to her and she held them with her own. "You need to release her," she told him. "She's only trying to avenge you, and rightly so."

After a moment, he opened his hand and Shea fell to the floor. She lay in a heap, coughing and trembling and trying to catch her breath. With a moan, she flopped over onto her back.

The other three males all bent over her, but were careful not to touch her.

"Are you all right?" Aiden asked.

Emma pushed her way through them. "Back off. Let me see her." She glanced up at Nik as she knelt down by her side. "I can touch her, right?"

He nodded once.

Ryan watched as she picked up Shea's hand and held it in her own. "Shea? Can you hear me? My name is Emma." She noticed that Nikulas stayed right next to her, his center of attention now on his female.

Shea's eyes fluttered open and she stared up at Emma. After a moment, she nodded. "I'll be okay."

"Good." Emma smiled. "So, I'd appreciate it if you didn't kill my sister. She didn't do those things to Luukas of her own free will. She did it to save my life."

"Doesn't change anything," Shea croaked.

It was Nikulas that spoke this time. "Yeah, well, how about this? Keira is Luukas' mate. Like, as in fated. Emma is mine. So, you might want to think about that before you go trying to off the females we not only love, but need to survive."

Shea pushed herself into a sitting position and Emma helped her, ignoring the glare the vampire gave her. "Are you fucking serious?" When Nikulas just stared at her with his steady blue gaze, she laughed nervously. "You're not serious."

"I am."

"But, they were just stories..."

"Yeah, we thought so too. But here we are."

Ryan stayed in the background with Christian, Grace, and Aiden, who had come to stand protectively in front of his "luv", arms crossed over his chest like a bodyguard. She had to hold back her laughter when Grace looked at her and rolled her eyes behind his back.

Shea got to her feet, shaking off Emma's hands as she tried to help, then apologized to her at Nik's warning growl. "I'm sorry I tried to kill your sister."

Emma laughed. "I don't think it's me you should be apologizing to."

She glanced at Keira and Luukas. "Sorry," she said.

Luukas stepped forward. "I love you like a daughter, Shea. But if you so much as send a threatening glance at my witch again, I *will* kill you before you harm her." He paused a moment to let that sink in. "Are we clear?"

Lowering her eyes with respect, Shea mumbled, "Yes."

"I can't hear you." Keira put a hand on his arm, but he shook her off. "I can't hear you," he repeated.

She raised her eyes and clenched her jaw. "Yes. I understand," she stated clearly.

"Good."

As he turned away to pull Keira under his arm, Shea turned to the group watching in silence from the kitchen. Her eyes lit on Ryan and widened in disbelief.

Ryan frowned. Why was she staring at her like that? Had she been talking out loud to the voices again? They were there, as always, although they weren't screaming for once. However, her head was beginning to ache between their mutterings and all of the commotion going on in front of her.

"What's up, Shea?" Christian asked.

She tore her eyes from Ryan. "You're bringing them home to hang out with us now?"

"What are you talking about?"

"Oh, like we're so innocent all of a sudden. Your dancers," she answered. "Don't tell me you've found one of those sluts that you actually like enough to fuck more than once."

Christian bared his fangs in a snarl, and only Ryan's grip on his hand kept him from leaping at his friend. "She's just lashing out," she started to say, but he talked over her.

"Shut the fuck up, Shea."

"Why? It's no secret that you go through whores like her so many times a night it's a wonder your dick hasn't fallen off."

Ryan looked up at Christian. "What is she talking about?" But he was still as stone as he glared at the other vampire.

"Did she just say what I think she said?" Grace asked Aiden.

"Seriously?" Emma asked Shea.

"Yeah, not cool, Shea," Nik muttered. "Not cool at all."

"SHEA!" Luukas' angry voice cut through the tension in the air. "In my office. NOW."

Visibly shaken and hurt, she stalked away from them and threw herself into a chair in front of his desk.

Luukas turned to Ryan, who was trying really hard to keep the tears in her eyes from overflowing. "Pay her no mind. I will deal with her."

But she just smiled and shook her head. After all, the female hadn't been wrong. She was exactly what she'd pegged her to be. And an addict to boot. "Don't worry about it."

"I will worry about it. You are a guest in my home. And you are Christian's. No one is mistreated in my home…unless it's by me." He kissed Keira on the head and then walked calmly into the office, shutting the door firmly behind him.

He was wrong. She wasn't Christian's. She wasn't anybody's.

"So," Keira broke the silence that Luukas left behind him. "Anyone hungry?"

As the girls started to bustle around the kitchen while the guys plopped back down on the counter stools to wait for them to eat, Christian pulled Ryan aside. "Ryan…" he paused and put his hands on his narrow hips, but he didn't seem to know what else to say.

She studied him, wanting to believe that Shea's accusation didn't mean what she thought it meant. But his body language told her all she needed to know. "Yeah, okay. I got it." Brushing him off, she wandered into the living room and sat down in the chair. When she looked up, Grace was there with a plate of food for her. She was nervous, and Ryan's skin prickled as she shared her agitation.

"I thought you might be hungry." Setting the plate down on the coffee table with a fork and a napkin, she stood there a bit awkwardly before asking, "Would you like something to drink?"

Ryan eyed up the stroganoff-looking casserole and shook her head. "I'm good. Thanks." Picking up the fork, she shoved a mouthful of noodles into her mouth, hoping the jittery woman would go away. She didn't even taste the food, and wouldn't be able to tell someone exactly what she was eating if they asked.

She didn't know why she was so upset. What did she expect? For him to profess his undying love to a junkie stripper that he wouldn't even have met if he hadn't been held against his will? For all she knew, they were probably both suffering from Stockholm Syndrome.

Shoving another forkful of food into her mouth, she chomped down so hard she thought she felt one of her teeth crack. It didn't matter. She didn't need to stay here. The monster that was after her was nowhere near here, he was down in Mexico. She'd eat, tell the girls thank you, and get the hell out of Dodge. She could make her way on the streets. She'd done it before. She'd be fine.

Her fork fell to her plate with a clank as the ever-present voices escalated to a fever pitch around her. They buzzed around her like a hoard of bees, getting louder and louder until tears filled her eyes and she pressed her palms to her ears. Like it would help.

"Are you okay?"

Shit. She was still there. Ryan lowered her hands, trying not to wince at the banshees screaming in her head. "I just have a headache." Understatement of the year.

"I can ask Keira if she has something that would help?"

But Ryan shook her head, "No, no. It'll go away. Thanks though."

Grace sat down on the couch cushion cattycorner to her. "I've only been here a few weeks myself."

Why are you still talking? Ryan thought. And then she mentally kicked herself. Grace was just trying to be nice. There was no need to be a bitch.

"Were you kidnapped too?" she asked. Okay, so she hadn't exactly been kidnapped. But she had been coerced.

Grace just laughed. "Uh, no. It's a strange situation, I know. Being the reason they live or die."

Huh? She waited for her to say more, but after a few minutes of watching her eat, Grace changed the subject instead.

"You have to be exhausted. Let me go see if it's all right for me to show you down to Christian's place as soon as you're done eating."

"Thanks." As Grace got up and walked over to the group in the kitchen, the good-natured teasing and pleasant conversation suddenly became hushed and secretive. Ryan ignored the uncomfortable feeling that they were all whispering about her and concentrated on not wincing from the noise going on inside her head. She felt a hand on her shoulder and twisted around to find Christian holding his hand out to her.

"Come on, it's been a long trip. Let's go get some rest."

Ignoring his hand, she rose from the overstuffed chair and picked her half-eaten plate up to return it to the kitchen, but he took it from her hand.

"I'll get that."

She handed him the plate and then stood there uncomfortably while he handed it off to one of the girls and told them that he was taking her "home".

Home.

Ryan pushed down the rush of tears that threatened to overwhelm at the word, but a few escaped in spite of her best efforts. She hadn't had a true home in years. To hide her hormone rush or whatever the hell this was, she went to wait for Christian in the foyer without saying goodbye to anyone. If she'd known where she was going, she would've walked right out of the apartment.

He found her there a minute later, calls of "bye!" and "see you tonight" following on his heels. She followed him out of the apartment and to the elevator where she stood just in front of him with her arms wrapped around her middle. She refused to look at him.

The bell chimed and the doors opened and they stepped inside. Christian punched the button for the floor below them. As the doors closed them in, he turned to her with that same half pitying/half ashamed look he'd had on his face since the female vampire had denounced him. He took a deep breath. "Ryan..."

"Don't." She cut him off before he could say anything else. She didn't want to hear his bullshit explanations. Hugging herself tight, she fought the urge to clamp her hands over her ears again.

"Ryan. Please. I'm asking you to listen..."

She rolled her eyes as the doors opened and practically sprinted out into the hallway. There were four doors on this floor, two on each opposite side of the hallway. A neutral grey carpet and light grey walls lined with colorful prints of the city led the way to each door.

Anger radiated off of him in waves as he followed her out and walked past her to the door on the right. Punching in a code on the panel on the wall, he flung open the door and waited for her to precede him inside.

She walked through the foyer and into the main room. The apartment was similar to the one they'd just come from, only smaller, and there was no office area. But the far wall was made of glass from floor to ceiling, and the lights of the city of Seattle provided a beautiful view as they twinkled in the early morning hours. Taking a quick glance around, she noticed Native American tapestries on the walls and furniture that reminded her of Arizona or somewhere else southwesterny with its warm colors and rugged geometric patterns.

Christian came up behind her and put his hand on her arm, but she twisted away and walked over to the windows. Her head was pounding from the voices, or entities, or whatever they were, but at least they'd calmed down a bit. "I'd like my own room, please," she tossed over her shoulder. She couldn't sleep in the same bed with him, if she could manage to sleep at all.

Her statement was greeted with nothing but silence. A wave of sexual hunger flowed over and around her in the next second, and her traitorous body responded eagerly.

"I don't think you really mean that," he said softly from right behind her.

She nearly jumped out of her skin and spun around to face him, steeling herself against those brilliant eyes. The way he looked at her never failed to get her heart racing and her panties wet, but she felt dirty enough as it was. She was just another one of his playthings, and things had already gone far enough. If she slept in the same bed with him, there'd be no turning back. She knew that.

"I've never meant anything more in my life." Her voice had a steely edge to it that surprised even her.

The muscles in his jaw clenched and unclenched. "I only have the one bedroom here."

"I'll crash on the couch."

Hands low on his narrow hips, he glared down at her. She glared right back. A moment later she felt a slight intrusion on her thoughts, and as the voices were pretty quiet, she assumed it was Christian poking around in her head. He'd already admitted that he could influence people's thoughts. As soon as she realized it was him, the walls slammed up, the same walls she used to try to block out the voices, and it must have worked, for she felt him retreat from her head again.

"You take the bedroom. I'll sleep out here." He walked through a door past the kitchen, and returned a few seconds later with blankets and a pillow under one arm.

"I'm not taking your room," she insisted.

"Ryan..."

"It's your room. I'll be fine out here." Her tone brooked no more argument.

He inhaled deeply, his clenched jaw belying his patient tone as he said, "The bathroom is there." He pointed to a door over by the foyer. "Or there's one off the bedroom with a shower if you change your mind."

"Thank you."

Dropping the stuff in his arms on the couch, he started to make up her bed.

"I can do that," she told him.

"I know." He tucked one blanket into the cushions and layered another one on top, folding back one corner for her to get in. He eyed up his handiwork, fluffed her pillow, and then shoved his hands into his front pockets and turned to face her. "If you need anything, I'll be right in the bedroom." He paused, started to walk away, stopped, and turned to her again. "I hope you change your mind and join me."

"I'll be fine."

His eyes ran from the top of her head to her bare toes peeking out from her sandal straps. When they returned to her face, she could swear she saw a moment of desperation flash across his face before his features became impassive.

"Thank you," she added.

He seemed like he wanted to say more, but finally, with a chaste kiss to the top of her head, he wandered off to his own room. She noticed he left the door cracked open.

Ryan sank down onto her makeshift bed and kicked off her sandals. Leaning back against the cushions, she pulled the blanket up over her legs and watched out the windows for the sun to come up.

As soon as it did, she was leaving.

33

Shea kept her eyes down as Luukas stalked past her to the window. An eerie stillness settled over him as he stared out at the city. Where was the yelling? The "I'm so disappointed in you's"? This brittle control he was exhibiting was more disturbing than his wrath.

Her happiness at seeing him home safe and sound after all these years was dampened by the abundance of other emotions she was feeling. Anger. Disappointment. Hopelessness. And a multitude of others that she couldn't even name. None of which were actually aimed at Luukas or the other Hunters.

She'd seen red earlier when he'd introduced her to that female. *His* female. Jesse had told her that he had mated with her, but she hadn't believed him. Hadn't wanted to believe him. She thought he had to be mistaken. It wasn't possible that Luukas, a male so full of strength and conviction, had given in to the wiles of a manipulative female. She was probably faking her feelings for him just so he wouldn't kill her, and had all the males here completely convinced. Her sister was probably in on it with her. And gods only knew who that was with Aiden. Another sister? A cousin?

Males were so easily manipulated by a pretty face.

And Christian! Bringing one of his whores home. What the hell was up with that? She knew right away what that female was, in spite of her more modest clothing. However, she felt bad now for lashing out at him like that. It wasn't him she was angry with. It wasn't Luukas either, if she were to be honest with herself. It wasn't any of them. She was angry because she'd been stupid enough to let hope in.

The moment she'd seen Luukas home safe and sound, she'd had to control her excitement. She'd thought, stupidly, that since this weird thing with her not being able to be touched by a male started when he'd disappeared, that his returning home would cure it. Of course, when he'd tried to crush her larynx for threatening his little bitch, she'd known immediately that that was not the case as all of her nerve endings starting shooting off, the pain unbearable.

Her thoughts were interrupted when she realized he was waiting for an answer to a question she hadn't heard. "I'm sorry?"

He sat back in his chair with a sigh, one elbow on the arm of his chair as he rubbed his jaw. He looked strong and confident and healthy, and in spite of everything that was going on, she was so happy to have him back.

"Did you happen to hear a word of what I just said?" he asked.

Lowering her eyes to hide the emotions there, she fiddled with the bottom of Jesses' shirt.

"Where were you, Shea?"

She looked up. "I told you. I was up at Leeha's stronghold."

"And how did you get there?"

"I was grabbed off the street as I left the apartment looking for Christian and Dante." Dante! "Is he here too? Dante? Did he make it back?"

"Not yet. We're looking for him. I'll fill you in after I'm finished with you. Who grabbed you?"

"Males in a van. Vampires." She described them for him. "They took me to a small plane, and we flew north to Vancouver. From there, they threw me in the back of a truck and we went to an abandoned barn until they got the call to bring me to her fortress."

A shadow darkened his grey eyes, and Shea watched as he sought out the little, brunette witch. He watched her laughing with the others, and the harsh lines softened from his face. After a moment, he closed his eyes and took a deep breath, and then turned back to Shea.

"Where are those vampires now?"

"I don't know. I haven't seen them since I first arrived there."

"Why did she bring you there and not the others?" He continued the debriefing.

"I don't know why the others weren't brought there. As for me, I was the one that she was originally going to use for the possession. But I was spared." She should tell him that it was Jesse that had saved her and kept her safe, if against her will. "I don't know why."

Liar, you know why. Just tell him about Jesse.

But she couldn't bring herself to say the words.

"She used Aiden instead." Her smile faltered as Luukas just looked at her, his expression grave. "But he's fine." She indicated the vampire in question on the other side of the glass wall. "Look at him. He's fine. Isn't he?"

"No. Aiden is not fine. Aiden did not escape the possession. He has a demon inside of him. Its name is Waano. But lucky for us, it hasn't shown its ugly face since we rescued him and killed Leeha."

"Leeha is dead?" she asked incredulously.

"You didn't know?"

She shook her head. It all became clear to her now. That's why Jesse let her go.

Because Leeha was dead, and he didn't have to protect her anymore.

34

Christian flipped over onto his stomach and punched the pillow into submission. Less than five seconds later, he was on his back again. Then his side. Then back to abusing his pillows. Finally, he gave up and jacked upright to a sitting position. Running his fingers through his growing hair, he thought about shaving it off again. He'd always kept it buzzed close to his skull, but it had grown out in the weeks he'd been gone.

Bending his long legs, he wrapped his arms around his knees and stared at the bedroom wall, wishing he could see through all that plaster and paint to the room on the other side.

He'd been tossing and turning for two hours, too antsy to sleep, listening to every little noise from the other room — of which there'd been absolutely none since he'd come in here. As a matter of fact, it was so quiet that he'd gotten up more than once and tiptoed over to the door to check that she was actually still there. But every time he did, he saw the back of her head over the top of the couch as she sat and stared at the rising sun. As far as he could tell, she hadn't moved. He wanted to go out there so bad, even if only to sit quietly next to her, but he didn't.

It wasn't because of all the windows. These apartments were specially made for their kind. All of the windows contained a layer of gas between the thick panes. It was activated by the sun and blocked the rays that would turn them into flaming infernos while still allowing them to enjoy the light. Plus, there were blackout curtains that would slide out from panels in the walls if need be. So no, it wasn't the light of day holding him back.

It was what Nikulas had said about Luuk and his female after Shea had tried to kill her. At first he'd thought Nik was just fucking around. He'd told him they all had females at the airport, yeah. But fated mates? Fated mates weren't real. They were just stories passed down by the elders to young vampires so their new immortal lives didn't seem quite so daunting a thing to take on all alone. Or so they'd always thought. So why would Nikulas say something like that? And why would he be dead serious when he did?

Unless it was true?

Christian shook his head in sympathy for the other males. Tied to a female for the rest of your life? Which was a long, fucking time when you were a vampire. Dependent on her blood for your very existence?

No thanks.

He shifted around on the bed uneasily, memories of his own possessiveness for Ryan coming back to him. But nah, it wasn't the same thing. The stuff he was feeling was easily explained. For one, she'd been the only female around for weeks, and she'd spent those weeks dick teasing him until he thought he would die from the agony of it. Second, it was perfectly normal that after all of that, it would take more than one roll in the hay to get her out of his system. And in spite of all the lusty stuff going on between them, he hadn't actually had intercourse with her yet. Not completely. So it stands to reason that he would want to keep her around until the deed was truly done.

But something else was nagging at him, something he'd been trying really hard not to think about. That ever since he'd laid his hands on her, ever since he'd first tasted the tiniest drops of her blood, the urges he'd been fighting for the past seven years had withered away and died. He no longer felt the need to fuck woman after woman after woman. His blood no longer burned in his veins. His muscles no longer cramped. His nerve endings no longer throbbed in agony.

He only wanted one female. And she was right on the other side of that door. What the hell was up with that? Not that he wasn't grateful to feel like a normal male again. He was. But why had it happened now? Was it because of her?

Christian gritted his teeth and shook his head. No. No, it couldn't be because of her. It had to be something else. Being dependent on a female would not work for him right now. He had a lot of making up to do already because of his dick: To Luukas and to his fellow Hunters.

If he hadn't run off half-cocked like he had, pun intended, he wouldn't have walked straight into that trap. And Shea wouldn't have been out looking for him and she wouldn't have gotten taken either. He would've been there to help them rescue Luuk from that psycho bitch Leeha. He would've been there to help Nikulas deal with him afterwards, and maybe Aiden would never have gotten taken by her and turned into one of her host bodies for her demons.

Which really creeped him out by the way.

No, he didn't have the time or the inclination to depend on a female for his survival. But how else to explain this need of his to keep her near him? How else to explain why he felt so fucking good ever since he'd met her? He'd been in a living hell every night since Luukas had disappeared, so why all of a sudden....

That was it!

Christian jumped clear off of the bed in his excitement. Wearing nothing but his boxer briefs, he paced around in a tight circle with his arms crossed on top of his head and a big smile on his face. Why hadn't it come to him sooner? The reason he was back to normal again wasn't because of the female on his couch. It was because Luukas was back! Whatever weird mumbo jumbo had brought it on while his creator was being gods' only knew what, now that he was back, it had gone away.

He headed to the door, wanting to share his joy with Ryan even though she would have no idea what he was so damn happy about. Halfway there, he remembered she was angry with him and he came to an abrupt halt.

Shit.

He didn't want her to be mad at him. He'd promised to help her with her addiction, and he would keep his promise. But he needed to be straight up with her, and tell her why Shea had said what she had. Maybe she would understand. After all, she'd done some pretty low things herself, and he didn't judge her for what she'd done. And now that he knew why things had changed for him, and if she was still willing, they could stick to their original agreement. He would help her, and when she was stronger and ready to be out on her own, he would set her up wherever she wanted to go.

He didn't stop to think why her opinion of him was so important.

Finding himself at the door to his room once again, he saw she was still sitting where she'd been the last time he'd looked. Her eyes straight ahead, staring out the wall of windows. Coughing discreetly so as not to startle her, he went out and sat down on the chair next to her and tried to figure out the best way to start this conversation.

Other than a quick once over when he'd first sat down, she'd turned away and proceeded to ignore him. But he knew she wasn't as unaffected by him as she tried to make it appear. Her spine had stiffened to show her irritation with him as soon as she'd realized he was there, but he knew it was only a bluff, because he could also hear her pulse speed up, could hear her blood quicken in her veins. Now that could be attributed to anger also, but the sensuous scent that rose from her in response to his presence was not.

He took a deep breath. "When Luukas was taken, some really strange stuff started happening to some of us. Me, Shea, even Dante. You haven't met him yet. He was taken too, and hasn't made his way back yet." She continued to stare out the window, but whether she realized it or not her head had turned towards him just slightly as she listened. He bit back a smile and continued his story.

"Dante, the scariest, toughest vampire I ever met, he kind of went off the deep end. He'd always been a loner, more old school, but he reverted back to the days when he'd first been reborn. He was living underground, and his hunting of humans escalated until the bodies were piling up." He hurried to explain, "Dante is very old, and lived in hiding for a long time to avoid being hunted himself. Horrific things were done to him by humans. But you don't have to fear him. He doesn't go after good people, only ones that deserve what he doles out. He wouldn't hurt you, or any of us." That didn't seem to make her less anxious, so he moved on.

"Shea and I had nearly similar symptoms, only we had completely opposite triggers. The day after Luuk disappeared, Shea discovered she felt horrific pain if she was touched by a male. Like she was being electrocuted or something. Even just a friendly touch on the arm or leg would have her wincing and jerking away."

"And what happened to you?" Her voice was so quiet he almost didn't realize she'd spoken.

"I had the exact opposite problem. I couldn't be touched enough. If I wasn't with a female on a regular basis, my entire body burned like holy fire. My muscles would start to cramp. My nerve endings short-circuited. And my thirst got completely out of control."

She turned to look at him then, concern wrinkling her brown. "That's why you were in such pain when I let you out?"

"Yes. Watching you dance every night was a beautiful kind of hell on earth for me." His voice became husky as he remembered. "I couldn't *not* watch you, *she'ashil*, no matter how much it hurt me. You're exquisite."

His lengthening cock was obvious underneath the thin material of his briefs, as were his elongated fangs, but he couldn't help it. The memories of her dancing for him were all it took for him to be hard and ready. Actually, her sitting there and breathing was all it took for him. And it really didn't make sense. He'd watched so many strippers that he thought he'd become rather immune to it all. The dancing. The nudity. The human women going through the motions physically, but not really there mentally. But Ryan had proven him so wrong. Her tired eyes flicked down to his lap and then immediately back up again, the musky scent of her rising desire proving that she had seen plenty with that quick look. But he needed to finish his story.

"I fucked a lot of human women, Ryan. Mostly dancers, because they were almost always up for it. Sometimes I went through four or five a night. But it wasn't because I wanted to. I hated it. Hated doing that to them. Hated doing that to me. But if I didn't do it, I became the creature you met when you first let me out of that room." He left out the part about how he'd nearly raped Shea that one time when he'd tried to fight his body's cravings, and he'd never liked Shea as anything more than a sister. "I became something even worse. Something dangerous. And so I did what my body drove me to do."

"So, I am just one of those many women." Her tone was flat, numb with acceptance.

"No, I don't think you are," he answered honestly. "Since Luukas has come back, I don't feel that way anymore. I just feel…normal. Like a normal male who wants to have sex with you because I want to, not because I'm afraid of what will happen if I don't."

She continued to stare out the window at the city, but her lips parted and her little tongue darted out to wet them. Christian felt a jolt through his groin as he watched it. Lowering himself off of the chair, he moved to kneel in front of her. She lowered her eyes, avoiding him. He found himself craving the sight of their turquoise color.

"Ryan, come to bed with me." His voice was a rough whisper.

Hers wasn't much better. "I don't want to become attached to you."

With a finger under her chin, he tilted her face up until she looked at him and repeated his request. "Come to bed with me. Let's enjoy each other. My blood will help you, and yours will help me. And when you're ready, when you feel strong enough, I'll keep my end of our deal and see that you're well taken care of, wherever you choose to go. And in the meantime, the other Hunters and I will take care of the vampire that threatened you."

Her eyes studied his face, lingering on his mouth for a moment. The sight of his fangs excited her, he could tell, so he bared them a little more for her. Her heart thumped in her chest, but her scent told him it wasn't in fear.

"Come to bed with me. Please."

"Okay," she finally whispered.

Taking her delicate face between his large palms, he moved in to kiss her as he'd been longing to do all night. But he took his time, savoring the anticipation: The rise and fall of her perfect breasts as she breathed him in. The way her beautiful eyes darkened with longing. And, he was male enough to acknowledge, giving her one last chance to turn him away if she so chose.

As he got closer, her eyes drifted shut and her lips parted slightly. Her small hands slid up his bare chest, lingering on his pecs, and then moving on to grip his broad shoulders. One side of his mouth lifted in a self-satisfied smile as she leaned in to meet him.

All teasing was chased from his mind when her soft lips met his and her tongue slid between them, exploring his mouth as she took control and deepened the kiss.

He let her play for a few seconds, but when she touched the tip of one of his fangs, he pulled away with a hiss. Her eyes flew open in confusion, but before she could move away or say anything, he growled deep in his throat and pulled her in again. Taking over the kiss, he buried his hands in her hair and ravaged her mouth until she was whimpering and scooting forward on the couch to get even closer to him.

Sliding one arm around her back and the other under her ass, he lifted her with him as he stood and strode into the bedroom. Setting her on her feet next to the bed, he yanked her shirt up and off. He wanted to strip her bare, but the need to feel her warm, supple skin against his was too strong. Pulling her tight against him, he kissed her again as she wrapped her arms around his neck and hung on tight. His cock kicked against her belly, his entire body shaking with the effort it was taking him to not spin her around, pull her shorts and panties aside, and plunge into her from behind.

"I need to be inside of you," he managed to grit out. He was barely hanging on to his self-control. His vampire instincts were taking over and he was becoming mindless with need for her. For her body, and her blood.

MINE.

She moaned and rocked her hips against him. He took that for a yes.

Her bra was on the floor less than a second later, his hands replacing the material that had covered her full breasts. Her stiff nipples tickled the middle of his palms, and he broke off their kiss to nip and kiss his way down her chest and pull one into his mouth. He teased her with his tongue and fangs until her back was arching and her fingers were digging into his biceps. Then he did the same on the other side.

She let out an anguished moan. "Christian," she breathed. "Please..."

The lady didn't have to ask twice.

35

Ryan's entire body yearned for him. Every touch of his tongue on her skin sent pulses of desire straight to the damp flesh between her legs. She longed to feel him touch her there, and felt another surge of wetness just thinking about it.

With an animalistic growl, he lifted her onto the bed and joined her there.

He nipped at her sensitive nipple, harder this time, and by the sounds of his moans she knew he'd drawn blood. But it didn't frighten her. Instead, she arched her body towards his warm mouth, encouraging him to take more. Her legs moved restlessly as he sucked harder, trying to ease the ache there. When that didn't work, she parted her legs and slid her hand between the fleshy folds, but he reached down and captured her wrist.

"That's *mine*," he told her.

Ryan squirmed beneath him until finally, he left her breast to work his way down her stomach. His hands and mouth were everywhere at once. The sounds he was making as he devoured her body only increasing her response to him, but still, she needed more.

"Christian...*please*," she begged.

Rearing up, he slid his hands into the waistband of her shorts and ripped them in half, pulling them from her body along with her panties. His briefs soon followed. Sliding one arm under her leg, he paused just a moment as he stared down at her womanhood. His other hand reached out to touch her, separating the fleshy folds and running his thumb up and down the crease.

Ryan cried out as the pressure in her groin spun out of control, leaving her teetering on the edge.

His upper lip pulled up in a snarl as he bared his fangs, and for a moment she thought he was going to bite her there, but he didn't. Eyes glowing like twin orbs, features harsh and strained, he lined himself up with her opening and impaled her with one strong thrust.

A tearing pain ripped through her, and Ryan cried out, this time in alarm and shock as he froze above her. She'd known it would hurt the first time, but he was so large, and the intensity of him inside of her along with the pain had caught her off guard.

His eyes went wide with shock and his mouth slackened as a look akin to horror came over his face. "Why didn't you tell me?" he demanded.

"Would you have believed me?" she scoffed as she fought back tears.

"Yes," he said simply. "Yes, I would have."

She felt the tears overflow as she looked up at him. "I don't want you to stop," she whispered.

Though his features were strained and his big body was shaking with the effort to hold himself still above her, he managed to give her a tight smile. She noticed his breathing was as harsh as hers was. "That's good. Because I don't think I could even if you asked me to." He suddenly got serious. "I'll make it good for you, love. I will. Just...bare with me."

He started to move inside of her, slowly at first, and then a little faster, watching her reaction the entire time. His forehead fell to her chest and she found herself responding to his thrusts as that heavy feeling came back. Pressing her head back into the mattress and closing her eyes, she moaned aloud. His mouth found her nipple again, and he teased it with his tongue and his teeth, nipping her and then soothing the bite with his tongue until she was once again writhing beneath him. When her nails were digging into his back, he lifted his upper body off her and sat back on his heels. Gripping her hips, he thrust up into her fast and hard.

Ryan's back was arched over his legs. In this position, he rubbed her in all the right places and she felt the waves of desire in her belly turn into a steady tightening. Everything else fell away as her entire being focused on that feeling. Christian watched her the entire time, the raw hunger on his face turning her on even more. Harder and harder he pumped, and then one hand left her hip and his thumb found that sweet spot between her legs. As soon as he touched her, she shattered around him with a cry.

He didn't stop touching her, dragging out her orgasm until she was senseless and calling out his name. Falling on top of her, he gathered her tightly underneath him and slammed into her over and over with long, hard thrusts until with a hoarse cry, his entire body shuddered and jerked and Ryan felt him emptying inside of her.

Long seconds later, he collapsed as his arms seemed to give out, then almost immediately rolled to the side and pulled her into his arms. "Are you okay?" he asked anxiously.

She took stock of her body and had to say, "Yeah. Yeah, I'm really good." And she was, other than a bit of soreness between her legs.

He let out a relieved breath, and hugged her to him. "I've been dreaming of doing that for so long."

Propping her head on her hand to look at him, she was taken aback for a moment by how…normal he looked. The harsh lines of his face were gone, his eyes lacked that glowing light, and his fangs had receded. He seemed truly at peace for the first time since she'd met him. "De-virginizing a stripper? Was it everything you dreamed of and more?" she teased.

"No."

She recoiled at his blunt answer and her face got hot with embarrassment, but then he said, "It was so much better than anything I'd ever imagined." Reaching up, he gently ran his fingers down her cheek. "How can one such as you still be innocent?"

She could understand how he felt. No one was more shocked than she was that her virginity was still intact after all this time, and all that she'd done.

"I wouldn't exactly say I was innocent. Just a virgin."

Rolling over on top of her again, he kissed her tenderly. "I'm glad. I'm glad I was your first. And I'm sincerely sorry that I didn't know. You should have said something."

Pushing those unpleasant thoughts of her past aside, she looked up at the male that had finally broken the barrier and gotten close to her, in more ways than one.

36

Christian stared down at the woman he'd just unintentionally deflowered. If he had known, he never would have brought her here.

Then he scoffed at himself. Who was he kidding? Yes, he would have. He'd wanted her. Badly. He still wanted her, even though he'd just fucked her. But if he'd known she was a virgin, he would have made sure she was more prepared for him. "Are you sure I didn't hurt you? You're feeling okay?"

Her blue eyes twinkled up at him. "I'm good, really. More than good. If I'd known what I was missing, I would've done this with someone a long time ago."

A sudden desire to shred open the torso of some unknown male tore through him at the mere thought of her being intimate like this with some nameless human. The urge was so intense he saw spots, so it took him a moment to notice that her mood had suddenly changed. "Ryan? What's wrong?"

"Nothing. I'm fine."

He cocked an eyebrow at her. Any male that had spent any time at all around the opposite sex knew that "fine" did not mean fine. The fact that she'd even said it meant she was not fine. As did the way she refused to look at him and the fine lines of stress that kept appearing and disappearing around her eyes and mouth as she tried not to let him see her wincing.

He rolled off of her to give her some space, pushing himself up on one arm to see her more clearly. A thin sheen of perspiration covered her skin and she was looking a tad bit green. "Is it withdrawals or the voices?" he asked quietly.

Her eyes flew to his mouth as he spoke, and he could tell she was trying to read his lips. "A little of both," she whispered. "Well, a little bit withdrawals and a lot of the voices." She winced again and raised her fingers to her temples. "They're screaming at me." Her voice broke at the end and a single tear slid down her cheek. "They'd been so quiet, but now they're screaming..."

He drew the sheet up over her waist so she wouldn't feel so exposed and ran his hand down her arm to get her attention. "What are they saying, *she'ashil*?"

"What?" Her voice was subdued, like she didn't want to add to the noise.

"What are the voices saying?"

Fingers still on her temples, she shook her head back and forth. "I don't know."

"Try to listen to them. What are they saying?"

"I don't know!" she said, louder now. "They all talk at once and talk over each other and I can't understand them." She struggled to sit up without using her arms. He reached out to help her but she brushed him off. Crossing her legs in front of her, she rocked herself back and forth. "I don't know if I can do this, Christian. I can't live like this," she sobbed. Her long, bright hair fell over her shoulders and hid her face.

He crossed his long legs, imitating her pose, and sat facing her. With one hand he brushed her long hair back away from her face so he could see her. "You can," he told her with more conviction than he actually felt. He'd never dealt with anything like this before, but he'd heard of people like her. "You're stronger than you think. You can do this." He rubbed her leg, and the fact that he always felt the need to be touching her didn't escape him, but he pushed the thought aside. He had other things to worry about right now. "Try to pick out one voice. Talk back to them if you need to."

She gave him a look, and he could tell she was worried about what he would think of her. "It's okay. I don't think you're crazy. Just try it." He kept his eyes steady on her face, trying to encourage her without breaking her concentration.

Taking a deep breath, she removed her hands from her head. She was listening to them. Really listening to them. Maybe for the first time. Patiently, he waited. Patience was something he was very good at, when he wasn't getting racked by his own withdrawal symptoms.

Ryan was shaking her head. "I can't. I can't understand them."

"So tell them that. They'll listen. Just like you told them to shut the fuck up at the hotel, remember? They listened to you."

A blush stole up her pale cheeks, but she did as he suggested. "Stop talking all at once," she told them firmly. "I can't understand you." Her hands went back up to rub her temples. "No. Stop! Only one. Only one can talk." She started to shake her head in defeat, but then she stilled and her hands fell from her head to grab his arm in excitement. "It's working," she whispered.

"What is it saying?" he whispered back.

Her head tilted to the side and her brow furrowed as she listened intently. "It's talking too fast, I...no...wait."

Christian was as still as she as he waited.

"Run," she said.

He frowned. "Run? From what? From who?" His spine stiffened indignantly. "From *me*?"

"Shhh," she scolded, holding up one finger to tell him to wait a minute.

It couldn't be telling her to run from him, he decided. Those things had thrown him off of her more than once before. If they were worried he was going to hurt her, they wouldn't hesitate to do so again. He was sure of it.

She let out a heavy sigh. "I don't know. All I can understand is the word 'run', and the rest is just gibberish."

"What do you think it's telling you to run from?"

"I don't know," she said. "But I don't think it's you. They wouldn't let you near me if they didn't like you."

"That's true. They've held me back from you before," he felt a little bit better.

An expression that was terribly haunted and yet somewhat self-satisfied at the same time passed over her features. It made a chill ran up his spine.

"But they didn't kill you," she said. "If they didn't like you, or if I truly wished it, you wouldn't be here right now."

"What do you mean by that?"

"Just what I said. I can't control them." She studied his face, looking for something. Whatever it was, she must have found it. Her voice was barely more than a whisper when she confessed, "They've killed for me before."

His mind flashed back to the dead woman he'd found in the cell at the club. "The woman at the club..."

"She was beating Josefina." Her tone was defensive, and this time it was her stiffening up defensively. "Jose is just a child. And she was beating her bloody, for nothing that was her fault! Just because she was angry at her disgusting husband and got her kicks from taking out her anger on young girls."

"Hey, hey," he soothed. "You don't have to defend her to me. I saw that room they kept you in. It was worse than a jail cell. They kept you locked up in there, didn't they?"

She nodded. "Yes. They only let us out to 'perform'." He noticed she was twisting the sheet in her hands. "Sometimes the *patron* would come in to our cell to get his payment for letting us stay there. His wife didn't like it, and she'd take it out on the girls."

Christian's blood began to seethe in anger and a red haze came down over his vision. He didn't feel quite so bad now for sucking the bastard dry. "Did he do that to you?" He barely got the words out from between his clenched teeth.

"No." Her hand covered his where it still lay on her knee, and he immediately felt a bit calmer. "No," she repeated. "He tried. The voices wouldn't let him."

Get a grip, asshole. She was a virgin up until a few minutes ago.

"That's good."

"No. It's not. Because he couldn't have me, he went after Jose. The only one I cared about in that place. He raped her. Brutally and repeatedly." She closed her eyes, turning paler at the memory.

"Why didn't the voices stop him if they knew you cared about her?" he asked.

"He did it when I was with you, and they never leave me. I'd come back from dancing for you to find her beaten black and blue and covered in his...covered in his..." Her voice broke and she didn't continue.

"He's dead," Christian informed her in a voice that was little more than a growl. "I sucked him dry when you ran out into the sun and I couldn't follow you."

She sniffed and looked up at him in amazement. "You did?"

"Yeah. As soon as your friends here released me, I tried to follow you outside. When I couldn't, I found him instead. I was starving. I practically ripped his throat out trying to feed. I felt bad about it at the time, but not so much anymore."

She hid behind her hair again. "So, if you'd been able to, you would've killed me when I let you out."

He wanted to tell her that wouldn't have happened. That there was no way in hell he could ever have hurt her. But he'd be lying. "I don't know."

She cleared her throat. "I wondered why you didn't come after me right away."

"Oh, I did. I wasn't going to let an exquisite creature like you get away that easy."

She gave him a tentative smile, and he smiled back.

"So, where did you come from?" he asked. "How did you end up in that place?"

"Um...Well...My life was nothing exciting. I was born in California to great parents. I have a younger brother. We had a nice house in a nice neighborhood. I went to a nice school, got good grades, had my college career all planned out." She shrugged. "For the most part, anyway. I was quite the nerd."

"What were you going to study in school?"

She smiled a bit sardonically. "I wanted to get my Masters in Political Science and study law. I wanted to fight for the immigrants in our country. Make their lives better."

The irony of where she was when he'd met her didn't escape him.

"When the voices showed up, I thought I was losing my mind. I told you about that. I ran away so I wouldn't get locked up. I hit the streets, and soon after discovered the magic of heroin. It made the noise in my head bearable." She paused, the look in her eyes far away as she remembered. "I had reached a new low point when the *matron* found me, scraped me up off the sidewalk, and brought me to their club to 'work' for them."

His heart was aching for her, for everything she'd been through, but he knew if he tried to coddle her now she'd shut down on him. "How long were you on the streets?"

She came back to him slowly. "Too long."

"Are you hungry?" he asked, hoping to distract her from her past, but she shook her head.

"What about you? What's your story? Your life has to be more interesting than mine."

Interesting? He didn't know about that. Longer, for sure, but not interesting really. "Not much to tell."

She dropped her chin and gave him a disbelieving look. "Yeah, right. I showed you mine now you show me yours. That's how it works. Now spill."

He grinned at her choice of words. "What would you like to know exactly?"

She thought about it for a second. "How old are you?"

"I believe I'd just turned twenty-seven. We didn't really keep track as much back then."

"No, I mean, how old are you now? When were you made into..." She waved her hand around in front of him. "This?"

Ah, that. "I was found by Luukas in the 1800's. I'm not certain of the exact date. I'd been mortally wounded during a buffalo hunt and was left to die among the animal carcasses. The buffalo had been stripped of their hides and their bodies were left to rot, as was I."

Ryan stopped him with a hand in front of her. "Wait. I thought you said you were half American Indian?"

"Yes. My mother was Navajo."

"And you were out hunting buffalo for their hides? Wasn't that something the Indian tribes abhorred? Wasting the animal like that?"

"I wasn't hunting the buffalo," he clarified. "I was hunting the white men that were decimating the herds and causing the tribes of the Great Plains to starve and freeze."

Her mouth dropped open. She snapped it shut a moment later. "That makes more sense."

"Not to my father," he told her. "He thought I was betraying my people. His people. He didn't understand."

"How did that even happen? Your mom and dad?"

She was still a bit pale, but his talking seemed to be helping her, so he kept going with his story. "My father loved my mother, and I think she loved him, but at that time, it wasn't acceptable to marry for either of them. So they would meet in secret, and I would imagine had quite the scandalous affair."

Her eyes were wide. "Couldn't they just be together?"

He shook his head. "My mother was married to a Navajo man, and what she'd done wouldn't be easily forgiven, to say the least. According to my father, when she gave birth to me and saw my lighter skin and my father's eyes, she snuck away from her camp and gave me to my father to raise. Her husband wasn't there at the time of the birth, and she told my father she was going to tell him I'd been stillborn. He said she was grieving heavily, and so he had high hopes that her husband would believe her. Neither of us ever saw her again. But she left this with him to give to me when I was old enough." He raised his arm and showed her the silver cuff bracelet he was never without. "As soon as I was old enough, my father told me all about her. I wanted to know my mother, so I taught myself about her people and tried to live by their beliefs. My father hated that. He wanted me to be a good Christian boy. We didn't get along very well. Of course, he was kind of an asshole. But I guess he did the best he could."

"What happened to your father?"

"He died of disease when I was fourteen. After that, I wandered from place to place, picking up work where I could, and trying to fight for my mother's people any way I knew how without actually being a part of their tribe. It was the only way I knew to try to know her."

"I'm so sorry, Christian."

"It was a long time ago. And I have a family now, thanks to Luukas. I owe him everything, and I have a lot to make for now that I'm back."

"What do you mean? Make up for what?"

"For not being here when he needed me these past years."

A look of confusion marred her brow. "But I thought you'd only been gone for some weeks?"

"Yeah, physically. But mentally, I've been checked out since he was abducted."

"But that was hardly your fault."

"It *was* my fault," he insisted. "If I hadn't been so worried about my dick, I could've done more to get him home sooner, and none of *this* would have happened." He waved his hand back and forth, indicating the two of them.

She dropped her hands and pulled away from him with a stiff little smile on her face. He was confused as to why, until he realized what he'd just said. "Ryan, *she'ashil*, I didn't mean..."

"It's fine," she cut in. "I'm going to go get cleaned up." Taking the sheet with her, she slid off the bed and headed to the bathroom. He heard the lock turn in the door, effectively shutting him out.

Dammit. He hadn't meant to make it sound like that.

37

A soft knock on the bedroom door woke Ryan from a fitful sleep. After her long shower earlier, she'd come out of the bathroom to find Christian curled on his side facing away from her. The daylight hours must have finally gotten to him, for she could hear his soft snores across the room. Tiptoeing over to the dresser, she'd found a cotton tank top and pulled it over her head. It was so big on her that it came to mid-thigh and showed plenty of side boob, but she didn't like going to sleep with nothing on. She'd never felt secure enough to be so free.

A quick survey of Christian's side of the bed showed he'd already gotten up, but there was a piece of paper on his pillow.

Ryan,
  I'm so sorry about what I said earlier. I

didn't mean for it to come out the way it did. I do NOT regret meeting you, she'ashil. Just the way it came about.

Had to go talk to the guys. Please help yourself to anything in the apartment. I'll be back soon.

Christian

The knock sounded again. She'd nearly forgotten that that was what had woken her up. Folding up the note and setting it on the nightstand beside the bed, she'd just swung her legs off the mattress when the bedroom door cracked open and Keira's dark head poked around the corner. She smiled when she saw that Ryan was awake.

"Hey," Ryan greeted her. "Sorry. I must have overslept."

"May I come in?" Keira asked.

"Oh! Yes, sorry. Come on in." Hopping up from the bed, she straightened her borrowed tank. "Let me just run to the restroom." Yanking the covers up on the bed to cover the specks of her virgin blood, she ran to the bathroom and shut the door firmly behind her. Lifting the toilet lid, she winced slightly as she sat down. She was still a little bit sore.

What was Keira doing here? Was she going to kick her out? Ryan had gotten the feeling that she was sort of the "queen bee" around here, being Luukas' wife, or girlfriend, or whatever. Maybe she didn't like the fact that he'd brought her here without asking.

Well, she wasn't going to find out anything hiding in the bathroom.

Finishing her business, she washed her hands, brushed her teeth, and braided her hair over her shoulder. She didn't have a hair band, but it helped contain the stuff. She really needed to cut it.

Enough stalling.

Taking a deep breath, she pulled open the door and left her sanctuary. "Sorry," she apologized again. "And sorry about the shirt." She plucked at the front of her tank top. "If I'd known you were coming, I would've found something else to wear."

"Ryan, if you apologize one more time, I'm gonna smack you." Keira's teasing grin took the sting out of her words. "I brought you some clothes. They're Emma's, so they should fit you pretty good. You guys are about the same size."

"Oh. Um...thank you." Walking over to the bed, she picked up the navy yoga pants and slipped them on. They fit her like a glove.

Keira got up and wandered over to the window, she assumed to give her a little privacy to change her shirt. Little did she know that Ryan could've cared less if she saw her tits. "Thank you for the clothes," she said again when she was decent.

"No problem," Keira said from the window. With a last look at the sparkling lights of Seattle, she turned away from the view and climbed up on the bed. "I think I need to start a donation closet," she laughed, but Ryan didn't get the joke. "Come sit with me."

She patted the mattress, so Ryan climbed up and settled back against the headboard. "What's up?" she asked her.

Keira studied her hands twisting in her lap for a moment, and Ryan could feel her indecision. When she looked up, all teasing was gone from her face. "Ryan, I don't know an easy way to go about this, so I'm just going to be straight forward. Okay?"

Sensing no animosity, Ryan agreed. "Sure. Okay. I prefer it that way, actually."

"Most of us Moss's do," Keira smiled.

Most of us...what? "What are you trying to say?" Ryan asked.

Keira held out her hand for her to shake. "Hi. I'm Keira Moss. We're cousins, I suspect."

Ignoring the outstretched hand, Ryan stared at her like she'd lost her mind. "That doesn't mean anything. Moss isn't an unusual name."

Dropping her hand back onto her lap, Keira continued, "My sister is Emma Moss, of course. Grace Moss, another cousin, I believe you talked to last night. We didn't know about her either until Aiden brought her back with him."

Ryan narrowed her eyes. "If you didn't know about her, how do you know you all are related?"

"Because we can feel it, mostly. Don't you feel it?"

She leveled those large hazel eyes on Ryan. The same eyes her sister had. Her sister that looked so much like Ryan. Did she feel it? She felt something, yes. Some kind of kinship with these women. But were they actually related?

"But also," Keira went on. "Because of the curse."

Ryan was jolted from her thoughts. "Curse? What curse? Christian's curse?"

Keira frowned. "Christian is still cursed?"

"Never mind," Ryan told her. "What curse are you talking about?"

She looked like she was about to say more, but she refocused and went back to what she'd been saying. "I don't know how much you know about me, or any of us."

"Just that Luukas had been abducted and was just rescued really."

"Yes, he was. What you don't know, is that I am part of the reason that he was abducted."

"What do you mean?"

"I mean I'm a witch, and to make a long story short, I was forced to use my powers to help a very evil woman keep Luukas prisoner." Her voice broke on the next part. "I kept him hungry and helpless, and I was able to do that because I can kind of suck his own power from him and hold it inside of me." She sniffed and wiped at her eyes.

Ryan felt like she'd just walked into an episode of the Twilight Zone. Not that she didn't believe her; after all, she had her own weird stuff. Which come to think of it had been awfully quiet since she'd woken up. But still... Luukas had powers? Other than being super strong and living off of the blood of mortals?

"Do they all have powers?" she asked.

Keira must have easily followed her thinking. "Not like Luukas. He's a Master vampire. And the more 'children' he creates, the more powerful he becomes."

"What can he do?"

"You'd kind of have to see it to believe it. But suffice it to say that he's a force of nature when you get him riled."

Ryan thought about that for a moment. "Is your sister a witch also?"

She nodded. "Yes. And so are you."

"What?" Ryan stopped fidgeting with the bottom of her shirt and laughed derisively. "I am no witch."

"You are. I can sense it, and so can the others. We come from a family of witches." She seemed so certain that Ryan was one of them. "What can you do?" Keira asked.

"I can't do anything," she told her. "Except strip and shoot opiates up my arm."

Her blunt words didn't have the effect she was going for. Keira just rolled her eyes.

"Christian told us a little about your life. But you have magic, Ryan. I can feel it in you. You just need to figure out what it is. Hasn't there been anything strange that's happened when you're around? Any weird premonitions? Anything?"

Christian had obviously kept his big mouth shut about her constant companions. Could it be that he was right? Did she hear them because she was sensitive to them and not because she was crazy? She supposed it wasn't such a far stretch. She was sensitive to the emotions of the living. Why not the dead?

"I can hear voices," she blurted. When Keira nodded encouragingly, she said, "They talk to me all the time. Well, most of the time. They're actually pretty quiet right now."

"When did you start hearing them?"

"When I was about fifteen."

Keira nodded again. "That sounds about right. Most of us don't come into our powers until we hit puberty. Your parents didn't tell you why you heard them or how to control them?"

"I didn't tell my parents," Ryan admitted. "I thought I was losing my mind and I ran away. They don't know where I am, or even that I'm still alive."

"We should call them."

But Ryan shook her head. "No. It's better this way."

Reaching out, Keira took her hands in hers and forced her to look at her. "Ryan, you're not alone anymore. You have family here. You're not crazy. You were just born into a family of witches is all. Your parents should have prepared you, but there are reasons why they didn't. We'll get into that later, though."

Ryan's head was starting to pound from all the True Confessions going on. First, trading life stories with Christians and now this.

"Ryan, we can help you learn about your abilities and how to use them."

Ryan laughed. "Well, I haven't had much luck controlling the voices up to this point. As a matter of fact, it's been the complete opposite."

Keira squeezed her hands. "Whatever has happened up till now isn't your fault. You didn't know."

Taking the focus back off of her, Ryan said, "So, tell me about this curse you were talking about." She pulled her hands from Keira's to discreetly wipe at the moisture in her eyes.

"The evil woman I mentioned, the one that was obsessed with Luuk, she was a former adopted member of his colony. Until he forced her to leave because she was one crow short of a murder, if you know what I mean. And she abducted me also. Had her minions grab me up as my sister and I were leaving a carnival back in our hometown in PA. Those things of hers nearly killed Emma. That's why she wears long sleeves and pants all the time." When Ryan frowned in confusion, she explained. "Em has scars. Horrible scars. The things that attacked her and took me are like monsters from a horror movie. They have rotting skin and fangs like vampires. They drink blood like vampires also." She shivered. "Emma barely lived through it."

"I'm so sorry," Ryan said sincerely. Monsters? There were real monsters in the world? Ryan's head was spinning.

Keira smiled. "She has Nik now, and he thinks she's beautiful. Which she is. And which brings me back to the curse that I assume is the one you're saying Christian has?" She didn't wait for an answer. "So, this woman that took Luukas, she made me do a spell, a curse, on the other vampires that are close to him. She was hoping to weaken them, and as they were all made by Luukas and he's affected by what happens to them, weaken him too. But I found a loophole in the spell, and when I cast it, I snuck it in there."

In spite of her better judgment, Ryan asked the obvious question. "What was the loophole?"

"That Luukas' Hunters would only be affected by the curse until they met their mates. I also put a little something in there to help those meetings along. See, years and years ago, witches and vampires used to hook up all the time, until a new High Priest took over the coven and forbid it. There's a little more to the story, but that's the gist of it. I just put things back the way they should be."

Ryan just sat there. Trying to take it all in.

"Oh, there's one other thing you should know. Christian is your mate."

"My mate?"

"Yes. Like penguins. Penguins mate for life. And so do vampires. I hope you like him, because he'll never let you go now."

She was teasing, Ryan knew, but that didn't stop the rush of anxiety that made her heart pound and her head feel woozy. "No. No. You must be mistaken. We're just...he just...I'm not staying here that long."

Now it was Keira's turn to frown in confusion. "Has he had your blood?"

"Yes, but..."

"And have you had his?"

"Yes. It helps with my withdrawals..."

"Ryan, honey. I hate to be the one to break it to you, but you two are now practically married. No, wait. More than married. You've exchanged blood. You're bonded."

"No. We can't be. I wasn't planning to stay," she argued.

But Keira just grinned at her and patted her leg consolingly. "Don't take it so hard. Christian is a complete stud. And a good male from what I've been told other than his behavior the last few years, which he really couldn't help." Hopping off the bed, she said, "Why don't you get some food and then come over to Nik and Emma's? It's right at the other end of the hall. We can start working on that entity problem you have."

"Um, yeah. Okay."

With a wave and a smile, Keira left Ryan sitting on the bed feeling like she'd just been hit by a truck.

She was a witch? That was why she heard voices? So, they really weren't just in her head. In spite of everything that they'd done, she hadn't really believed it until now.

And she had family she hadn't known about. Women with weird abilities like her. Because she came from a family of witches.

And Christian. That stuff Keira had said. What the hell was up with that? Ryan jumped off the bed and began to pace around the room. No. He would've told her if that were true. He wouldn't have given her his blood. Except he'd had to do it to save her. Or so he said.

But if that were the case, then he wouldn't have had hers. He'd never taken from her out of thirst or hunger or whatever. Only little sips here and there when they had sex. She liked it, and from the sounds he made and the way he lost control when he took from her, he did too. But it wasn't like he'd *needed* her blood. So, she would think that he could've controlled himself if need be.

She couldn't be tied to him. This was only supposed to be short term. Until they found the vampire who had attacked her.

Yes, she'd also agreed to let him try to help her with her addiction and to deal with the voices, but deep down, she'd always known it wasn't going to work. She'd always known she would go back to the drugs. If she were completely honest with herself, she didn't really want to learn to deal with the voices.

She needed the dope to function. Needed it to keep her sanity. Besides, he didn't want her around long term. He'd made that pretty damn clear.

She didn't need him either. Or the others. She would be fine.

38

Josiah stood across from the high-rise apartments in downtown Seattle. Craning his head back on his neck as far as it would go, he watched as a powerful figure paced restlessly in front of the window on the top floor. His vampire eyesight even allowed him to see the male's dark hair and tall physique.

Luukas.

He'd filled out more since Josiah had last seen him. But that didn't matter. It wasn't the Master vampire that Josiah was here for.

He was here for his fucking witch.

Actually, he was here for all of the females. After his visit from Leeha, he'd done a lot of thinking. She wanted him to prove himself? Fine. He'd fucking prove himself. And he didn't need the demons or anyone else to help him.

His plan was simple. So simple that he was amazed he hadn't thought of it before. He would watch and wait. The witches had to leave that fortress sometime. And when they did, he would catch them unaware and take them out quickly and efficiently. No more games. No more playing around. He would prove to Leeha once and for all he was worth sticking around for. She wouldn't agree with his plan, she liked to play with her victims too much. But he would accomplish what she never could. And he would do it without her help.

Once the females were dead, their mates would soon follow them. It was so simple, he didn't know why he hadn't thought of it before. Josiah wouldn't have to do anything but watch and wait.

Game over.

39

Christian was antsy as he sat in the corner of Luuk's office listening to Nik lay out plans for their next move in the quest to find Dante. Something felt off, but he couldn't figure out what it was. At first he thought it was because Luukas was finally home, or because of what all had happened the last few weeks to all of them. But it wasn't because he'd been gone, or Shea had been gone, or Aiden was possessed, or Luukas was unstable. As a matter of fact, if Dante had been over in his usual corner, it would be like none of it had ever happened.

Glancing out towards the other room through the glass wall divider, he saw Keira had returned from talking to Ryan and was grabbing another bottle of wine out of the cabinet. She gave him a thumb's up as she headed back out the front door. The girls were practicing down at Nik and Aiden's tonight, as they wanted to work on some heavier stuff and Nik had told him that too much magic in the air made Luukas "jumpy".

He'd been surprised but not shocked when he'd shown up tonight and Keira had pulled him aside and told him that Ryan was a Moss witch, and that she was going to go down and talk to her if that was all right with him. He didn't know why he hadn't figured it out earlier. But with everything that was going on, it just hadn't clicked.

He wondered if the fact that she had family here would make her want to stay. Not that it mattered. What they had between them was just a fling. A fling that he was thoroughly enjoying because for the first time in seven years he wasn't being forced to fuck her just to relieve the agony of his body. No. He was fucking her because of plain old normal lust for a female. And he was helping her because she had helped him get out of that damn room. He owed her at least that much before she went off to the next chapter in her life.

"Maybe we should go back up to the mountain." Luukas spoke up from where he was pacing by the window. His body was tense but his voice was firm. "Shea can lead us inside..."

"No!" Shea blurted. They all turned to look at her except for Luukas, who remained at the window looking out at the cityscape. "I mean, we'd be wasting our time. Dante isn't there. The demons aren't there. There's nothing there to see. Everyone is gone."

"Leeha wouldn't have just left that altar unguarded," Aiden argued.

"But Leeha is dead," Nik pointed out. "It makes sense that her followers would no longer be there."

"Who was watching you, Shea?" Luukas asked. "Someone had to be there to keep you there for so long."

"No one was there. I was locked in a cell and it took me a while to get out is all."

Aiden frowned at her and opened his mouth to say something, but Shea frantically shook her head at him to keep quiet. "Besides," she continued. "Dante could be anywhere. I mean, look at Christian, he was all the way in Mexico."

Christian had only been halfway listening to the exchange, his mind on the woman downstairs in his bedroom, but the sound of his name brought him back to the conversation going on around him.

Luukas turned from the window and studied him with bright silver eyes. "Do you recall anything else about your little vacation?" he asked. "Anything at all that may be useful to me?"

Christian could feel his face turning red at Luukas' implied accusation. "Vacation", indeed. "No," he said shortly. "I've told you everything I could remember as soon as I came upstairs tonight."

Nik broke the tension in the air, as he was so good at doing. "And you didn't recognize the vampire that attacked Ryan down there? Before you chased her into the street to get hit by a car?"

Aiden laughed and smacked him on the arm as Christian rolled his eyes. "I didn't make her run into the road. She panicked and ran out there all on her own, and I found her later at the hospital." He kept her little friends to himself for now. He wasn't sure how Luukas would react to her bringing spooks into his home. But as soon as he got the chance, he was planning to sit down with Nik and Aiden and fill them in, see how they thought he should handle it. They'd been around the new Luukas longer than he had.

Maybe the girls would have more insight as to what Ryan could do after they hung out tonight. They could probably help her better than he could.

"Surprising, really," Aiden mused. "My Grace barely flinched when she found out I was, shall we say, enhanced. And she enjoys it immensely. And I know for a fact that Emma doesn't shy away from Nik's manly teeth. I can hear her clear on the other side of the apartment."

"Shut up, Aiden," Nikulas growled.

"Really, mate. You should try a ball gag…"

"Aiden!" Shea scolded.

"Fucking hell!" Nik shouted as he shot up out of his chair. "I fucking warned you, man."

"Nikulas. SIT." Luukas had watched the back and forth between them with a tolerance usually reserved for rowdy children, but apparently his tolerance level had been reached. "Sit down," he repeated. "And Aiden, stop instigating."

"But he's so fun to rile up." He dodged the swing Nik took at him and laughed.

"Nikulas." Luukas' tone would brook no argument.

Nik sat back down but pointed at Aiden. "I'm not forgetting about this."

Aiden grinned and winked.

Happy that the attention had been diverted away from him, Christian rubbed the center of his chest. Something was wrong. Something was very, very wrong.

"...won't hurt to look. If we head out now, we can be there and back by dawn."

Christian had only caught the tail end of what Luukas had just said, but he was quick to figure out what he'd missed. They were going to Leeha's old fortress. The place where Luukas had been held and tortured, where Aiden had been possessed, and from where Shea had just escaped. The four of them exchanged anxious looks as Luukas turned his back to them and said, "We can stop at Nikulas and Aiden's and let the females know that we're leaving on the way down to the garage." Glancing at them over his shoulder as they stood up to leave he added, "Bring weapons."

"Everything is ready down at my place," Shea told him. "I'll take the guys to collect them and we'll meet you at Nik's."

"Yes. Good. Thank you, Shea."

They filed out of the office and out of the apartment. No one spoke until they reached Shea's place. Aiden stopped her before she could open the door.

"You're keeping him a secret and I want to know why."

"I don't have a secret," she insisted. "I just don't want to upset Luukas."

"But he should know."

"Uh, what are we talking about here?" Nik asked.

"The warlock. The one that put the bloody demon in me. Shea is protecting him."

"I'm not protecting him."

"Holy shit. Is he still up there?" Excitement shone in Nik's eyes.

Christian looked from one to the other of them and crossed his arms over his chest. "What the fuck are you all talking about?"

Aiden filled him in. "When we got to Leeha's mountain fortress to rescue Luukas, I went with Leeha when she ran from the werewolves that came along to help."

"They weren't there to help," Nik grumbled. "They were there to save Mark and to fuck with us by stealing Emma in the middle of the day."

Aiden rolled his eyes. "They were just having a bit of fun. I don't know why your knickers are still in a twist about it all."

"Fun?" Nik looked like he wanted to hit him again. "They nearly got Emma killed!"

"They didn't know what had happened to her..."

"All right, all right," Christian interrupted them. "Get back to the story."

Aiden quirked a brow as Nik glared at him, but he continued where he'd left off. "So, I went with Leeha down into the bowels of her mountain, and after walking for what seemed like miles through tunnel after tunnel, we came to this cozy little altar room. And lo and behold, who is already there in silver chains? But our little Shea. Apparently, *she* had been the one Leeha wanted the demon in, and not me. Which makes sense, as Leeha has always had her cap set for me."

"So, why was it put in you instead?" Christian asked him.

"Because the warlock with the dark magic has the hots for Shea and refused to use her."

"He does not have the hots for me," she scoffed. "But he did protect me from her, and he let me go. We owe him for that much at least."

"We don't owe him fucking shit," Nik said. "He tried to kill my brother."

"But did he? Really?" Aiden asked. "Seems to me that someone with the power to call forth beings of hell would have no problem defeating a vampire. Even a Master vampire like Luukas. And yet he let him and Keira go."

Nik was shaking his head. "No. I don't believe it. I think he just got bested by my brother the bad ass. And, he was a bad ass that was protecting his female. That right there is a scary fucking combination."

"He's probably long gone by now in any case," Shea said. "So, can we all just agree that Luukas doesn't need to know that I was with him all this time? Please?"

"I agree," Aiden said after a moment. "He doesn't need to know. At least not right now."

"I don't like this," Nik told them. "I don't like keeping stuff from him."

"We're not keeping it from him, mate. We're just not mentioning it for right now. If it becomes pertinent that he should know, then we will tell him. All right, Shea?"

After a moment, she gave a reluctant nod.

Nik crossed his arms and looked like he was about to argue some more, but then he sighed. "Fine. But the moment that information becomes something he needs to know in any way, shape, or form, you're telling him, Shea."

"I will. I promise."

"You good with that?" Nik asked Christian.

"Yeah. I'm all right with that."

Aiden unblocked the door and Shea set about entering the code to let them into her apartment so they could gather up the weapons she'd gotten ready all those weeks ago, when they were supposed to go meet Nik and Aiden and rescue Luukas.

As her place was right next door to Christian's, he told them, "I'll be right there, I just want to change clothes," and punched in the code to get inside his place.

Shutting the door behind him, he rushed into the bedroom. "Ryan?" The bed was made and the bathroom was empty. Nothing was out of place. Everything was as it should be.

Hands on his hips, he stood in the middle of the room and chewed on the inside of his cheek. He didn't know why he'd expected her to be here. She was probably down the hall with the others.

So, why couldn't he shake this feeling that something was horribly wrong?

40

Ryan approached the dealer without a hint of hesitation in her step, in spite of the pandemonium going on in her head and the tugging pain in her chest. Both of which were urging her not to do this, and both of which she wanted nothing more than to shut the hell up.

The city of Seattle, like most large cities, was a hotbed of dealers, users, and pushers. Ryan walked down the sidewalk with no fear of the people around her, stepping around a homeless man carefully so as not to wake him. Being on the streets was as familiar to her as being home. She was way more comfortable here than sleeping in the soft bed of a practical strangers' apartment. *This* was her life. This was where she should be. And this was where it would end.

Not playing house with some supernatural creature that she didn't even know existed a week ago. She didn't belong there. She didn't belong to him. No matter what they all seemed to think. They barely knew each other. And although she appreciated him taking care of her and his offer to keep helping her, the fact of the matter was that she didn't want to live with the dope, and she didn't want to live with the voices. She hated them. Hated what they'd made her become. And she was going to shut them up once and for all.

Approaching the dealer she had spotted a mile away, she gave her a friendly smile. "Hey."

"Hey," the woman said, and took a long drag off her cigarette as she looked Ryan up and down. Average looking, with lanky dark hair and sun worn skin, she wouldn't attract much attention if a person didn't know the signs.

"I'm looking for some stuff," Ryan told her. "Tar...whatever you have."

"Haven't seen you around here before," the woman stalled.

"Seattle is a big city," Ryan retorted. She knew the game the woman was playing. She wanted to make sure she wasn't a nark. "Look, I need something. I'll take all you've got. I can pay." She couldn't pay, at least not with money.

The woman glanced around, and then eyed up Ryan's new clothes and clean hair. She must have decided she wasn't a threat, for she nodded and tossed the cigarette into the street, hitting the windshield of a passing car. She flipped the driver off when he honked at her. "All right, come on."

Ryan followed her into a doorway. Less than five minutes later, she walked back out with tears streaming down her cheeks and the woman's bag slung over her shoulder. She walked for a good five blocks until she hit the waterfront by Pike Market. Finding an empty bench, she sat down and rummaged through the goods she'd just stolen. Inside was everything she needed. Even a spoon and a lighter.

She sat there for a few minutes with the bag held tight against her side, staring across Puget Sound and wishing she could see the Olympic Mountains, but it was too dark. The voices were quiet; as if even they couldn't believe where she was at as she sat there contemplating what she'd just done, and what she was about to do.

A misty rain began to fall, and Ryan lifted her face to feel the cool wetness against her skin. She contemplated putting off what she was going to do until tomorrow, so she could feel the sun one more time, then she laughed to herself. She was in the Pacific Northwest; the chances of her seeing the sun anytime soon were slim to none. It was probably why the vampires liked it here.

Vampires. Ryan's laughter died on her lips and she lifted her hand, touching the side of her neck. It still seemed so surreal to her that she'd been spending her time with a real live vampire. He'd bitten her, drank her blood. And she'd drank his! The thought almost made her gag in spite of the memory of how good it had tasted. And the way it had made her *feel*... words just couldn't describe it. The way *he* had made her feel.

But it didn't matter. None of it mattered. If Keira was to be believed — and Ryan did believe her — he had only kept her around because he knew she was his mate.

Well, he'd just have to find some other chick to bond with. He shouldn't have any problem with that. Not with his history of women.

The rain started to fall heavier now, and the people that had been wandering past her began to run for cover. Holding her bag closed and gathering it close to her side, Ryan stood up to go find some shelter herself where no one would find her until it was over. Heading towards the giant Ferris wheel, she walked past it and ducked down a side street. She kept going until she was far enough away from the attractions that the pedestrians thinned out and the streets were mostly empty. Just down the street, she saw a sign pointing to an underground garage.

Getting into the elevator and punching the number four, she twisted her wet hair into a ponytail, wringing out the water as best as she could. Her clothes were also soaked through and she shivered as the doors opened again. Peeking out, she only saw about four or five cars and absolutely no people. Perfect.

Ryan found a dark corner far away from the elevator and slid down the wall to sit on the dirty pavement. Dumping out the contents of the stolen bag, she picked through the loose change and tampons until she found everything that she needed. As she gathered her supplies, the voices returned with a vengeance. They whizzed around her, some screaming, some sobbing, and some begging her not to do what she was about to do.

Hurrying now, she lit the lighter under the spoon and heated up the tar. Her hands were shaking so badly, it took her twice as long as it normally did. When it was ready, she filled up two of the needles. She didn't bother with a filter this time even though there was some cotton in the bag. It didn't matter. She didn't plan on being here long enough for it to matter. Taking off her wet coat, she used one of the sleeves as a tourniquet and tapped out the big vein on the inside of her elbow. Track marks didn't matter at this point either.

She stuck one of the needles between her teeth and picked up the other one. She'd have to hurry to get them both in before she nodded off. Hopefully, it would be enough to do the job.

Pricking her skin with the first needle, she put her thumb on the plunger...and stopped. Her head fell back against the wall and tears streamed down her face as she left the needle hanging in her arm, the plunger still up. The voices quieted, as if they knew what she was thinking and didn't want to take the chance of distracting her now.

What the hell was she doing? She didn't want to die. And being with Christian these few days...she'd actually felt a surge of hope, the first one she'd ever felt, that things might be okay. No, it wasn't the type of life she used to envision for herself before the drugs had taken over. And no, he wasn't the kind of man she used to fantasize about sitting in English class as a teenager.

Actually, he wasn't a man at all. He was better. He was good to her, he wanted to help her, and he made her feel amazing. Better than she'd felt about herself in a long time. And all he asked in return was that she let him do it.

But he doesn't want you like that. Not for the long haul.

Or did he? He'd told her he didn't regret meeting her. How would either of them know if they didn't give this relationship a chance? If she didn't give Christian the chance to help her? Maybe she really could learn to control the voices, and maybe it wouldn't be so bad being tied to a male that made her blood pound until the only thing she needed was him. If not? Well, they still had their deal.

She was reaching to pull the needle out of her arm when she heard a man's laughter not ten feet in front of her. Her hand froze in mid-air and her eyes widened in disbelief as she stared up at the guy that had tried to rip out her throat back in Tijuana.

How was he here, in this place? How was this possible?

She blinked and he was no longer ten feet away but squatting down directly in front of her. His eyes fell to the needle hanging out of her arm.

"You're making this way too easy for me. It almost takes all the fun of it." His lips turned up into a wide grin, exposing a row of white teeth and two long fangs. "But it's been awhile since I've gotten high." Grabbing her wrist in one hand and the needle in the other, he depressed the plunger before Ryan realized what was happening.

"Nooooo!" The denial shot from her lips to blend with the voices in her head, only to end in little more than a whisper as the heroin flooded her system.

Her sight was already glazing over, her body lifting from the hard concrete, but she managed to lift her head just enough to see his dark eyes light up with anticipation as he brought her wrist to his mouth and bit her.

41

Christian tucked the pistol into the back of his jeans and followed the others down the hall to Nik and Aiden's apartment. Vaguely, he wondered why they still roomed together. Dante hadn't used his place across the hall in years, and Aiden could probably have easily moved in there or to one of the other apartments on the floor below.

He shrugged internally. Maybe they liked the company. They were like an old married couple. Nothing but bickering but unable to leave each other after so many years together.

Luukas came out of the elevator just as they arrived, and while they waited for him to walk the short distance down the hall, Christian tried really hard to ignore the unrest that was growing by leaps and bounds inside of him. The feeling was similar to how he'd felt when he'd needed to be with a woman, that same kind of pull, but without the crippling pain.

You can't fuck this up. You can't fuck this up. Everything is fine. Just do your job.

Looking over at Aiden, he saw him frown and rub his chest. "Are you all right?" he asked. Nik's head whipped around and he took a step towards his best friend, but Aiden held up his other hand and warded him off.

"I'm fine, mate. Just a bit of rumbling is all."

"Is he..." Nikulas didn't finish the sentence.

Aiden shook his head. "No, no. Don't think so. Just a bit restless with all that's going on and where we're going. He senses these things you know, even when he's not listening."

Luukas walked up then and narrowed his eyes at Aiden, his body visibly tensing. Although he had of yet to get the full story about what all had happened to his creator while he'd been gone, Christian knew enough to know that Aiden was lucky that tensing up was all he did.

"I'm good," Aiden assured him without being asked.

Luukas studied him for a moment and then turned and rapped on the door before he opened it. The cloud of magic that rushed from the room was invisible to the naked eye, but powerful nonetheless. They all cringed when they felt it, Luukas stepping back so fast he rammed through the others behind him and didn't stop until his back hit the opposite wall.

The chanting they'd heard within abruptly stopped and the air cleared almost instantly.

"Almost," someone mumbled from inside.

"Sorry," they heard Keira call right before she rushed into the foyer. Her large hazel eyes swept by the others in the group and landed on Luukas where he stood with his back against the wall, chest heaving, eyes darting around the hallway. They landed on her as she walked towards him and stayed there.

"Witch," he growled.

Christian half expected her to stop, give him some room to calm down, but she didn't. She walked right up to him and wrapped her arms around his waist and leaned her body into his. Luukas' arms shot around her and pulled her in tight and held her, his face buried in her dark hair. Bit by bit, the tension left his body and his breathing returned to normal.

"He'll be okay in a minute," Nik whispered. "This stuff freaks him out."

"Who are you kidding?" Aiden said. "It freaks us all out. Let us all hope and pray that we stay on their good side, or we may find ourselves waking up as toads or some such nonsense someday."

As they continued with their bantering, Christian followed them inside and looked around for Ryan, but he didn't see her. "Where's Ryan?" he called out. He realized he'd perhaps spoken a tad too loudly when everyone stopped talking and turned to stare at him. Clearing his throat, he tried again. "She wasn't at my place, I assumed she'd be here. Is she in the other room or something?"

Emma was the first to speak up. "She hasn't shown up yet, but she told Keira she'd be here. Maybe she just ran out for coffee or something."

That tight feeling in Christian's chest constricted until he couldn't breathe. "Something's wrong," he said to Aiden.

"I'm sure she'll be along, mate. Don't panic. It's just the bond."

Christian barely heard him. Sucking in deep breaths of air, he tried to calm his pounding heart. They were both right. She probably just stepped out for a minute, maybe went out to get snacks for everyone or something.

Except she had no money to do something like that, even if she'd thought of it.

Well, maybe she'd just left. Taken off. Decided she didn't want to be here with him after all. If he knew Ryan at all, and he felt that he did even in the short time he'd known her, she wouldn't care about the money he'd offered her to help her get a new start. If she decided to go, she would just go. And he should be relieved that there wasn't some big break-up scene or hard feelings between them. She was a grown woman. She could take care of herself.

Then why did he have to purposefully restrain himself from running out the door after her?

As the others said their "goodbyes" and "be carefuls", Christian took deep breaths and tried to focus himself. He wasn't going to run out on everyone over a female. Not again. He could already feel that their trust in him was tentative to say the least, especially Shea's. She stared at him from across the room where she'd taken up a stance well away from all of the hugging couples. She seemed to be waiting for him to pull something.

He wasn't going to give her the satisfaction. He'd prove to her and everyone else that they could depend on him and he could be trusted. He'd earn back all of that respect that he'd lost.

"Let's go, everyone," Luukas ordered from the doorway. Giving Keira one last look, he ran his fingers down her cheek and then abruptly turned and marched down to the elevator.

Christian filed in between Shea and Nik and joined his maker. Crossing his arms over his chest, he could feel Luukas' eyes on him, but he didn't acknowledge the look. He knew what Luukas was thinking, what they all were thinking. And they were wrong. He was fine.

The doors opened and they all crowded inside. No one spoke as the elevator made its way down to the parking garage. Forty years later, the little chime went off and the letter "G" lit up on the panel. Eons after that the doors opened up.

Christian shot out of there and into the fresh air. Instead of getting better, the tightening in his chest got worse, and this time it was accompanied by a buzzing inside his head. He was beginning to wonder if he wasn't better after all, but maybe the symptoms had only changed. The funny part was, he wasn't craving the touch of just any woman. He was hungering for the sight of only one.

He noticed that Shea was holding the door of the SUV open for him and he quickened his steps. Lifting one foot up onto the floorboard, he started to lift himself up into the vehicle but stopped as the buzzing in his head turned into something more like a wailing.

"Are you kidding me, C? Come on. You can't do this again."

Christian looked up and realized that Shea was talking to him. Everyone else was inside the vehicle, waiting. "I'm sorry. Something's wrong. I have to go." Turning on his heel, he strode towards the exit door that would take him up to street level.

"Dammit, C! Come back here!" Shea yelled.

"Christian! What the hell?" Nik's voice joined hers.

Yelling back over his shoulder, "I'll meet you there!" Christian slammed through the door and took the stairs three at a time. A few seconds later, he was on the street. He started walking as fast as he could without drawing undue attention to himself from the humans, and soon found himself down by the water at Pier 57 staring up at the giant Ferris wheel. But no, this wasn't right. Continuing on past the wheel, he picked up speed as a sense of panic hit him that was so strong his heart nearly stopped beating all together. He took off at vamp speed, uncaring now who saw him or what they would think, and tracked the call that had his blood singing in his veins.

A sense of déjà vu hit him like a sledgehammer as he ran down a set of steps and burst through another door. He found himself in the nearly empty level of another underground parking garage. Ryan was standing directly in front of him, facing him. The vampire from the park in Mexico was holding her in his arms from behind, and his mouth was at her throat. She stood passively in his arms as he drank from her, her eyes rolling around to land on Christian, just like they had the last time she'd shot up. And just like before, a single fat tear escaped and ran down her cheek. She lifted one hand in front of her, reaching for him...

In the space of a heartbeat, the sense of panic and fear that had brought him here was replaced with a rush of fury. Everything went red and a roar of rage echoed through the barren space as one word pounded through his mind:

MINE!

The next thing he knew, he was behind the other vampire. The fingers of one hand were sunk down to the second knuckle through his eye sockets as the other hand pried open his jaws from his female's throat. He wanted to sink his fangs in and rip the male's jugular from his throat, but the thought of tasting all that blood wasn't as appetizing as it once had been.

The vampire screamed in pain and rage and clawed at Christian's forearms. Christian barely felt his frantic attempts to free himself. His only concern was that Ryan was out of harms way.

As soon as she was free, Ryan stumbled away and fell to her hands and knees on the floor.

When she was far enough away, Christian started to slowly pull the vampire's face apart with his bare hands. The vampire kicked and screamed as he tried to get Christian to release him, but it was like trying to get a crocodile to release his dinner. Bones cracked and blood spurted as Christian separated the young vampire's jaw from his face, then he smiled as he let go and watched him bounce off the concrete wall and fall on his ass.

Strolling up behind him, Christian reached down and wrapped his hands around what was left of his face. With a hard twist to the right, he broke the bones in his neck. For good measure, he yanked the pistol out of his waistband and holding the head by its tight, curly hair, he pulled the trigger. Brain matter splattered the wall in front of him. He barely glanced at it before he shoved the pistol back into his pants and wiped his hands off on the body.

It wasn't enough. Christian stared down at the body, the rest of the world forgotten as he dropped down, about to tear it into tiny pieces.

A quiet groan shattered through the blood lust, and his head whipped around to his female. She had slid forward onto her stomach and was lying there with her limbs twisted awkwardly beneath her. The other vampire was instantly forgotten. He was no longer a threat.

Very carefully, he rolled her over and pulled her onto his lap. "Ryan? *She'ashil?*" Her eyelids fluttered but didn't open. That sense of déjà vu continued as Christian brought his own wrist to his mouth and bit down until the blood flowed freely from the wound. This time he had no second thoughts as he put his wrist to her mouth and softly urged her to drink.

She did, weakly at first, and then with stronger pulls as her strength began to return. His cock responded instantly, punching up painfully in his jeans, but he didn't even bother to readjust himself. He just wanted her to keep drinking.

She stopped all too soon. Blinking up at him with tear-filled turquoise eyes, she said, "I'm so sorry."

He brushed her hair out of her face. "Shhh. It's all right, *she'ashil.*"

"No, it's not." She pressed the heel of one hand against the side of her head and squeezed her eyes shut. "I need to tell you..." Her face scrunched up as she winced. "I need to tell you. I was going to do it, but I changed my mind."

"Do what?" he asked.

Instead of answering him, she straightened out her right arm and showed him the ragged needle mark. The hole was beginning to close, but he could tell it had been ugly before the healing powers of his blood. Faced with the evidence of her weakness, he didn't know what to say to make her feel better, so he said nothing. Just took her hand in his and held it until her voice brought his eyes back to her face.

"I'm not lying," she whispered. "I changed my mind."

"Why did you change your mind?" he asked quietly.

She only hesitated a moment before she confessed, "Because I want to stay with you."

Christian's heart expanded until the last remaining remnants of tightness were pushed from his chest, leaving only a space full of so many feelings that he couldn't even begin to describe them.

"So, what's it gonna be, Christian?" she whispered. "Red or blue?"

He frowned down at her. "Red or blue?"

She swallowed hard, but her blue eyes were steady on his when she said, "Red I stay, blue I go."

The mere thought of her going anywhere had pure panic rushing through his veins again and he pulled her up tight against him. "Red, *she'ashil*. I choose red."

"That's good," she mumbled into his shirt. "Because according to Keira, we're mated. It's worse than marriage she says."

Christian recoiled in shock. "What?"

But Ryan just shrugged and gave him a small smile. "Can you take me home, please?"

A black SUV pulled up next to them and doors opened and closed. "Yeah," he said as he watched his four friends and fellow Hunters pile out of the vehicle.

Luukas gave him a questioning glance as he walked past to check out the body. With a snarl, he gave it a vicious kick. "Gods, I hated that son of a bitch."

Christian paid him no mind. "Yeah," he told her. "Let's go home."

42

Christian sat sprawled in his favorite chair as he watched Ryan play with Mojo. They were hedgehog-sitting while Grace and Aiden and the others went back up to the remains of Leeha's fortress. Luukas was determined to dig his way through the rubble to the altar room, and Keira had finally convinced him that having some witch power there was better than not. The three girls together had been working really hard, and together, they were becoming a force to be reckoned with.

This was their fourth trip up there since he'd been back. He had wanted to go with them this time, but Luukas had told him to stay and he hadn't argued. Although Ryan was doing really well, she was still fighting off the addiction, and he worried about her being left here on her own for too long.

The other girls had been working with her though, and come to find out he'd been correct. She wasn't crazy. The voices she heard all the time were entities that only the most truly powerful witches could hear and control. Kind of like her familiars.

His female was a bad ass. Or at least she would be.

She'd already gotten much better at communicating with the beings that sought to protect her and do her bidding, especially as they were completely ecstatic that she was off the dope and trying to talk to them. They'd given her such a hard time about doing the drugs because they had rendered them useless. That was why they couldn't protect her when she was really high. It broke their connection with her.

Ryan was cooing to Mojo. The goofy rodent was lying on his back getting his belly rubbed. She shot him a gorgeous smile and Christian held back his groan as his cock kicked up and his fangs dropped. He'd been trying to take it easy with her while she recovered, but his hunger for her was about to rage out of control.

Her smile faltered as she processed the look on his face. Her eyes dropped instantly to his groin and he did groan then, his hips rocking up of their own accord just from her looking at him. He didn't try to hide his lust for her. It would be impossible anyway.

She bit her bottom lip and her eyes darkened as they travelled from his groin, across his stomach, up his chest and back to his face. "Mojo, honey, I think it's time for bed." Scooping up the bristly thing, she put him in his temporary house in the kitchen and came back to where Christian sat waiting for her.

A steady rain fell outside, enclosing them in their own little world. Ryan switched off all the lights except the lamp and flicked on the stereo. "Closer" by Nine Inch Nails pulsed through the speakers and she smiled a small, secret smile.

Then she started to move.

Christian's heart stopped completely, then suddenly started beating double time as the stunning female in front of him began dancing for him. She'd gained a little weight while here with him, and her curves had filled out perfectly. She was barefoot, wearing jean shorts and a tee shirt, not a ridiculous stripper costume, and she was the most erotic thing he'd ever seen as she lifted her long bright hair and moved her hips like a belly dancer.

When she took off her shirt, he took off his. And when she bent over in front of him and slid her shorts down her long legs, leaving her in nothing but a lace bra and a thong, he had to clamp his hand down over the head of his cock so he didn't come. He'd never been affected like this just by watching a female dance. But they'd never been Ryan.

Strutting over to him, she dropped to her knees in front of him and moved his hand so she could undo his jeans. His cock sprang free, jerking eagerly in her hand when she wrapped it around him. He was so jazzed up, her small hand barely covered a portion of him. Leaning forward, she ran her tongue along the large vein that ran up the length of him. When she reached the head, she lapped up the small bead of come that had escaped.

Christian's hips jerked up as she closed her mouth around his head, but he dug his fingers into the arms of the chair and resisted the urge to lift her onto his lap and impale her. "Ah! Gods. *She'ashil...*"

His blood pounded in his ears and he ached to sink his fangs into the throbbing pulse in her throat. He resisted as long as he could as he watched her fuck him with her mouth. But as the beat of the song rose stronger and stronger, so did his need to come. "I need to be inside of you." A predatory growl rumbled in his throat when he scented her body's response. "Now, Ryan," he ordered.

Gripping her under the arms and ignoring her sound of protest, he lifted her up and onto his lap. He reached behind her and unhooked her bra, exposing her luscious breasts to his hungry gaze, then ripped her thong in half and threw it on the floor. By the time he had her naked, she was panting and making little sounds that were driving him mad.

He pushed his pants down to his knees and reached between her legs. She was soaking wet and ready. Her nails dug into his shoulders and she cried out as he slid two fingers inside of her, stretching her and trying to get her ready for him. "You're so tight," he gritted out. His cock throbbed and his hips were rocking up and down uncontrollably, he couldn't help it.

"Please, Christian," she begged. "I'm ready. I want you so much." Pushing his arm away, she wrapped her small hand around him and guided him to her.

"I don't want to hurt you," he moaned. And then he cried out as she sat down and took him all. Her little body hugged him in a tight grip, all wet heat and soft curves. He'd never felt anything so good in his entire life.

And then she started to move.

Christian threw his head back against the chair and gripped her hips, thrusting up into her every time she came down. He tried to slow her down, but she was having none of it, so he opened his eyes to watch her ride him. So not a good idea if he wanted to make this last.

Her head was thrown back and her back was arched, her soft hair tickling his thighs. Her gorgeous breasts were bouncing in rhythm with his thrusts. He leaned forward and captured one large, dusky nipple in his mouth and sucked. With a cry, she threaded her fingers in his hair and slowed down the rolling of her hips. When he pulled away to give the other side the same attention, she brought his mouth up to her throat instead.

"Drink," she said.

He tried to pull away, worried that it would be too much for her. He didn't want to weaken her in any way while she was battling her own cravings. "No. I don't need to yet."

Looking him right in the eye, she said, "I want you to drink from me." Tilting her head away, she brushed her hair away from the throbbing pulse there. "Do it," she ordered, and rolled her hips again.

Christian growled as his eyes zeroed in on that pulse. His entire body ached for her blood. With one hand around the back of her neck, he pulled her into him. The erotic scent of her rose around him and he inhaled deeply, then ran his tongue along the artery there much as she had.

"Yes," she whispered. Her hips began to move in a steady rhythm. "Take me, Christian."

And he was lost.

A feral sound came from him as he reared back and struck hard, sinking his fangs deep into her throat. Her blood filled his mouth, the sweetest thing he'd ever tasted, and he began to drink in earnest. Ryan cried out, her body convulsing as she came. Holding her still with one hand behind her neck and the other around her hip, he curled his hips up and down and pounded into her faster and faster until his own orgasm rocked through him so hard he cried out against her throat and pushed up inside of her as far as he could go while his body jerked and spasmed.

When his vision cleared again, he carefully removed his fangs and licked her wounds closed. Wrapping his arms around her, he pulled her in against him, enjoying the feel of her new curves against his hardness.

Taking her gently by the arms and setting her away from him, he wanted to make sure one thing was perfectly clear. "You don't dance for anyone but me, *she'ashil*."

She took his face between her hands and her turquoise eyes stared directly into his. "I only ever danced for you, Christian. Only for you. I just didn't know it for a while."

Leaning in, she kissed him until his cock stirred inside of her.

"Dance for me again," he whispered.

And she did.

The Series Continues With
<u>A Vampire's Submission</u>.
Keep reading for a sneak peak!

CHAPTER ONE

Dante's hand was on fire. Literally.

Instinctive self-preservation was the only thing that saved it from incinerating in the mid-day sun. As he pulled his hand inch by slow inch down into the grave he'd dug, the desert sand caved in on itself, dousing the flames.

His breaths were soft and shallow, so much so that a human would not have been able to survive the lack of oxygen. He didn't really need to breathe. It was more a habit than anything else, even after hundreds of years. The hot, dry air did little but burn the inside of his lungs, yet he continued the struggle.

He lay absolutely still in his grave. So still, in fact, that he could feel the movement of a creature slithering across the sand above him, tracking it with his heightened senses and by the vibrations in the fine grains. Arresting his breath, lest the serpent sense the predator lying in wait just beneath the

CHAPTER ONE

desert floor, he forced himself to be patient. If he struck prematurely, before it got close enough to his hand, it would get away. Dante had learned this the hard way.

But this time his skill was dead on. The snake had no time to defend itself or escape before it was pulled down into the grave with him. His fangs—larger than the serpent's own—sliced effortlessly through its protective scales. When he finished draining it of its lifeblood, he pushed the corpse away to join the pile of partially decayed reptiles above and let the burning sand settle over him again.

Dante had no sense of time as he waited to heal. He had no idea how long he'd been there, buried under the hot sand to protect him from the sun by day and insulate him from the freezing cold at night. How long he'd lain in the grave he'd dug for himself with bloodied broken fingers. After he'd jumped from the plane, he'd landed in a heap of shattered bones and lacerated skin, the pain such that he'd never felt before. Not even when he was a young, cocky vampire that had been put in his place more than once.

What he did know was that his bones were nearly healed now, in spite of the meager offerings from the desert. And that he'd been damn lucky the sun had already descended below the horizon, or he would have burned to ash before he'd been able to burrow into the sand.

And he was ravenous for more blood.

Hours, or years, later—he honestly didn't know or care which—he felt the heat of the sun begin to wane. The sand that protected him cooled as quickly as it heated. In the distance,

CHAPTER ONE

he heard a yip, followed by a howl. Threads of the coyote's voice still hung in the night air when it was joined by others, together forming an eerie, beautiful song.

Dante worked his arm up through the heavy sand, cautiously breaking a few fingers through the surface. He waited a few seconds, and when he felt nothing but a cool breeze caressing his desiccated skin, he pulled his arm back in to his body and clawed at the grains in earnest.

It seemed a losing battle at first, for with every handful of sand he moved, more fell into the pocket of air he'd just created. But over time he made his way to the surface, unearthing himself like something out of a human's nightmare with a little help from the night winds.

The effort exhausted him.

Once free of the heavy weight, he collapsed face first onto the sand and rolled over onto his back. He gathered his energy as he ran his tongue over lips, cracked and dry with thirst. He couldn't even swallow.

Squinting his eyes against the brightness of the moon, he let his head fall to the side. All he saw was sand, sand, and more fucking sand. Turning the other way he saw much of the same. Wait, no. There were a few patches of creosote, and just beyond it some type of round cactus.

Neither of which would ease his particular type of thirst.

Dante studied the bursts of light above him. It had been a long time since he recalled seeing so many stars in one place before. As his eyes followed a particularly fascinating

CHAPTER ONE

constellation spanning across the never-ending expanse of blackness, they were drawn down to a portion of the night that was brighter, more illuminated than the rest. Only one thing lit up the night sky like that.

A city.

And where there was a city, there were humans. And humans were full of blood. Much more than the scaly creatures he'd been surviving on up until now.

Dante burst to his feet in a flash of movement that belied his exhaustion of just a few moments ago. The thirst burned his insides like the sun burned his skin, and his fangs shot down, readying to feed. Pure vampire instinct took over, and Dante became the predator he had been reborn to be.

Read **A Vampire's Submission** now.

NOTE FROM THE AUTHOR

Heroin addiction is one of the saddest things I've ever seen, and like many people, I've had it hit very close to home. The addict in my family is out of rehab and doing well, and for that I am so very grateful. But that addiction will be a constant struggle for them for the rest of their life. And they don't have access to any vampire blood to magically heal them.

This book was very hard to write in many ways, but it was something that was clamoring inside of me and I needed to get it out. I hope I did justice to the people who have suffered from this addiction. And I hope it never, *ever*, comes near any of you.

Thank you for reading.

ABOUT THE AUTHOR

L.E. Wilson writes romance starring intense alpha males and the women who are fearless enough to love them just as they are. In her novels you'll find smoking hot scenes, a touch of suspense, some humor, a bit of gore, and multifaceted characters, all working together to combine her lifelong obsession with the paranormal and her love of romance.

Her writing career came about the usual way: on a dare from her loving husband. Little did she know just one casual suggestion would open a box of worms (or words as the case may be) that would forever change her life.

On a Personal Note:

"I love to hear from my readers! Contact me anytime at le@lewilsonauthor.com."